THE Makedown

Gitty Daneshvari

NEW YORK   BOSTON

5 Spot
Hachette Book Group
237 Park Avenue
New York, NY 10017

Visit our Web site at www.5-spot.com.

5 Spot is an imprint of Grand Central Publishing.
The 5 Spot name and logo are trademarks of Hachette Book Group, Inc.

Printed in the United States of America

First Edition: February 2009

10 9 8 7 6 5 4 3 2 1

Library of Congress Cataloging-in-Publication Data

Daneshvari, Gitty.
    The makedown / Gitty Daneshvari.—1st ed.
        p. cm.
    Summary: "A tale of average girl lands hot boyfriend, girl fears losing hot boyfriend, girl embarks on the opposite of a makeover to render him unattractive to the opposite sex"—Provided by publisher.
    ISBN: 978-0-446-69988-4
    1. Man-Woman relationships—Fiction.   2. Mate selection—Fiction.
I. Title.
    PS3604.A5174M35 2009
    813'.6—dc22
                                                        2008031355

To my parents—thank you for everything.

Acknowledgments

I would like to thank the following people: Caryn Karmatz Rudy, Petersen Harris, Laurel Heren, Howard Abramson, Sarah Burnes, Shari Smiley, Breda Carroll, Jen Kleiner, Lucy Punch, Jessica Fantini, Shamsi Daneshvari, Stefanie Markman, Neosha Kashef, Keith Sweitzer, Lucy Rimalower, Swanna MacNair, Pam Silverstein, Marley Shelton, Beau Flynn and everyone at Contrafilm, Mara Jacobs, Amanda Coplan, Rosanna Bilow, Margo Klewans, Stir Crazy, Victor Levin, Tanny Gordon, Theodore Gordon, Jonathan Gordon, Nicole Terry, Shirley Nagelschmidt Bessey, Candace Lilligren, Mike Carnes, Ann Cherkis, Claudine Auguste, Johanna Mawdesly, Judee Ann Williams, Kallie Shimek, and everyone else who supported me along the way.

makedown

pronunciation: 'māk-"daùn

function: noun

definition: The lessening of external beauty and innate confidence as a means of leveling the playing field.

etymology: Modern English, derived from the work of Anna Norton, a pioneer in the field of dating beyond one's reach.

PART

I

Hello Fatty

Chapter One

I was born into the sovereignty of nerds, from which few have escaped and of which even fewer have had sex. For thirteen harrowing years, nerdiness reigned supreme, leaving me unattractive and socially awkward with little more than a stellar report card to call a friend.

Life didn't start off that badly for me. For my first decade, I enjoyed an utterly average existence: unremarkable brown eyes, brown hair, average height, and a tendency toward chubbiness, but nothing too dramatic. In these years, I was notable only for my proclivity to answer teachers' questions with long and pedantic responses. For example, when asked the capital of Ohio, I couldn't simply respond *Columbus*. No, I was compelled to explain that Chillicothe served as the capital from the state's inception in 1803 until 1816, with a two-year sojourn in Zanesville from 1810 to 1812. This particular personality trait was irritating but tolerable to my peers. Well, at least until the age of ten, when I began the steep descent into ugly.

Puberty literally walloped the ordinariness out of me. My medium-sized lips, medium-sized brown eyes, and medium-sized nose became distorted with cystic acne and unruly eyebrows as my hormones surged. The coffee-colored locks that hung above my shoulders wilted dramatically as a result of my scalp's excessive oil production. And as for my body, the bones, muscles, and organs were completely unprepared for the onslaught of weight, which ascended as my metabolism slowed to a crawl.

The rapid physical deterioration coincided with my classmates' indoctrination into the art of Cruel and Unusual Punishment. They seemed hell-bent on escalating their insults, locked in a fierce competition to be the first to make me cry. Oddly, the more they antagonized me over my slovenly state, the worse I let myself become. Instead of propelling me to exercise and cozy up to the local dermatologist, the comments merely increased my sense of helplessness. The one with the longest staying power came from a fifth-grade despot, who thought it would be fun to give the entire class bear nicknames in honor of her peculiar ursine obsession. In a class of "Cute Bear," "Smiley Bear," and "Beauty Bear," "Weird Fat Bear" rather stung. I prayed nightly for a coup that would overthrow the bear regime. Sadly, by middle school, I would have deemed Weird Fat Bear a compliment.

The girls' bathroom at Paul Revere Middle School was my unhygienic haven, where I escaped prying eyes to scarf down lunch alone. Hunched over on the damp tile floor, I furtively hid behind a metallic trash can to avoid notice. When girls did happen to wander in for a smoke or to apply makeup and caught a glimpse of my Cro-Magnon eating habits, laughter and ridicule always ensued. My response never varied; I would silently stare at my bologna, mayonnaise, and Wonder Bread sandwich and wait. To pass the time while enduring the torture, I would inspect the amount of mayonnaise lathered on the bread. The importance of mayonnaise in my youth simply cannot be underestimated. I even created a litmus test for the correct amount of mayonnaise a sandwich required. The creamy substance had to squeeze out the sides of the bread while the sandwich was being heaved into my mouth or satiety did not occur. Subsequently, my shirts were littered with unsightly pea-sized oil stains. Even more distressing were the yellowing particles of white bread that decorated my braces, prompting students and teachers alike to turn away in disgust. But my eating habits were only a minor contributor to my appalling physical appearance.

My hair and clothing were the worst. The oily brown locks plastered around my face provided a stark contrast to the tangled rats' nests occupying subprime real estate on the back of my head. My eyes watered with pain every time Mother attempted to brush out these dreadlocks. After all, some of my rats' nests had been with me almost as long as my arms and legs. They were literally seminal parts of my childhood. Nostalgia and agony aside, hefty dandruff flakes also dislodged in the process, further deterring me from brushing. Any friction against my scalp resulted in a sprinkling of white on my fluorescent-colored T-shirts. These objectionable shirts, often with factory mistakes, were frequently paired with faded black stretch pants. In an era of flannel shirts and light denim jeans, these garments cemented my status as a fashion pariah.

My single-minded pursuit of academic success did little to alleviate my lowly status. Without pesky friends to drain my energy, I was able to concentrate solely on school, and here I did excel. Frankly, my academic aptitude was something of a genetic anomaly, having been raised by parents who reserved reading for the bathroom. My mother often commented on my father's willingness to read anything from a shampoo bottle to a box of tampons while on the toilet. She considered her *Reader's Digest* selection vastly superior. Mary Norton was a plump five feet six with short, shellacked brown hair and glasses that she considered the height of 1970s fashion. Of course, it was the 1990s then, but she cherished them nonetheless. Mother freely admitted that she didn't need glasses but claimed them necessary to be taken seriously in "business." Given an extra few seconds, Mother would explain that "glasses are to women what ties are to men; a standard in business, a sign of excellence." This, of course, like most of Mother's life lessons, made no sense, especially since she was a retired travel agent. Regardless of her ignorance, she freely offered her opinion on everything from ordering in restaurants to what "black people are really mad about." And to emphasize a statement, she would lower the phony glasses to the tip of her nose. Mother had a limited worldview, although she would dispute that, citing her knowledge of Western Europe's airport codes as evidence to the contrary.

My father, Fred, was a simple man and one of few words. He was a manager at Allstate Insurance, a company he had been with since graduating Ohio State. For all intents and purposes (or, as Mother would say, "intensive purposes"), he was an undiagnosed mute. My father's quiet manner allowed us a "happy" home life, diffusing Mother's madness through silence. While neither of my parents admitted regret over the twenty dollars spent at the justice of the peace, it was clear that the marriage was not a love connection. Or for that matter even a *like* connection. The fact that the marriage spawned Barney and me was rather surprising.

Two years my senior, my brother Barney was the only person in Norfolk, Ohio, further ostracized than I was, but to his credit, he never cared. He played Dungeons & Dragons, masturbated excessively, and felt generally satisfied by life. Barney was also challenged in the looks department and spent the majority of his teenage years in the hall bathroom with the school yearbook, much to Mother's annoyance. "What are you doing in there with the yearbook, Barney?" she would ask suspiciously pulling her glasses to the tip of her nose. "Learning my classmates' surnames," Barney would reply. I thought she bought it, but her invariable response of "Dinner is in an hour, and don't forget to wash your hands" leads me to believe Mother might actually have been clued in.

Luckily for my surprisingly small bladder, the Internet was invented. For Barney, it was life changing, and he literally divided his life into BI (Before Internet) and AI (After Internet). For those living in social isolation, hiding behind a screen is nothing short of a miracle. His trips to the bathroom with the yearbook petered off after he received his own computer, and so began the era of him locking his bedroom door. "Barney, why is the door locked?" Mother would demand as she cocked her ear against the hollow wood. "I'm exercising in the nude. It's supposed to burn more calories." "Don't forget to wash your hands."

But if Barney excelled behind closed doors, I was determined to shine in the classroom. In addition to my aforementioned knack for displaying my encyclopedic knowledge on any given subject, I was known for taking notes regarding everything from the school's fire exits to class attendance, just in case the teacher needed them. Not surprisingly, this increased my peers' interest in me as a target.

One cold November day in eighth grade social studies, I stood before the class in my favorite black stretch pants and lime green T-shirt, reading my paper on the Chumash Indians. While pleased that Mr. Van Leeuwin had chosen my paper as the best, I was uncomfortable speaking in front of my classmates. During my conclusion, a note passed from student to student, filling the room with laughter.

Naïvely, I assumed it to be about Mr. Van Leeuwin; after all, he did wear tie-dyed clothes, and surely that was enough to elicit some chuckling. I finished, carefully sucked in my fat rolls, and returned to my desk. From two seats away Kyle Mander, the most popular boy in school, passed me the note.

I had secretly harbored a crush on Kyle since I watched him make the winning shot at the state basketball finals. As the clock ticked, Kyle coolly lobbed the ball in the air. He didn't wait to see if the ball went in; instead, he raised his hands overhead and unapologetically chanted his own name. Kyle's confidence seduced me, producing a detailed fantasy sequence.

Fantasies provided the bulk of my adolescent entertainment. This was understandable, considering how often I was told I resembled a young Roseanne Barr, "only with acne and really bad hair." The comparison to Roseanne Barr doggedly followed me until *The Rosie O'Donnell Show* debuted, and everyone decided that I looked like her "only with acne and really bad hair." I actually sent my local congressman a letter asking for a countywide moratorium on unflattering celebrity comparisons. I am still waiting for a response.

Fantasy was my sole refuge from a life of rampant humiliation and self-loathing, and I gave myself plenty of time to construct elaborate make-believe scenarios, like one in which I resembled Alyssa Milano and hung with such high-octane acts as the Backstreet Boys and 'N Sync. The celebs had come calling after witnessing my superslick Britney Spears–inspired dance moves on a Malls Across America tour. On break from touring, I stopped by to watch Kyle score the winning shot at the state championship. He ran to me in the stands, pushing away parents, popular kids, and semipopular kids by the handful, pulling my size-six body into his arms. Gasps filled the auditorium as Kyle gave me the most romantic kiss any eighth-grader had seen outside of Cinemax. "Anna, that shot and every other shot I make is for you. You're my girl." "Oh Kyle, you're more romantic than Michael Bolton." "That's right. I even wrote you a song. Anna, I'm your man-na," Kyle sang as he possessively slung his arm around my shoulders.

I shivered in excitement, but hearing a loud "Hey look, fat Anna is trying to dance," I returned reluctantly to my eighth-grade social studies reality. I unfolded Kyle's note, allowing myself to contemplate the possibility that it held a confession of his feelings as opposed to a joke about our teacher. My heart crawled up my throat, restricting my oxygen intake and reddening my face. At first sight, the words were indecipherable, a jumbled mix of letters. The phrase I yearned to see, "Anna, I like you. Can we go steady forever?" was not there. Nor was there anything regarding Mr. Van Leeuwin's hippy attire. No, the note read "Anna Norton has a camel toe because she masturbates with superglue." For the record, I did not have a camel toe; it was merely a thick seam in my stretch pants. As for masturbation, I was deliberately unaware of my body and therefore centuries away from learning how to use it for my own satisfaction. In shock, I dropped the note to the floor, nearly suffocating on my own self-loathing.

To my right sat fellow nerd Sally Worthington. Clearly aware of the contents of the note, she watched me suffer. Her face didn't offer compassion or understanding but rather disgust and repulsion. Unlike plumbers, truck drivers, or teachers, nerds had no union. "Anna, if you brushed your hair and wiped the dried food off your face, they'd stop being so mean to you," Sally said with a level of irritation that surprised me. At the time, I couldn't figure out why she even cared, but in retrospect I realize she saw me as bad press; I was giving nerds everywhere a bad rap. It was one thing to be socially inept and painfully out of style, but ignoring society's grooming standards was unforgivable. Unable to respond to Sally, I ran out of the room to seek refuge in the relative privacy of the girls' bathroom.

Middle school is cruel; I was not to be given the luxury of a quiet cry. "Hey Norton, I think I can solve your problems," Jordan Marins, the Dense Princess of eighth grade, jeered as she passed by. "Go home, stick your face in peanut butter, and let your dog chew it off!" She and the gang of idiots trailing behind her burst into laughter. I wanted to tell Jordan that I was sorry I got 100 percent on the history exam, while she received a class record of 7 percent after confusing the Civil War with the Vietnam

War. Instead of calling out her stupidity, I mumbled, "I don't have a dog."

"Yeah, maybe that's because you *are* a dog," Princess Jordan retorted. I consoled myself with thoughts of her working the counter at McDonald's after failing out of cosmetology school. I loved these fantasies, and this one was so powerful that I didn't hear Jordan bark in my ear before trotting off victoriously.

As the years passed and the insults increased, my beloved make-believe ceased to protect me with the same virility it once had. During this decline, a voice emerged within me more vile and putrescent than anything I encountered in the school hallways. Meticulous student that I was, I created a log to capture the criticism hurled my way. I named it Hello Fatty and began tracking the insults I received in addition to my own assessments. It was of the utmost importance that I remained ahead of the mudslinging curve, attempting to callus my emotions and create a protective barrier from others' verbal attacks. "Hey Norton, you know you got a rat's face and a pig's body?" Kyle would yell across the crowded hall between classes. Pity was all I could offer Kyle. That was his best shot. Rat's face? Pig's body? I was performing on a much higher and nastier level of insults; it almost wasn't fair.

Hello Fatty,
Cellulite curds swarm the tires of lard on your legs like bees to honey. So deep are the rolls of blubber that mold and fungus have grown, creating a rancid-egg smell. Pus-filled sacs form because of your massive thighs rubbing together. As you enter history class, the sores explode, staining your pants and making you look like a child who

has soiled herself. Students barf uncontrollably at the sight
of you, because you are the foulest of all beasts.

xoxo Anna

Hello Fatty was an important part of the rigid sched-
ule I maintained throughout high school. Every day after
school, I studied, ate dinner, danced with my imaginary friend, and logged insults. Due to Mother's habit of
"cleaning my room"—code for "looking for dope"—I
took great care to hide Hello Fatty. Mother became convinced that I was smoking "grass" after watching a special
on the local news. She settled on drugs as the only logi-
cal explanation for my abundant appetite. She confronted
me the next afternoon. As I studied, Mother eyed me
suspiciously, watching crumbs descend from the front of
my shirt. Finally, when I could take no more, I yelled,
"What?"

"Anna, I need to ask you a serious question."

"Mmmhmm?" I grunted, licking my fingers clean of
remnants from my afternoon snack.

"Are you partaking in the illegal narcotic known as
grass, dope, or marijuana?"

"What?" I asked with outrage. "No. Why would you
ask me that?" I said with all the defensiveness one expects
from an overweight teenager.

"Look at yourself, covered in Doritos dust and Pringles
crumbs! It's called the munchies!"

"Mother, how dare you! You know damn well I'm
just fat!"

Fat. The word had haunted me most of my life. I
didn't want to be fat anymore. Actually, I didn't even want
to be *me* anymore. All my fantasies and Hello Fatty one-

upmanship proved insufficient protection. I needed more. I needed a Fairy Godmother. While my advanced age led me to reject the possibility of a real Santa Claus, Tooth Fairy, or Easter Bunny, I accepted Fairy Godmothers (FGs for short) as incontrovertible truth. The FG job description was simple: intervene when parents were unable to see that their children's clothes and general demeanor were causing them to be exiled to nerd-dom. Admittedly, the aforementioned definition of FG was not directly lifted from a fairy tale. After reading countless fairytales, I took it upon myself to create a modern translation. Then, while perusing *People* magazine's weight-loss issue, I happened upon a high school student's transformation. Her before looked like...well, me. Her after was a stunning, slim, and desirable teenager. How could she have pulled it off? The young woman had morphed into an entirely new person through an extensive makeover, the likes of which could only have been accomplished by a devoted FG. Soon, everywhere I turned, FGs' exertions grabbed my attention, bolstering my belief.

While scientifically unsound, my theory held enormous emotional protection. This devout belief in FG shielded me from an everyday regimen of spitballs, loneliness, and mockery. Technically, all those horrid afflictions still plagued me daily, but I wasn't bothered by them. It was impossible to be leveled by the horrors of my life while simultaneously believing that FG could transform my exterior, endowing me with self-confidence. Obviously, FG didn't have time to intervene on just anyone's behalf. Lightweights crying over being stood up at prom or having fat ankles need not apply. Long-term catastrophic social and emotional annihilation were prerequisites for an FG intervention, so I welcomed them. What didn't kill me made me a better candidate for FG's limitless transformative powers.

As high school waned, I dared to believe that everything would change in the next year. College. That was where FG would make her long-awaited appearance, guiding me through a makeover to average looks and modest happiness. For clarification's sake, I didn't actually think an old lady with a wand was going to show up, a gaggle of mice in tow. FG could come in many forms; hell, she could even come as a rabid hyena with a taste for virgin blood, for all I cared. She simply needed to come, and as quickly as possible.

Chapter Two

I wish I could say FG found me at the University of Pennsylvania, but try as I might, I couldn't seem to find her anywhere. She did not arrive in the form of a roommate, excited as I had been to meet the oft-imagined Jane Zelisky. I had spent days dreaming up our interactions—at last, I'd have a friend who would look beyond my off-putting exterior and adore hanging out with the real me, and I envisioned us together in every possible scenario—late-night pizza parties, midmorning chocolate bar hunts, afternoon sugar cereal binges—the full gamut of interpersonal adventures. My dream was shattered mere hours after arriving on campus by a geeky RA who bore an eerie resemblance to Howdy Doody. "Anna Norton?" the lanky redheaded boy asked cautiously, eyeing a clipboard and my room number. "I'm your resident advisor, George Macadamia, but everyone calls me Nut on account of the whole Macadamia thing. They're really popular in Hawaii—macadamia nuts, that is. I haven't been to Hawaii, but that's what I read online," he babbled without making eye contact. An ease fell over me; Nut surpassed me in terms of both awkwardness and randomness. "I'm here to talk to you about Jane," Nut said with a strained face.

"Oh no! Is she okay? Was there an accident?" I screeched dramatically, covering my mouth with my hand as soap opera actors often do.

"Uh. I think she—"

"Is she dead? Is my friend dead?" I screamed, milking the whole "friend" thing for all it was worth. I bent over, clutching my stomach as if poisoned, then straightened to beat my breast in anguish.

"Um…um…," Nut stuttered, visibly uncomfortable with my emotional outburst.

"I knew it! She's dead! Oh God, why? Why did you take my friend?" I wailed, tears in my eyes. My belief that Nut was on an equally nerdy playing field freed my inner drama queen and then some.

"Actually, she deferred a year, so it looks like you're going to have the room to yourself."

It would have played better if she'd died, I thought ruefully.

"Um, isn't there someone else who needs a room-mate?" I managed to pull myself together enough to ask.

"Nope, but I'm across the hall if you need anything."

Again channeling my inner actor, I regurgitated a scene from many a made-for-TV movie. I slid down the door to portray my complete and utter misery. Slumped over on the floor, visions of the girls' bathroom at Paul Revere played through my mind, making my tears all too real. Friendship, that ever-elusive mistress, had once again duped me, leaving me with nothing but a weird resident advisor named Nut. Although there was something else to consider. Did Nut tell all the dorm residents where he lived? Or was that a play for friendship? Perhaps even more than friendship? Nut was an übernerd, but that didn't diminish my desire to win him over with my feminine wiles. No one had ever liked me. In twelve years of formal education, not one boy ever engaged in a crush on me. Girls missing limbs, girls with moustaches, girls with halitosis, and girls with chronic nosebleeds all experienced the sensation of being liked, yet I never made the cut. I yearned to believe that my past was no longer relevant at Penn. Nut would be my white knight! Was he the first sign of FG's intervention? While devastated by the loss of my friend Jane, my focus had already shifted to my boyfriend Nut.

> *Hello Fatty,*
> *I've met the man who will take my virginity, starting FG's long-awaited makeover. His name is Nut, and, well, all I can say is I'm NUTS for him. One nerd to another, this is love.*
>
> —*Anna*

The following day I entered the dining hall at 7:30 a.m. for the express purpose of launching my relationship with Nut. I deemed a breathy voice necessary to aid in the seduction. "Um, hello Nut," I offered in my best Melanie Griffith imitation. Of course, he had already heard my awkward real voice. Visibly affected by my new voice—or so I hoped—Nut could barely respond.

"What?" he said without making eye contact.

"I said hello, Nut," I whispered.

"Um, okay. Hi, I guess," Nut said while chewing.

"You guess?" I squawked indignantly before remembering my stage directions and seductively moving my tongue back and forth across my lips.

"Okay, hi."

I sat down across from Nut and continued my journey

to humiliation. "You know I've always loved macadamia nuts."

"Really?"

"Yeah, they're my favorite nut."

"Mine, too," Nut said, finally making eye contact. "I used to be allergic to nuts as a child, but around the time my peeps in high school started calling me Nut, the allergy disappeared."

"Wow, you're a medical miracle," I exclaimed, not even bothering to use my sex kitten voice.

"Kind of. Well actually, not at all. People can develop and lose allergies at any time," Nut responded with his mouth full of food. "I got to go; I'm rushing. I'm a senior, so this is my last shot; I really want to get in—be with the boys—you know, have brothers for life—"

"Um, yeah, completely. I'm rushing, too. I only have a brother. I thought it would be good balance to get some sisters. Go girls! Hey sisters! Anna's in the house!"

Sororities evoked images of girls with Sharpies circling fat pockets on my body while laughing maliciously. I doubted those "sisters" would even let me buy their sweatshirt. However, I desperately wanted something to share with Nut, and my freshman orientation packet—a seventy-page document I'd immediately highlighted and taken notes on, as well as committed to memory—recommended rushing as an excellent way to meet people. I figured there had to be a nerdy sorority, this was the Ivy League, after all. Penn was filled with nerds; surely there was an appropriate group for me.

I opened the packet to the section on student life and surveyed my options. Why did I have to be born a godless white chick? Hadn't I suffered enough? My lack of religion and ethnicity barred me from some very nerdy groups, which listed studying and watching television as activities. After contemplating some very unethical alternatives, I decided to try Delta Beta, a dry sorority that prided itself on academic standards, conservative politics, and the protection of women's virtues. As an intelligent virgin, Delta Beta was a good fit, barring the conservative politics. I had always considered myself a nonpracticing liberal due to my prochoice stance. However, I was far more desperate than I was liberal, so I registered for Republican groups online. Rocking Repubs, Teens Against Terror, and My Elephant Is an Honor Student But Your Donkey's Not all listed Anna Norton as a member. I picked the most cutting-edge of the Republican youth groups in an effort to diminish my feeling of selling out.

A mere twelve girls showed up at Delta Beta's orientation; apparently, its no-alcohol policy hadn't done much to help boost its appeal. I rejoiced in its unpopularity, since it exponentially increased my odds of acceptance. The evening began with Maureen, the Delta Beta leader, asking us about our personal heroes. As luck would have it, I went first, naming Jesus Christ as my personal hero. The candidates that followed responded with Ronald Reagan, Richard Nixon, Gerald Ford, and George Bush. It quickly became clear that my choice of Jesus Christ was a bit unusual in the context of this politically obsessed group. After hearing everyone's responses, Maureen decided to dig a little deeper, starting once again with me.

"Anna Norton?"

"Yes," I responded cautiously.

"You chose Jesus Christ as your hero."

"That's correct, Mr. Christ," I intoned, attempting to sound pious.

"What are some of Jesus's teachings that have influenced you?"

"Um...um...," I stuttered nervously before spitting out the first thing that came to mind, "Thou shall not vote Democrat...or smoke cigarettes?"

"I'm sorry, what did you say?" Maureen asked.

"Um," I said, racking my brain for some Jesus-ism. Damn Mother. Why hadn't she taken me to Sunday school?

"Well?" Maureen prodded me.

"Thou shall not covet my neighbor's wife."

"What does that mean to you?"

"Um, no lusting after ladies...who belong to...," I stammered desperately.

"Moving on." Maureen sounded irritated. I sounded like a lesbian, or at the very least a phony Jesus lover, especially once the rest of the group described their heroes with terms such as *family values, patriotism, liberty,* and *freedom.*

My opportunity for sisterhood was evaporating, so I decided to convey both my regret over my inappropriate answers and my longing to be included to Maureen by staring at her with expressions that alternated between sorrow and enthusiasm. This was an ill-advised plan; Maureen watched me with a perturbed expression before asking if I needed medical assistance. When I assured her that I was perfectly fine, she snorted, "That's a matter of opinion," and turned on her heel to confer with her "sisters" on first-round cuts. I crossed my fingers, arms, and legs and prayed to FG. Even if I wasn't ultimately accepted into the Sisterhood of the Traveling Twin Sets, I yearned to make it to the second round. If I made it to the second round, I would break my lifelong streak of exclusion.

After about thirty seconds, Maureen reentered the room with her sisters and a smug look of power. My stomach clenched painfully as I fought to stay positive. "First, I want to thank you all very much for applying to Delta Beta. Unfortunately, it's impossible for us to accept everyone because"—Maureen paused to think of the best explanation—"Well, we didn't like one of you...at all. Now, the following girls are advancing to the second round: Jennifer Fantini, Laurel Harrison, Theodora Marshall, Jane Murray, Harriet Nielsen, Judith Green, Bree Wallis, Marie Gordon, Alexa Hardin, Susie Coplan, and Stephanie Benedict." Maureen had accepted everyone except me. Once again, I was rejected. I didn't bother thanking her; instead, I stood and walked out. Screw you, Maureen, I thought as rage tempered my crashing self-esteem. Why had I even tried to be part of a sorority? They represent everything I despise about girls and society. I headed straight back to my dorm, hoping an evening of fantasizing about Nut would eradicate any memory of Republican fascist sisterhoods.

As I approached my dorm room, I spotted Nut knocking on my door. Was this a blessing from the god of nerds? The first sign of FG? "Nut, are you looking for me?" I asked, trying unsuccessfully to keep the amazement out of my voice.

"Hey, can I watch *Felicity* in your room? My TV's busted, and no one else will let me in."

"Yes, I would love to have you over."

"I brought Doritos," Nut added. He sat next to me on the bed, acting as the official Doritos holder.

"How great is Ben?" Nut sighed happily as *Felicity*'s theme music filled my cramped little abode.

"I love him almost as much as I love Doritos," I shot back with what I hoped was a flirtatious giggle.

"Definitely," was Nut's clever reply. We both sat contentedly pushing Doritos into our mouths.

Television was the foundation on which we would build a friendship. The two of us enjoyed weekly dates to watch *Felicity* and *Dawson's Creek* while gorging on a variety of junk food from the local minimart. As episodes progressed, I squeezed closer and closer to Nut. One night, deep into the Felicity-hairgate, I decided it was time to take our relationship to the next level. Nut was a fan of OP corduroy shorts, which exposed his long and freckled legs. Under the influence of hormones and pent-up sexual aggression, I yanked up the hem of my maternity denim jean skirt, revealing my pale and flaccid thigh. A shiver ran up my spine, and not in a good way. Still I persevered. I raised my left leg onto Nut's, washing over it like a tsunami swallowing a dingy. Spectacularly monstrous, I found it hard to look away as I brushed my leg back and forth over his. Nut stared at the screen, eyes locked on Ben Covington. My lack of exercise soon slowed my leg thrusts to a crawl. On the verge of a muscle spasm, I was greatly relieved when Nut leapt off the bed. "I think I should let you know something." Nut paused as if waiting for a drum roll. "It's really important. I am . . . a big fan of Ben's. Do you understand?"

"Yeah, I know what you mean," I cooed seductively.

"No, I don't think you do. I mean...I mean...this is harder than telling my parents...I'm gay."

"Gay? But, but that's impossible," I cried out, wounded.

"You must have known," Nut said.

"No, I didn't," I muttered. How could my boyfriend—okay, pretend boyfriend—be gay?

"Anna, I spend my nights watching TV with you. Don't you think if I was straight I would be out chasing hotties like other guys?"

He was right—I was the Liza Minnelli of the dormitory, only less attractive. It was too painful to process.

"*Dawson's* is starting. Wanna watch?" I offered, bringing the summit of humiliation and sexuality to an end.

For the duration of my freshman year, Nut and I watched a minimum of eight hours of television together a week. He was my social life, and I was incredibly grateful for him. For the first time since its creation, I didn't write anything in Hello Fatty. In June, I attended Nut's graduation, to which he wore his small OP corduroy shorts under his graduation gown. He waved to his parents as he got his diploma. I beamed back from my place a few rows behind them, imagining he was waving to me. Nut's only postcollege plan was to move to California to live in San Francisco.

"Nut, we're two hours from New York. Why do you have to go all the way across the country?"

"Anna, look at me," he said dramatically. I gazed into his eyes, wondering if he would have even liked me if he were straight. "If I am ever going to get laid"—Nut paused, prompting me to salivate—"by a man, I need to be with my own people."

I sighed and honestly wished I were gay. It would be such fun to be part of a "people."

The following fall, with Nut in San Francisco, I fell into a deep depression. He had been my only friend at Penn (technically, anywhere in the world). Unkindly stationed in a single dorm room again, my loneliness soared, engulfing my every thought and causing me to fill whole volumes of Hello Fatty. I missed companionship as I watched show after show on my tiny TV. Short of hiring an escort, I only had one option: Barney. It was actually an ingenious idea, since Barney had an active fantasy about university life. He had dropped out of community college for a variety of reasons, most of which originated from his laziness, but still clung to the idea of being the big man on campus. Dressed in the Penn sweatshirt and cap he bought online, Barney hit the quad while I was in class. He sat alone on the lush grass and waited patiently for someone to talk to him, but no one did. Frustrated, he took matters into his own hands. "What are you studying?" Barney asked a mousy brunette seated alone on the quad.

"Astronomy," the coed replied with a bored affectation.

"Wow, I bet a lot of people ... tell you ... you look like a star ... 'cause you're so beautiful and shiny."

The girl gave him a look of disgust, stood, and walked away.

Barney was genuinely depressed when he relayed the conversation to me. I understood his pain all too well, offered him a bag of frosted cookies, and turned on the television. We were definitely related, and we were definitely nerds.

Chapter Three

E very former nerd has a defining moment that acts as the catalyst for change. For me it was my twenty-third birthday, a night that was filled with embarrassment, racial slurs, and general infamy. Included on this special occasion was Harry, my first boyfriend. He suited my family perfectly with his porky frame, flannel shirts, and jeans with tapered ankles. His hairline started midway across his scalp, a side effect he ascribed to his acne medication. Perfect skin came with a price.

Life was all about compromise, or so Harry liked to remind me. He certainly wasn't telling me anything I didn't know; I ate all the Little Debbie I wanted but had Harry as a boyfriend. At twenty-three, I was seventy-five pounds over what Mother called a "healthy" weight and was plagued by acne that traveled from my forehead to my shoulder blades. This was puberty—adult puberty—at its worst.

Three and a half years after I attempted to seduce Nut, I met Harry in quantum physics. Technically, we didn't meet in class but at Denny's, studying over hash browns and eggs.

"Hey, can I borrow your ketchup?"

"Sure," I said, barely looking up from my physics textbook.

"You've got Professor Shapiro with me."

The shock at someone's noticing me in a class and admitting to it outside of that class was enough to render the chapter I was reading on eigenvalue incomprehensible, so I shifted my focus to that someone. Of course, he was exceptionally unattractive, his poreless complexion notwithstanding. "Yeah, I do. I'm cramming for tomorrow. I'm a little nervous," I confided.

"I made flash cards; want me to quiz you?" It was the most romantic thing anyone had ever said to me. Harry joined me at my booth and immediately flagged the waitress.

"We'll have two deluxe breakfasts and a side of fries with ranch dressing."

I loved that he knew to order ranch dressing with the french fries. The synchronicity of our relationship continued when we learned we grew up two counties away from each other in Ohio. What more could we want in a partner? We both loved to study. We both loved to eat. And considering our lack of options, we both deemed that enough.

Unlike our hormonally crazed peers, ours wasn't a highly sexual relationship. Occasionally, we kissed with tongue, but we didn't go much further than that. Harry may have grazed my boob while leaning for the Lay's ruffled-cut potato chips, but that hardly counted as second base.

Two weeks before graduation, Harry and I watched *Star Trek: Voyager* while doing whipped cream shots. As I lifted the canister to my mouth and squirted a load, Harry turned to me with a serious expression. "I really like you, Anna, but if we don't have sexual intercourse soon, I fear I could turn to . . . porn," Harry said shamefully.

"Porn?" I asked with surprise.

"Yeah, and I'm talking about the hard stuff," Harry said, averting his eyes.

Porn clearly held a much more negative connotation for Harry than me. Having grown up with Barney, I assumed that all men spent most of their waking hours trolling the Web for nudie pictures. "Well, I certainly don't want to be the girl who drove you to porn," I remarked dryly.

"So you'll do it?"

"Yeah, okay."

"Right now?"

"Um, sure."

"You don't need any prep time?"

"No, do you?"

"I don't think so," Harry said, unsure of himself. "Well, maybe a minute to get a mint and a . . . condom."

"Good thinking; can I have one as well?" I asked before quickly clarifying, "A mint, that is. Why would I need my own condom?" I was pretty sure I wouldn't need one, but to be honest, I was not positive how the mechanics of sex worked.

Harry ignored me and grinned. "I'm so excited to do it."

I smiled back gamely, but I can't say that I shared his enthusiasm for sex. It was more that I was about to turn twenty-three and I was embarrassed by my virgin status. Women are more like men than they realize, or at least dorky women are.

"Should I turn off the TV?" Harry asked as he popped an Altoid.

"No, leave it on," I said strategically, knowing a little eye candy in the form of Tom Paris would be helpful. Five minutes later, it was over. It was surprisingly painless and inconsequential. I didn't feel like a woman. I didn't have an orgasm. I didn't even take my bra off. However, on the bright side, I didn't graduate a virgin. Perhaps I did have an FG after all. Technically, she had delivered a boyfriend and sex. Maybe she just needed her meds increased or her glasses fixed. A farsighted FG—it kind of made sense, in a pathetic sort of way.

Within a few weeks of graduation, both Harry and I returned to our parents' homes in Ohio. Harry still hadn't found a job to his liking, while I was lucky enough to have been offered an apprenticeship in the lab at Werner Research Institute analyzing human and primate DNA. Harry wasn't at all bothered by his lack of employment; he was far too preoccupied with trying to have sex with me. He mentioned at least twice a day that he could borrow his mother's car any time the mood hit me. Not surprisingly, in the two weeks leading up to my birthday dinner, that mood never made an appearance.

Mother chose Benihana for my birthday dinner. She loved "exotic" cuisine, and for Ohio, Benihana is as exotic as it gets. The evening began with Mother's standard cocktails of strawberry wine coolers and a Costco vegetable platter at the house. After licking ranch dressing off celery sticks, Mother, Dad, Barney, Harry, and I piled into the brown Chrysler station wagon and headed for the "Hana." Once seated around the sizzling tabletop grill, our chef chopped, diced, and fried as we "oohed" and "ahhed." We didn't bother talking, as that was half the treat of the Hana; the chef's presence allowed us to comfortably ignore one another. Unfortunately, Mother broke the cardinal Hana rule of silence and tapped her glass to make a toast. She wobbled slightly while standing, mostly due to the vodka tonics she had consumed. Mother wasn't an alcoholic, but about three times a year she would induce the madness. My most vivid memory of her alcohol-induced insanity occurred when I was sixteen. Dispatched to pick up my parents from the airport after two weeks in Mexico, I discovered Mother drunk in a wheelchair. Dad followed silently behind her as the steward from Mexicana Airline requested that she never fly "Air Beano," as she referred to them, again. Alcohol tended to bring out the bigoted facets of her personality. Actually, any form of human contact did; alcohol simply provided a convenient scapegoat.

Smiling in a way that only drunk people can, Mother began the toast, ignoring the copious amounts of liquid swishing out of the tumbler and onto the sizzling grill below. "My daughter, a University of Pennsylvania graduate. I couldn't be more proud. I am so excited to have you back home in your old room with a real job. It's wonderful." Mother paused, allowing her joyful air to morph into a harsh expression. "Of course, as we celebrate, we must also prepare for the destruction that is coming." Mother sipped her vodka tonic loudly and then continued, "A quiet plague is sweeping this country; an epidemic so vicious that it could destroy the very fabric of the American family."

We stared at her, wondering if this was to be another say-no-to-drugs conversation. Mother was a staunch Republican who truly listened when Nancy Reagan told the country to "D.A.R.E. to say no." Mother even coined her own antidrug phrase: "Stay clean; try soap, not dope." She thought it was ingenious since it advertised both good hygiene and the antidrug sentiment. She was dumbfounded when Ivory, Jergens, Irish Spring, and

Dove failed to respond to her queries about adopting this marketing campaign.

Mother prepared to continue her speech, pulling her fake glasses to the edge of her nose. Then, in a dramatic gesture we had not seen before, she took off her glasses.

"All across this beautiful bastion of democracy there are middle-aged, overweight, balding men who understand that their glory days are over. Up until now, they have been satisfied with their wives, their families, their suburban existence."

At this point, we realized that even for Mother, the toast was bizarre. Barney, who rarely showed emotion away from his computer screen, looked genuinely concerned.

"Tiny, little, flexible Orientals are descending upon this country, stealing our middle-aged men. We are in the throes of a geisha invasion. They don't want the young ones. They want the ones with retirement funds. So you can look the other way, but believe me, they are coming and they are armed!"

The first question that came to mind was "Armed with what?" I imagined an infantry of sexy Asian (I have told Mother many times that *Oriental* is only used to describe carpets) women landing at Cleveland International with garter belts, heels, and maybe a dildo or two. Before I could even finish the perverted thought, Dad interrupted in his usual monotone voice. "I'm leaving Mother for Sarah."

"Who's Sarah?" Barney screeched. "Did you meet her online? It's all my fault! I shouldn't have brought DSL into our lives," he cried as he banged his fists on the table.

Ignoring Barney's flair for the dramatic, I mumbled, "Ming. He's talking about Ming." Sarah was Dad's secretary at Allstate Insurance. She was Filipina, but Mother believed her to be Chinese and, therefore, called her Ming. Mother thought it was particularly funny to tell Ming that life should be taken with "a grain of rice" every time she called the office.

There wasn't enough rice in the world to make the situation any better. Barney asked for the check. Harry, who had continued eating throughout the speech, asked for a doggy bag. He hated to waste food, especially when someone else was paying. As we walked to the car, a family destroyed, Harry whispered in my ear, "I've got Mom's minivan for the night."

"That really isn't...," I started to respond before giving up. I couldn't articulate a response for such an insensitive and inappropriate invitation.

"I'm talking removable seats," Harry continued.

I wanted to scream in his face, but I couldn't. A profound sense of loss had settled over me since Dad's announcement. This was it. This was my life, and no fantasies or dreams could change it. For the first time in over a decade, I looked at my reflection in the car window. I expected to see a stranger. After years of avoiding mirrors, surely my face must have changed and matured, but it hadn't. I was the same. The round contours, saggy skin, and acne remained. I was still Weird Fat Bear, and it was clear that I always would be.

Hello Fatty,
FG isn't coming. I have no faith in me, in my parents, in Harry, and certainly not in FG. If FG hasn't stepped in by now, she must not exist. I am alone.
                                                              —Anna

Silently weeping on the crushed velvet seat cover of my parents' car, I knew I had to change or die. I couldn't allow myself to rot away in Ohio. I needed to reinvent myself as best I could. I didn't have a list of places to go, but I had seen enough movies to know that New York was the Mecca of reinvention. Even if I failed, it had to be better to fail in New York than in Norfolk, Ohio.

That night, Dad packed his stuff while Mother screamed and Barney cried. Barney had never been good with change, which explained his inability to move out of the house. Harry and I sat on the curb in front of my house, pretending not to hear the implosion of my family. The fact that it was my birthday had completely slipped my mind in light of the current situation.

"You know, I haven't given you your gift yet."

"That's okay, I'm not really in the mood," I sighed.

"Are you in the mood for anything else?" Harry asked with particular emphasis on the word *anything*.

"I don't think so," I mumbled, staring at the concrete beneath my ugly brown shoes.

"The third row pulls right out, makes it feel like a real bed back there."

He simply could not comprehend my lack of interest in seven minutes of screwing in the back of his mom's minivan. He didn't care that my birthday had been ruined by my parents. He didn't care that I was emotionally destitute. He wanted to get his needs met. A quiet rage bubbled in me, directed at Harry, my family, and all of Ohio.

"Harry, we're breaking up, effective immediately."

"What? I don't understand!" Harry exclaimed. "We're perfect for each other, Anna." That was the sad part. Harry really thought this was the whole me, a pliable, easygoing girl who enjoyed eating, studying, sex, and little else. To Harry, this was the good life. To me, it was a one-way road to obesity and suicide. Looking into his large and incredibly vapid eyes, I didn't have the heart to tell him that I hated him. I hated him for being a mirror, showing me exactly what I had become.

"I'm moving, Harry. I can't bear to be here."

"Where are you going?"

"New York," I answered, knowing that voicing it aloud would make it so. I watched his mind work over-time to comprehend the situation. I noticed a flicker of hope in his eyes and immediately felt the need to snuff it out. "I can't do the long-distance thing. It's too hard...too painful," I lied.

"*Oh, Mr. Fred, more plum sauce,*" Mother hollered from inside the house in a horrendous Chinese accent.

"What about your job?" Harry asked, ignoring Mother's screams.

"There are research facilities in New York, too."

"Okay," Harry said quietly.

"Okay," I nervously reciprocated, unsure if Harry was hurt, angry, or ambivalent.

"*Do you have rice in your ears? Hello? Can you hear me?*"

"Thank you for taking my virginity."

"You're welcome," I replied, embarrassed.

"Can I still keep the doggy bag?"

"Of course."

"*I bet your penis is already yellow!*"

Harry hugged me tightly before giving me a spastic kiss good-bye that felt like he was having an epileptic sei-zure in my mouth. I wanted to pull away and tell him he tasted like teriyaki sauce, but I didn't. He deserved this "romantic" good-bye. He deserved to think that he had really known me, even if the person he knew was merely a stand-in for the vibrant soul hidden beneath thirty layers of lard. If this was the best FG had to offer, then I would simply have to be my own FG.

PART

II

Finding FG

Chapter Four

Three days, eight slices of pizza, fourteen egg rolls, and one epiphany have passed since moving into my one-room studio in the Bushwick neighborhood of Brooklyn. With its communal bathroom down the hall, it isn't even as nice as my dorm room. Nothing says home like wearing flip-flops in the shower and using seat covers on the toilet. It is, however, cheap, and for an unemployed recent college graduate, cheap trumps all other considerations. Fortunately or unfortunately, I am on a block laden with junk food: six Chinese dives, four pizzerias, and two Spanish bodegas. I have ordered more delivery in the last three days than I have in my entire life combined. At home, Mother always worried that the deliverymen would return to ransack the house or sexually assault her. Even in my late teens, Mother didn't deem me worthy of being sexually assaulted by burglars. But I digress. The point is, I have holed up in my one-room snack parlor with saturated fats. This behavior is counterproductive to the whole change-my-life thing. However, the brutality of my epiphany necessitated a few days of emotional eating.

After securing my studio apartment, I wandered the streets of Manhattan, eyes wide, brimming with optimism. I walked under the arch in Washington Square Park, remembering all the times I had seen it in films. I salivated over cupcakes in Magnolia Bakery's window, ate a very expensive salad at Cafe Cluny, which I was disappointed to hear had nothing to do with the actor, and perused reading material at McNally Jackson books before exiting to continue pretending to be a New Yorker. A few blocks down, at the corner of Chunky and Lard Ass, I paused to look up and assess the civilians. Within three seconds, it hit me: I was never going to fit in because I was fat. F.A.T. Obviously, I have long been aware of my status as a fatty. The fact that my stomach acts as an awning for my lower body is hardly news. The epiphany was not that I was fat but rather how incredibly fat I was. By Midwestern standards, I am fat, but by Manhattan standards, I am a card-carrying member of the Obese Ladies Who Make Richard Simmons Cry Club. The female population of Manhattan is so thin that they have raised my body mass index level by 50 percent. And to make matters worse, they are a great deal more sophisticated and better dressed. How could such rampant skinniness be possible? After a day of looking at apartments and periodic window-shopping, the only rational conclusion I could come to was that women must forgo food in this city for rent and clothes. While digesting the information, I realized the only rational reaction was to drown my inadequacies in a three-day food bender.

Hello Fatty,
If you see FG, if she exists, tell her to go fuck herself!
—Anna
P.S. Sorry for the profanity. It's the junk talking.
And if FG does actually exist, tell her I am
sorry and that I love her—and need her.

On the second day of my junk food bender, I woke to a gurgling stomach, one of many ramifications of digesting my body weight in processed foods with artificial colors and unpronounceable chemicals. Somewhere between kung pao pork topped with Funyuns and pizza dipped in ranch dressing, I sent a half-coherent e-mail to my former statistics professor, Tom Steterson. Having been his TA for two years, he knew me personally, but more important, he too struggled with lard. Cruelly, students often referred to him as Professor Cantseehisownfeeterson. Clearly, I did not participate in such taunting. Anyway, with my newfound understanding of Manhattan's strict weight and fashion requirements, I was in dire need of professional guidance. As a hefty man with an impressive career, I assumed he was well versed in navigating the business world as a fatty. In an effort to keep Steterson on my good side, I smartly removed the "fatty" reference from my e-mail.

Two days later, I rub my bloated stomach, reminiscing about the three full days of solitary competitive eating. If only I could be proud of such an accomplishment. I check my e-mail while stifling a Cheetos-scented yawn. My inbox has two messages, both equally important. The first is from Phatbands, an innovative lap band that curbs appetite while sending sonar pulses to the muscles' memory cells, toning the body without exercise. For a brief moment, I believe that science has finally caught up with my needs. Then I remember that medical achievements aren't typically announced through spam. Moving on, slightly dejected, I open Mr. Steterson's response. "Anna, I am thrilled to hear that you have landed in New York and admittedly am not surprised that you are struggling a bit to get your foot in the door. It's a tough city for introverts. I have taken the liberty of calling Martin Johnson, the head of the New York City Penn Alumni Group and a vice president at Goldman Sachs. He's a sharp man with an excellent eye for talent. He's expecting your call. All the best, Tom."

I am thrilled that Mr. Steterson felt comfortable enough to sign his e-mail Tom. More than the introduction at Goldman Sachs, I am energized by the thought that "Tom" can now be considered a friend. Addressing each other on a first-name basis is the foundation of friendship, or so I've heard. Bolstered by my new friendship, I call Martin Johnson's office, and to my surprise, they know who I am. The assistant even suggests an interview with human resources regarding an entry-level position. I accept, ecstatic. I'm heading to Wall Street! My business card will soon read *Anna Norton, Badass Broker.* I like the sound of that, and while I had always set my sights on a career in science, I have come to New York to change, so surely this is a step in the right direction. Now I can relax a bit and celebrate the new brokerage-bound, friendship-rich Anna!

Three semi-junk-food-filled days later, I travel down Broad Street in the Financial District, entering Goldman Sachs in a cheap, ill-fitting navy suit. The suit is less than stellar, but I don't mind. I have a job to claim. Once I've earned the right to answer phones and fetch coffees, I'll start amassing a sexy and sophisticated wardrobe. I will buy clothes that store clerks refer to as investments for their ageless style and high price. I am intoxicated by my life and my prospects. I'm not sure that this has ever happened. A small part of me wants to call my family and let them know that we aren't serotonin challenged and incapable of experiencing optimism, as previously thought. However, I think better of it.

A weathered and grumpy human resource executive sits across from me, skeptically perusing my résumé. The deep crevices below his mouth speak to his proclivity for frowning. Normally such a persnickety old man would be enough to make me turn on my scuffed pumps and dash out of the building. But not today. I'm far too excited about my future to care about some near-suicidal executive. I don't even mind if he offs himself, as long as he puts my start paperwork through first. Lowering his glasses to the end of his nose as Mother does, Scott Lantern looks up at me with a scowl. "Most of our trainees have a business or finance background."

"Yes, I assumed as much, but with all due respect, Mr. Lantern, a degree in molecular biology from the University of Pennsylvania along with a 4.0 grade point average undoubtedly demonstrates my superior work ethic and intellectual abilities. I have no doubt whatsoever that I am equipped to analyze market trends and compose investment strategies."

Scott Lantern continues to stare at me over his glasses, his face a mélange of misery and resentment. "How are your interpersonal skills? This can be a very stressful environment; sensitive people are not encouraged to pursue employment here, as they rarely last the day, if you get my drift."

"I definitely get your drift," I say enthusiastically. "My nickname at Penn was...Lizard Skin. I take nothing personally." Why did I choose Lizard Skin as a nickname? It's so unflattering. He probably thinks I have psoriasis. I should have claimed to have a high-functioning form of Asperger's syndrome.

"Uh-huh," Scott says, nodding. "Well, I feel the need to warn you that the boys here can be a bit rough."

"I can handle it," I say with a confident nod that sets only a few chins aquiver.

"All right then, before I begin the formal interview, I like to take prospective employees to meet a few of the trainees. It lets you get a feel for the place. Follow me."

Scott Lantern walks like a boxer preparing to enter the ring: strong, hard, and aggressive. Assistants and brokers move out of his way as he navigates a maze of cubicles and ringing phones. He pauses before an open door, grunts something, and enters the office. I follow him, but not before noticing an assistant's sleek and wireless headset. I yearn to stomp around my corner office with a headset, yelling mean and nasty things in between the requisite "buy!" and "sell!" Scott nods toward three attractive and well-dressed young men.

"Morgan Atterson, Jonathan Door, and Eric Smith," Scott smiles. "Three of our top trainees, all Harvard graduates. This is Anna Norton, a candidate for traineeship and a recent graduate of Penn."

"Nice to meet you," Morgan, Jonathan, and Eric offer flatly, holding out their hands.

"Nice to meet you as well," I say, shaking hands with each one of them.

"Scott," Morgan says with a snicker, "is this because of the Tiffany thing?"

"No," Scott responds sternly before turning to me. "Anna, wait outside. I have a few more people for you to meet, but I need to make sure they're in."

"Um, okay." I turn to the trainees. "Bye. Hope to see you guys around real soon," I trill optimistically while heading for the door.

The three men don't respond. Instead they smile insidiously, as if enjoying an inside joke. Oh, how I will love being part of an office, sharing jokes and smirks about bosses. I can see it now: hordes of smartly dressed men and women stopping by my cubicle to share lighthearted gossip. They will even call me Annie as a term of endearment. Occasionally while walking the halls, I will hear people whisper, "I can't wait to tell Annie." Distracted by thoughts of my new life, I lean against the office door.

"If you don't stop boning all the hotties, Scott's going to keep hiring fatties," Eric's voice carries into the hallway from the office.

This brings me back to reality quickly, dare I say too quickly. I have the emotional bends.

"That last chick was definitely to punish me. I've never seen anything quite so hideous," Morgan says.

"Barely even human!" Jonathan chimes in, and the three men dissolve into laughter and high fives.

Here marks the spot where Miss Anna Norton dies of mortification. My face flushes, and a thick sweat moustache grows above my lip. Scott returns and beckons me to follow him. "Okay, Anna, they're ready."

I can't move. I can't respond. Scott stares as a tsunami

of misery engulfs me. Tears poke through my mascara-covered lashes. I'm not even fit to be used as a form of punishment; I'm a fat ass crying in public. It's pathetic, a testament to my weak character and inability to hack it in this city. Scott rubs his forehead with a look of resignation; he's clearly been here before.

"Lizard Skin," Scott says while handing me a tissue, "there's another elevator around the corner."

I want to say thank you, but I can't. My voice box disappears along with all remnants of self-esteem. Moving quickly toward the elevator, every inch of flaccid skin electrifies, confirming the awful truth. I am disgusting, not just to myself but to the world. I am ashamed to exist and mortified to have thought that I could survive in such a place. I am the person who people mock and sneer at behind her back. People like me can't change; we can only hide. I must return to Ohio and the heartbreaking truth I have tried to escape. I must own my caste and the arranged marriage with the misery that comes with it.

After putting down a deposit and first and last month's rent on the cheapest apartment in four papers, charging large quantities of junk food to my "emergency only credit card," I am nearly broke. I never entertained the possibility of wanting to return home, so I took no measures to plan for such an occasion. I am totally alone. A phone call to Mother is out of the question. She would fish my overwhelming failure out of me, then force me to listen to her gut-wrenching disappointment. The phone call is more than I can handle. I would rather temp for two weeks and return home with stories of job offers and an epiphany about the importance of living near your family. I simply cannot stomach watching my failure reflected back in her eyes. I will lie with grandeur about my New York escapades before squirreling myself away to recover from this horrible ordeal. Then, when ready, I will reach out to Harry with the promise of a meal at Red Lobster and sex in his mother's minivan. I pray that his cellulite-ridden arms haven't found a new fatty to hold.

Chapter Five

In a state of extreme stress and mild hysteria, I waddle out of the Financial District in search of a temp agency. Thoughts of FG and the sliver of optimism I clung to earlier make me cry even harder. There is a pain in my chest, a physical manifestation of melancholy. "Please... please...please...," I mumble, pushing past people on the crowded street. Next to a bodega, I spot my saving grace, Apple One Employment Agency.

Barging through the door without a résumé or semblance of mental stability is rather imprudent, but I cannot control myself. An older woman sitting behind a cheap fake wood desk spots me and immediately states, "No public restroom. Try Quiznos."

"I'm here to get a job...any job. I graduated from the University of Pennsylvania with a degree in molecular biology," I say, wiping the snot from my nose onto my hand.

"I'll let you know if I hear of any molecular gigs," the woman deadpans.

"I'm serious," I plead. "You can call them."

"Them? All those molecular scientists out there?"

"University of Pennsylvania."

"Sure, I'll just call the dean. He'll know you?"

"Actually, he doesn't know me, but the office has

records. I usually have a résumé on me, but I left the last copy at Goldman Sachs."

"Ah, at Goldman Sachs? Let me guess; they needed a molecular biologist?"

"They called me fat," I wail, taking a seat in front of the woman's desk.

"I always get the crazies," she mutters to herself.

"I'm sorry, I need a job. Really, I'm not crazy, just fat."

"Stop crying...please...no one hires crybabies."

"Or fatties," I stutter, holding back tears.

"So, you'll take any job?" the woman says with a smirk. I nod, and the woman stands and turns the corner. Tears continue to well up in me, exploding down my bulbous cheeks every three to five seconds. My vision blurs desks, lamps, and people into one crazy color scheme as I choke on my sadness.

"Lady?" I hear the woman say. I immediately wipe my tears and swallow my spit. Before me is the same large woman I had only seconds ago spoken to, but oddly it's not her that my eyes focus on. Down the hall, bathed in a flood of afternoon light, complete with a golden halo, a woman approaches. Dressed all in white, she raises her left hand in the air and points to the sky with a pen. In that moment, the woman's sleek silver pen eerily resembles a wand. Well, at least to me.

"Lady? Hello?" the temp woman hollers, breaking my focus on my possible FG. "Here's a piece of paper. Write me your résumé, include that Harvard stuff—"

"I went to Penn, not Harvard, although I did get in there," I say proudly through my haze of humiliation.

"Just write it down. Company policy: no résumé, no job. And you can commit to a year?"

"Of course," I respond, imagining disappearing after cashing my first and only paycheck.

"I may actually have a place that's right for you," she says with a hint of menace. "I think you're just what she's looking for. You're willing to work for minimum wage, right?"

"As long as no one calls me fat, sure."

"Excellent."

"What's the job?" I ask tentatively. Not that it would matter—I'll take anything, especially since it's only a temporary humiliation en route to a lifetime of the same.

"Caterer's assistant. You're meeting her at the kitchen in thirty minutes."

"I should change and get a real copy of my résumé—"

"You don't have time," she interrupts. "I'll photocopy this; it will have to do," she says, holding up the legal pad on which I wrote my résumé. "Here's the address. And if she doesn't hire you, don't come back—and that goes for her, too."

"For her, too?" I repeat back with surprise.

"Yeah, you're the eighth placement we've made this year."

That can't possibly be a good sign.

Two weeks, I remind myself while riding the industrial elevator in a Lower East Side building. I only need to stay here two weeks, and then I can quietly recede into my familial misery in Ohio. It's less time than most kids stay at camp. I can do it. Plus, my placement in a food-related industry is very reassuring. If necessary, I can steal food and engage in secret eating in the bathroom to calm my nerves. I stop at a steel door with a small plaque that says D&D Catering. I wipe away any remnants of mascara from beneath my eyes and knock. I hear someone walking on the other side of the door, stopping to gaze through the peephole. "I'm from the agency," I blurt out. "My name is Anna Norton."

I hear the familiar sound of a deadbolt turning.

"Hello," the woman says, eyeing me up and down.

I take a breath and step back, shocked. "You're... you're... you're my FG," I stammer ridiculously, staring at the woman I watched from afar at the temp agency. She's casually sophisticated, dressed in a white linen dress with her soft golden brown locks pulled into a bun, displaying large diamond earrings.

"Your what?"

I continue to stare at her, dumbfounded. In a city this big, to see the same stranger twice in one day. Could this be the celestial sign I've been waiting for?

"Weren't you... aren't... you, did I just see you back at the agency?"

"Yes, I came back to meet you. What did you just call me? FG?" she asks suspiciously.

"It's an abbreviation for... fute grane. It means 'interview' in Dutch," I lie poorly.

"Are you Dutch?"

"No... I thought you were Dutch..."

"My name is Janice Delviddio. Does that sound Dutch to you?"

"Must have been the woman's accent at the temp agency... sounded very Flemish..."

"Where's your résumé?"

I hand her the photocopy of my "résumé."

"Is this some kind of a joke? I get it, they're punishing me for having high standards." Exasperated, Janice opens the door wider and motions for me to come in. A strange calm settles over me as I accept the presence of FG. I can't shake the image of her bathed in warm light and carrying a wand.

"So you went to Penn?" Janice says, inspecting the scrawled document before her.

"Yeah. I don't usually handwrite my résumé, but you see . . . ," I say before pausing to inspect the woman's expression. My FG suddenly looks decidedly disappointed in me, as if she deserves better. What is going on? My FG is rejecting me.

"Is everything okay?" I stutter under her harsh glare.

"Not really, but I don't have much of a choice."

Behind Janice is a professional kitchen with stainless steel appliances and miles of counter space. There is a small sitting area set up between two framed vintage posters. The large loft space looks remarkably similar to a set for a cable TV cooking show.

"Nice place. I, um, well, I don't know a lot about cooking," I manage to get out, hoping that Janice will stop dissecting me with her emerald green eyes. "But I eat a lot, if that helps. Actually, not a lot, I may have a metabolism issue," I burble maniacally, "or maybe something with my thyroid."

"A thyroid condition, you say?" Janice asks warily.

"Or a slow metabolism."

"Interesting. And your doctor told you this?"

"Well," I swallow hard, wondering how much worse my day could possibly get, "um, not exactly."

"What exactly does 'not exactly' mean?"

"It varies, but in this case it means...no."

"Do you have a problem with lying?"

"Not at all. I didn't technically lie. I said that I may have an issue with my metabolism or thyroid—"

"And you came to this assessment because you're fat."

I don't think I want an FG anymore. At least not one who calls me fat.

"She said you wouldn't call me fat. She promised."

"Sweetie," Janice says with sudden compassion, "I'm an FF."

"A what?" I ask, astonished. Is she owning up to being my FG but disguising it with a different letter?

"A Former Fatty. I've been there. Please don't cry."

"It's just that this is the second time today I've been called fat. First the guys at Goldman Sachs, and now you."

"Anna, I used to be fat, so I can call you that. Making fun of your own kind is an exception to the rules. I promise."

I gape at the stylish woman before me, unable to process her remarks. Did she just tell me she used to be fat?

"This is America; eating is the national pastime," she continues, smiling at my confusion as if to say "yes, I know, hard to believe someone as stunning as I once looked like you." She says, of course, nothing of the kind, merely continues her sociological discourse. "We think the land of plenty refers to eating Carl's Jr. and McDonald's in our cars."

"I love Carl's Jr.," I mutter.

"I used to eat two Western Bacon Cheeseburgers, onion rings, and french fries for lunch. Trust me, I understand the appeal. Where are you from?"

"How do you know I am not from here?"

"You're wearing white socks with a navy suit and black shoes."

"I guess I'm not very stylish." She doesn't disagree. I wipe my face, feeling outrageously self-conscious and exhausted after the crying marathon.

"I was born and raised in Ohio," I say quietly.

"Okay, Anna, here's the deal. I need an assistant, someone to pick up stuff, chop, and basically help me do what I do. I specified someone with a college degree, because after eight assistants, I know that a base level of intelligence is needed to follow my instructions precisely."

I stare at her, unsure if she expects me to say something. I graduated from Penn with a degree in molecular biology. I am sure I can comprehend her directions.

"So if I write out directions, you would feel comfortable taking a short walk to pick up a few items?"

Two weeks, I think. "Yes, I can handle that."

"Excellent," Janice says softly as she grabs for a pen. "Let's begin."

Chapter Six

Janice is a liar. A big, massive liar. Perhaps even the largest liar in the five boroughs. Plus she has the geography skills of a blind man. I have stained my pits yellow following these directions. Fortunately, you can't tell because my suit is navy, but I can feel it. I'm a mess of perspiration from traipsing around Manhattan, walking in a series of interlocking circles as I faithfully follow her maps. It's almost as if she's trying to confuse me. These directions took me around Tompkins Square Park three times, each time in a wider circle, before heading to the West Village, then back to the Lower East Side. All the while, these damn plastic bags cut into my arm, stopping the circulation. I wouldn't be surprised if my arms were the color of eggplant by the time I finish. *Two weeks,* I chant as my mantra, *two weeks.*

The bags of venison, Polynesian basil, and Napa Valley wines fall to the floor of the elevator as I slump heavily against the wall. I stare longingly at the control panel, salivating over the large red stop button. I would gladly spend the night in here so I could cool down and take a nap. The doors open, setting me free to trudge down the hall with my arms full, stopping only to throw my body against Janice's front door. "Uhhhh," I grunt at Janice as she opens the door, wearing a pristine white apron. What kind of a chef keeps an apron clean while cooking?

"Oh, Anna, you must be exhausted. Drop the bags. Come sit down; I've made you a snack."

The wine clinks against the cement floor, miraculously remaining intact as I collapse on a wooden chair with hair pasted to my forehead. Janice places a chilled bottle of water and a bowl of fresh fruit and yogurt in front of me. I guzzle the water untidily, droplets flowing out both sides of my mouth. She watches me with the love of a concerned parent, which weirds me out, especially considering how harsh she was earlier.

"Great job, Anna! Water is good for your digestive system. You know, people often eat when they're really just dehydrated."

"Good to know," I pant. "By the way...your directions...fucking sucked! When did you move here?" I ask.

"Must be fifteen years now."

"And you still haven't figured out your way around the city? I was walking in circles, attempting to decipher your convoluted directions."

"Listen, Anna, I'm going to level with you."

I recoil in terror, squinting my eyes and hunching my shoulders in preparation.

"Don't worry, I am not going to call you fat...again. However, if you're working for me, I see it as my job to...well...to improve you. Smooth out the edges. And I say this as a Former Fatty—someone who's walked in those size-eighteen pants. I've been turned down for jobs because my ass was too big. They didn't say it, but I knew it, so if you're working for me, I see it as a disservice to let you stay this way. The world can be pretty mean."

Technically, this is what I've always wanted—a beautiful woman to take me under her wing and make me over in her image—but something about it makes me uneasy.

"I know you can't believe me right now, but this is for your own good—and mine—since it doesn't really look good for caterers to have...you know...bigger employees. It makes people think the food is fattening."

"But really, you're doing this for *my* good?" I say to Janice, unsure what to make of this Betty Crocker crackhead.

"I used to be at least one and a half times your size. Trust me; I know what I am talking about. The world is a hell of a lot meaner to people with weight issues, and I'm not talking about simply calling you the *f* word to your face. I'm talking about all the stuff they say behind your back. I want to rescue you from all that, Anna. Now then; take another liter of water, and I'll see you tomorrow at nine a.m. sharp."

I allow her to push me toward the door, wondering what all this water is supposed to do, other than make me uncomfortable on the way home. I'm too tired to care. I don't even bother saying good-bye; I just wave from the hallway.

My legs are sore. With each step, I remember that building muscle is achieved through tearing tissue. Red and stringy masses of flesh, from my heels to my groin, pound under the pressure of minuscule fissures. Most notably painful are the soles of my feet, covered in quarter-sized blisters. Running a close second are the red sores caused by the rubbing together of my thighs. These raw spots sting as they scratch against the rough polyester of my pants. I hobble toward my front door, lusting for the opportunity to lie down and take off my clothes. My muscles, skin, and mind desperately crave stillness. Slamming the door behind me, I remove my clothes and collapse facedown on the futon. Without moving the rest of my body, I extend my left arm, grab the phone, and hit redial.

"Hello, Wong's Garden."

"I need egg rolls, about fifteen . . . no, make it twenty . . . and some ribs. This is an emergency, so make it snappy," I say, lying naked, spread-eagle on the bed.

All life-changing plans have been abandoned, allowing me to gorge without any guilt. In a sense, I am on vacation for the next two weeks. A respite before I return to my humble origins. As any good travel magazine will tell you, sampling the local fare is half the fun. Plus, I won't be able to partake in any Chinese cuisine once back with Mother. Post Dad leaving Mother for Ming, Chinese food is frowned upon heavily in the Norton house. Any consumption of kung pao chicken, Szechuan beef, or hot and sour soup is considered fraternizing with the enemy.

I wake the next morning and begin my preparations to avoid the agonies of the day before. I treat the sores on my upper thighs with Neosporin before pulling on a pair of black stretch pants and a baggy sweatshirt. Band-Aids are applied liberally before I place my never-before-worn running shoes on my feet. Much to my surprise, the shoes still fit. I bought them during a bout of optimism at the mall freshman year at Penn. By the time I returned to my dorm room, all interest in running had died, and the shoes remained in my closet for the next four years. They will definitely come in handy now.

After exiting the subway near Janice's Lower East Side kitchen, I pause to allow strangers to scrutinize me.

I welcome their judgment of me as a poorly dressed tourist because that's exactly what I am. I no longer strive for more; I was born a fatty in the Midwest and I will die a fatty in the Midwest. I have seen the light, and it is sending me back to the dark, because that's where I belong.

"Wow," Janice says as she opens the door, "are you going to the gym, 'cause I think you're late for the step class—in 1985. This outfit is . . . awful. It's worse than yesterday's suit."

"Nice to see you again, too. And yes, I am sporting a casual look today, but I felt it more appropriate considering all the running around you made me do yesterday. My body is not quite . . . used to it, so—"

"Fair enough. This level of movement is new to you. I understand that," Janice says matter-of-factly. "But stretch pants?"

"Well, they're comfortable," I say as my cheeks darken dramatically with shame. I can't bear the idea of crying in front of this woman again, yet I can't stop the water from welling beneath my eyelids. I am so tired of the indignity of being me. This is why I must leave New York; I need to go where fat asses in stretch pants don't surprise people. I need to be allowed to hate myself quietly without people bringing my inadequacies to my attention.

"Oh, no. Why are you crying?" Janice asks with a wrinkled forehead.

"I'm not," I protest before realizing that I am. The tears I tried valiantly to hold in have exploded onto my face. I am powerless. Powerless to control my tears. Powerless to control my weight and body. Powerless to fit into, let alone afford, appropriate clothes.

"Anna? Anna! You're freaking me out. What is it?"

I can only point to my pants and speak unclearly, "They're all I have. The other stuff gives me blisters. I'm so ashamed..."

Janice looks simultaneously annoyed and heartbroken. "Never, ever, cry over stretch pants. Actually, never cry over clothes. Come on, I'm going to teach you a trick," Janice says, grabbing her quilted handbag off the counter.

"Please, don't make me go out in public," I whine. "Everyone will point at me."

"Okay, you need a reality check. You are not Michael Jackson or one of his freaky kids with the veils on their heads; people aren't going to stare at you. They may look and wonder where you're visiting from, but that's it. Trust me, whatever happens, I will handle all interaction with the outside world. Here, put on my sunglasses. Let's go," Janice commands.

I follow Janice out of the building, staring at the nearby Williamsburg Bridge through her expensive glasses, wondering if she'd be so kind as to push me off it. Unfortunately, we head in the other direction.

"You're not taking me to Jenny Craig, are you?"

"No."

"Weight Watchers?"

"No."

"Anywhere with a scale? I don't think I could handle that."

"No scales," Janice says firmly.

If she's lying, so help me God, I'll smother her smooth face in my flabby stomach. Rage boils within me as I imagine Janice smiling patronizingly as she points to the group scale at Fatty Fucks. She will beg for air, but I won't stop until her body falls limp, suffocated to death by my fat rolls. Janice abruptly turns onto East Broadway, intersecting throngs of iPod-listening, chicly dressed people before detouring into the Gap. Immediately, remorse over my plan to kill her takes hold. I hover on the verge of a breakdown, both physically and mentally. This is how I live my life.

"Regardless of whether you're heavy or not, everyone should stick to solid, basic colors: black, white, gray, beige, and navy. However, given your body type," Janice says delicately, "white and beige should only be used as accents, understand?"

I nod my head, still reeling with disgrace from my previous thoughts. Janice absorbs my nod, then takes off, pulling dark-colored items off the racks like a sniper. My eyes trained to the floor, I follow Janice's black flats around the room. I simply cannot handle making eye contact with any of the other patrons. Recognizing their stifled laughter or curiosity over my dated outfit would break me.

"Anna?" Janice asks nicely. "Are you ready?"

I pull my head up slowly, noting we're in the dressing room. My heart drops to my stomach, landing in a nasty bath of bile. I don't want to take my clothes off, even if I'm alone in the room. All those mirrors allow me to see what others do when walking behind me.

"I don't think I can do it. I just, I—"

"Yes, you can. I purposely chose items with some give," Janice says sternly, handing me the first outfit. Unable to fight her, I agree and enter the dressing room. My eyes stay focused on the dirty gray carpet as I remove my clothes. Not once do I lift my gaze to see my reflection in the mirror. I merely pull on the black, low-waisted trousers, white T-shirts, and plain black sweater. Exiting the room, I hear Janice gasp.

"Yes, now we're talking," she says happily.

I look up, gaining encouragement from her voice and turning toward the mirror. I am still fat with bad skin, but I admit, I appear more dignified. "Wow," I say stupidly.

"It's a simple trick. Never try to hide the flaw, just dress it better. Even after I started dieting, I had months and months of fat left on me. It became more painful as I started really looking at my body, so I decided if I was going to be fat, I would be well dressed and fat."

"Yeah, you're right," I say with a grin before something dawns on me: money. I can't afford these clothes, never mind how much better I look. To the best of my knowledge, Gap doesn't offer scholarships for the weight- and financially challenged.

"Stop, stop worrying. I'm buying. Consider it a signing bonus."

"Oh, no . . . I was—" I begin to lie.

"Stop. It was all over your face. Just say thank you."

"Thank you," I say.

I've decided to give Janice and New York another chance.

Chapter Seven

The Janice regime consists of walking everywhere, from the newly gentrified Battery Park to the stuffy Upper East Side in search of spices, organic produce, and occasionally her laundry. Mostly, I contemplate ways to ask Janice for a raise while trudging through the streets in all-black ensembles of trousers, loafers, cotton T-shirts, and cardigans. Shockingly, the job is much easier now that I have appropriate clothes for blending into the monochromatic city. Janice has also introduced me to the mind-blowing line of Spanx tights and body shapers. They make my fat smooth, ironing out the unsightly lumps. I remain an overweight girl, but an improved one. Every day, I roll my eyes as Janice monitors my snacks, insisting that I follow her protein and vegetable regimen. I follow it when I am with her because frankly, it's easier than handling the guilt she piles on. Janice behaves like a highly involved parent, which is simultaneously comforting and annoying. As long as I can recall, I have been solely responsible for the monstrosity I have made out of my body. It's a relief to have another name on the deed to my distended ass. On the other hand, I profoundly resent being told what to do by someone who doles out paychecks like an allowance.

My desire to be a self-sufficient grown-up often bumps into Janice's controlling generosity. She genuinely enjoys having me around as a project, pal, and employee all in one. However, I see another self-serving motive beneath her perfectly microdermabrasioned skin. She needs me. No one else with my education, or even half my education, would do this job for minimum wage. I often picture Janice at home in her apartment in a chic West Village pre-war brownstone, translating my salary into Indian rupees. Surely she sleeps better knowing that my salary could support a family of twenty in rural India. It's not to say that Janice is cheap, because she's not. She's supplied me with multiple outfits from the Gap, all her choice, of course, and many accessories. She feeds me healthy foods and unlimited supplies of bottled water, all of which I appreciate. The bottom line is that Janice is a taskmaster who sticks to her ways, even outdated ones, such as paying people minimum wage to toughen them up and suss out their interests. The reality is that my ability to survive at the job has more to do with my cheap rent than anything else.

Feeling virtuous after eating a grilled chicken breast prepared by the health food Nazi, I board the L train with throngs of funky yet successful-looking Brooklynites. Most of them get off the L in Williamsburg, giving me room to regret drinking that last liter of water. Janice constantly pushes water on me, marking a chart every time I finish a bottle. "Do you really need to write down how much water I drink?" I ask in my "you're so lame" tone of voice.

"You are an investment. I keep track of all my investments. Stocks, bonds, art, and Anna."

"I feel so—"

"Important?"

"Not exactly," I respond honestly. "More like com-modified."

"Come on, Anna, you're part of my team now. You reflect on me and I reflect on you. Plus, you'll be happier. I cry a lot less now that I'm thin," Janice says with a wink of the eye.

Clearly, she realizes how asinine her "investment" conversation sounds, yet she says it. Part of me thinks I have wandered upon someone as lonely as I am, regardless of the fact that she's married to some supposedly fantastic guy. She enjoys me, and the focus I bring to her life, a little too much. Janice has found a safe and productive manner in which to channel her control issues. And I have found an FG and mother figure.

My own mother, it should be noted, always elicited a certain rebellion in me. Small things such as calling her the formal "Mother" were intended to irk her, although they didn't. Numerous times, I pointed out the uselessness of her glasses in front of strangers, but again she paid me no mind. In Janice, I have an involved guardian, one who my rebellions would deeply upset. Therefore, when falling off the wagon, I go to great lengths to cover it up. An estimated two times a week, I indulge my love of junk. Today as I charge up the subway stairs, a strong aroma dazzles my olfactory glands. I breathe out sharply, trying to regain a semblance of composure. Now that I am staying in New York for an extended period, I have made the decision to at least try to be a bit healthier. When I thought I was leaving in two weeks, it was a free-for-all of fried foods, but after the introduction to inexpensive style at the Gap, I'm pushing myself to lighten the burden of self-loathing. It's much more exhausting to hate myself and my body when my job forces me out in the world on a daily basis.

After hopping up the stairs from the subway, I stop in front of my favorite pizzeria. I have come to know many of the junk food dealers on the street personally, and as I peer through the plate glass window, I spot my man with the mole. He's the one who adds extra cheese to the pizza. Don't, I tell myself, picturing how remorseful I will feel after stuffing my face. On the other hand, this is a special occasion; the man with the mole is here. This doesn't happen every day. It's better than a sale. And no one passes on their favorite items when they're on sale, do they? If I don't eat the mole man's pizza, I will regret it. Maybe I'll only eat half the slice. Yes, that is a fabulous compromise. I won't feel quite as guilty, but I will still get to enjoy mole man's extra cheese. Of course, I will have to buy the whole slice, since they don't sell halvsies. "A slice of pepperoni," I tell the mole man, my mouth dripping with anticipation. "What days are you here?"

"Every day."

Why did I ask? I felt so much better when I believed this was a special occasion. Well, it's too late now; he's already handed me the slice. The tantalizing aroma of pepperoni, crisp cheese, and tangy marinara sauce distracts me. Dazed, I sit on a stool and fold the slice in half, letting the oil drip onto the paper plate. That must save a lot of calories. Buoyed by my calorie-cutting idea, I shove, swallow, and repeat. Drunk on pizza, I immediately order another slice. Once again, I fold the slice in half, drain the oil, shove, swallow, and repeat. When the second slice is done, I feel full.

Hello Fatty,
You are full. Actually, you were full before you even

started with the pizza, you fat ass. Stop eating. Stop eating. Stop eating, Fatty!!! Think of FG!! She'll be so disappointed, you nasty cow.

—Anna

I override my body's voice and order a third slice. I am now inebriated on fat. I've lost the ability to speak. I hit the counter with my fist, nod at mole man, and lay down three dollars. I fold the slice, drain the oil, shove, and swallow. After three slices, my stomach is swollen and painful. I wobble home with thoughts of mutilation and vomit. Ill, mentally and physically, I set my alarm to ensure I have enough time to wash off the pizza smell. The situation is analogous to a cheating man washing away the scent of his mistress before his wife gets home, except not nearly as exciting.

The communal bathroom is empty at 7:00, when I begin my degreasing session. I stand naked except for the shower sandals, massaging my hair and body aggressively, rinsing away any lingering pizza aroma. Seated on the L train, I perform a quick breath check. I worry that a burp or hiccup could ruin everything in a second, exposing my terrible lapse. I immediately decide to keep myself outside a four-foot radius around Janice.

"Hello," Janice yells out as I enter D&D.

"Hi," I meekly respond, watching her lay out fruit and black coffee. I look over my list of errands for the day, excited to leave as soon as possible. Janice watches me suspiciously, invisibly shelving her maternal role for that of the food bitch.

"Anna, what did you have for dinner last night?" she asks with studied casualness.

I should have prepared something; I was too preoccupied with the smell factor. "Oh…a lot of water…and
steamed…broccoli…with rice…brown rice," I stammer.

Janice places a piece of pineapple into her mouth, all
the while keeping her eyes trained on me. "How long did
you cook the rice?"

"Um…I would guesstimate that it was about ten
minutes," I stutter awkwardly. Rice! Why would I choose
rice? I've never made rice except for Uncle Ben's, which
cooks in the microwave.

"How many cups?"

"Um…three."

"Anna, if you ever get married, don't cheat. You are a
terrible liar."

Ignoring the true meaning of the comment, I ask, "Do
you think I'll get married?"

"What did you really eat for dinner?"

"Not that I'm obsessed with getting married, because
I'm not. I've never even bought a wedding magazine
before. I was just wondering if you thought I would…," I
trail off timidly.

"Chinese?"

"What? No!"

"Pizza?"

"Wha—"

"Pizza? Really?"

"Let me explain. I was tired after all the walking—"

"Fat people often struggle with exercise at first," Janice says directly.

"Janice, please don't use the *f* word!"

"The fact that you don't want me to say the word

fat shows how many issues you have with your fat. But hey, it's your fat, and if you want to pretend it's not there, adding to it with pizza, negating all the hard work we're doing, fine. Go ahead," Janice says patronizingly. "All I know is that when I was fat, I would have loved to have someone like me to help."

I don't have it in me to argue with her; there's no point. I mainline fruit as quickly as possible, answering with a hunk of pineapple hanging out the left side of my mouth.

"I'm sorry; it will never happen again."

"Hey, don't apologize to me. It's your ass," Janice replies coolly, adding to the errand list. I can already tell that she's going to punish me with an extra-strenuous day of walking. I hate her. I loathe her for making me feel bad and I despise myself because she's right. I hope she chokes on a piece of fruit so I can lecture her on the importance of chewing food properly. Who am I kidding? I have a history of swallowing food whole; I am in no position to discuss the importance of chewing. Somehow, my lack of chewing makes me even more annoyed with Janice, sparking a rebellion.

Two hours later, a lovely yellow cab drops me in front of Janice's building with grocery bags in hand. My thighs aren't raw. My heels aren't aching, and I am back an hour and a half early. Instead of the usual afternoon snack, I am greeted with a curious scowl.

"Drop the bags," Janice demands harshly.

"What?"

"Turn around and go back to each store and take a picture. My digital camera's on the desk. And leave your wallet here."

"Why?"

"I sent you out on walking errands, not cab errands."

"I paid for the cab myself, if that's what you are worried about."

"Anna, for the last time, I am trying to help you. Trust me, the world is a much nicer place without four chins and saddlebags, okay?"

Chapter Eight

F ood interrogation has become a regular part of the job, and as a result, I've actually lost a little weight. For someone of my girth, fifteen pounds doesn't translate to much; fewer indentations on my legs after removing my pants is the highlight. Most important, throughout the dietary cross-examinations, my ability to lie has not improved at all. And certainly not for a lack of trying. On nights I've been naughty, I toil tirelessly to perfect the cadence of my lie. In bed, I hold a mirror to study my facial expressions as I repeatedly tell the lie. By the end of the night, fatigue lulls me into believing that the fib is plausible. None of it matters, since Janice has a sixth sense with my stomach. I am convinced that Janice has x-ray vision, allowing her to discern the contents of my digestive track. That is the only explanation for her deft ability to tell when I've gone astray.

On this particular morning, Janice radiates an angelic beauty, with her golden brown locks falling neatly to her shoulders. In a black cashmere cardigan and a pencil skirt, she emanates kindness, but I know it is a front; Janice is searching for a small fissure to crack open and expose my food register. A tight knot forms in my stomach, but I force myself to stay calm. I breathe deeply through my nose, concentrating on my "truth." I read that sociopaths pass lie-detector tests by believing their own lie. I'm not a sociopath, simply a strong believer in method acting.

"Good morning, Anna," Janice says coldly.

Stay calm, I tell myself. Act normal. What do I usually do when she says hello? Greet her. Speak slowly. Keep my voice even. Remember, she can't prove I'm lying without a stomach pump.

"How are—" I begin to inquire, but Janice cuts me off.

"Dinner?"

This is it. The moment I have been waiting for, time to speak my "truth."

"Angel hair pasta. I diced some fresh tomatoes and added a drop of olive oil. Really delicious...and healthy. I didn't put any garlic in...because...I didn't want my breath to smell," I babble.

Silence. More silence. And even more silence. Does the silence speak to her disbelief or belief in my lie? Has my lying improved? Has all the practice paid off? A miniscule wave of relief passes over me as she crinkles her nose and beams caringly at me. She is going to congratulate me. Remember, don't act too surprised or grateful.

"Anna, sweet, lovely, Anna, your nose."

"My nose?" I ask curiously.

"Your nose is growing," Janice says firmly.

Janice's comment causes a sweat 'stache to form on my upper lip. With each passing second, her eyebrows rise a little more. I am at a crossroads; I can either continue the lie or admit my deception. I question whether I have what it takes to maintain the angel hair pasta position. Of course, facing Janice's wrath is hardly appetizing either.

"Fettuccine Alfredo," I mumble with shame. Why do I even bother? It's futile.

"Did you eat the whole thing?"

"Yes," I say guiltily.

I feel quite full as I swallow chunks of self-respect.

"Are you mad at me?" Janice asks with genuine concern.

"No, why would you say that?"

"We made it past the fifteen-pound mark, and now to go out and do this. It feels personal."

"Not at all. But Janice, losing fifteen pounds depressed me. I look exactly the same. Do you realize how fat you have to be to look the same after losing fifteen pounds?"

"I know, I know, but people are noticing. At the Adelman benefit, Juan told me you were starting to look like a heavier Janeane Garofalo. Now if that's not progress, what is?"

"Who is Juan? And how is being a fat Janeane Garofalo good?"

"He's the dishwasher, and he's about the height of your breasts, so he has a pretty good vantage point. For someone with no friends, you sure don't make much of an effort to learn anyone's names."

"I'm sorry, I thought his name was...okay, I never knew his name. Sorry."

"I understand, I do. However, you're still going to drink an extra liter of water and jump rope for as long as it takes me to prep the enchiladas."

"Okay, Janice," I say contritely.

Janice's obsession with my eating habits ceases while cooking, as she encourages me to taste everything. Of course, jump rope is mandatory on food-prep days. Only where pastries are concerned does Janice enforce a hardline policy of no tasting. Moreover, if a tray of baked goods is out, she watches it like a hawk, often re-counting the items several times an hour. It's silly, since I would never eat anything naughty while she is in a five-mile radius. I don't even want to *think* of what cruel and unusual punishment she would send my way.

Janice's uncanny ability to tell when I'm lying has forced me to contain all binge eating to Friday nights. The weekend is required to practice my "truth" before Monday morning's inquisition. The remorse of junk food and lying overwhelms me, filling pages in Hello Fatty on Saturday and Sunday.

> *Hello Fatty,*
> *It's been exactly seven days since my last grotesque bender of nachos with extra cheese, sour cream, and guacamole plus two strawberry milkshakes and a side of fries. I stare down at my stomach, imagining all the lumps of lard clogging my arteries and destroying my chances of ever having sex again. I worry that they will need a garbage can to contain my ashes after I am gone. I am thinking of specifying saving only a tiny amount of ashes in a small urn. I may not fit into much in life, but I sure as hell am not letting that happen in death.*
>
> *Sincerely,*
> *Anna, the Fattest Girl in the Tristate Area*

It's a sad state of affairs, but unfortunately, I can't stop. Sometimes late into the Friday feast, it actually hurts to cram food into my shrinking stomach, but I continue. Like an addict using to maintain, I balloon one night a week as part of a recurring exercise in masochism. Even the threat of Janice's examination doesn't stop the shove fest.

"Friday night dinner?" Janice asks, eyeing my lower body closely.

"Salad bar at Whole Foods," I say without any affectation.

"Which one?"

"Union Square," I respond without skipping a beat. Having the weekend to digest my crimes makes all the difference in the world.

"Paper or plastic?" Janice asks quickly, hoping to catch me off guard.

"Paper. Better for the planet."

Janice nods and rubs her chin like a character in a cartoon, perplexed by the situation. "Saturday breakfast?"

I passed the Friday night test! Onto Saturday! Stay calm. Show no emotion, or I will blow my cover.

After enduring an elaborate inquisition on my eating and drinking habits over the weekend, I begin my daily errands. I pass through the Village, before making my first stop at Balducci's, in Chelsea, then stopping at the organic produce mart, then onto a small butcher next to MSG, then Zabar's on the Upper West Side, and finally back to the Lower East Side. Janice wants me to exercise. All the time. Well, except when I'm drinking water. By the following Friday night, I'm salivating at the thought of my junk food bender. Seven days without junk is hard. By day four, I've got cramps; by day six, cold sweats; and by day seven, all of the above. I realize my weight loss would increase if I stopped binging, but I can't. Beyond the physical repercussions such as delirium tremens, total junk food eradication would leave me with a bleak mental reality. Without the promise of pizza, donuts, Doritos, and Oreos, what would I have to look forward to? As it is,

I have trouble making it to Friday evening, often twitching with anticipation all afternoon. By 4:30 or 5:00, the tantalizing proximity of the drug makes it near impossible to concentrate.

"Um, hey, I'm going to leave a little early today. You know, beat the Friday traffic," I mutter quietly.

"Is everything okay?" Janice asks skeptically.

"Yeah, of course."

"You seem a bit nervous. Paranoid, almost."

"Paranoid? Nervous? Me? Not at all. I don't want to be sandwiched between two smelly emos on the L train. Nothing paranoid about that. I'm protecting myself. I mean, really, who wants to rub elbows with stinkers."

"Okay," Janice says distrustfully. "Enjoy the roomy ride home. See you Monday."

Janice is onto me, I'm sure of it. My palms sweat intensely, causing my hand to slip off the subway's metal pole. Passengers crash into me as the car rocks along the tracks before stopping in the dark tunnel. Hundreds of feet below the East River, we wait, dripping all over one another. People moan with frustration and simmering panic as seconds turn to minutes. I remain lost in my own world, even as the train starts up again and my fellow riders cheer; I am unable to think of much beside Janice's peculiar expression when I left the office.

Once in my apartment, I think of all the different options available: pizza, eggplant parmigiana, donuts, egg rolls, and more. My fingers ache to dial, but something stops me. I am torn between two mes—the one who's emerging and the one I've always been. Even though I vowed to give up on the transformation, I can't deny that the tiny improvements I have seen have lit the torch of faith again. Maybe not a torch, but at the very least a match of faith is burning. I still yearn to be a regular girl eating cake on her birthday but declining the rest of the year. To be this girl, I must break up with junk food. However, I wonder if breaking up with food warrants one last night of sex before moving on. A farewell dinner, if you will, to signify the end of an era. I must share this monumental moment with someone. A close friend would be appropriate; unfortunately I only have one. It's moments like this that I wish I hadn't lost contact with Nut; then I wouldn't have to force my brother into the role of friend. Honestly, he's not very good at being an older brother, let alone a friend, but he's my only option for "sharing this moment."

"Hello?"

"Barney? It's Anna."

"Anna who?" Barney asks doubtfully.

"Anna your sister, Barney."

"What month is your birthday?"

"Why?" I respond with frustration. This is exactly why I don't call home more often; my family is far too weird.

"This is a security question; if you want to talk to me, you'll have to answer it."

"May."

"Hey Anna, what's happening?" Barney says warmly, immediately changing his tone.

"What's with the security question?"

"I had to abort a relationship with a lady, and she's been pretty desperate to get her man back," Barney says proudly.

"You were seeing someone?" I ask jealously.

"I've been seeing a lot of people, if you know what I mean."

"Wait, you mean you've been dating people? Did you get a standing reservation at Olive Garden for this parade of women?" I ask bitchily, suffocating on a mixture of shock and envy.

I guess all those years of practicing by himself have really paid off. It doesn't say much for me that a porn-obsessed fat dude living with his mother in suburban Ohio dates more than I do.

"I'm taking my time; don't want to rush into anything. Lots of talking and typing," Barney says cockily.

"Barn, have you *met* any of the women you're dating?"

"Anna, don't get bogged down by semantics. I'm a playah now; I gotta roll."

"Barney, don't talk like that, please. I'm embarrassed for you."

"I gotta go. Mother and I have a date at the cineplex."

"Wait, don't you want to know why I called?"

"Anna, I can't miss the coming attractions. It throws off the whole experience."

"Barney, I'm quitting junk food tomorrow," I proudly declare.

"10-4, Anna. Over and out."

My brother shouldn't be allowed to use the phone, as he is utterly incapable of communication. He cannot disengage from his own world of madness long enough to take in the magnitude of what I said: I, Anna Norton, have quit the junk! Well, I will be quitting the junk as soon as I finish my farewell dinner. Since Chinese food always leaves me craving more, I deem this the perfect first course.

"Wong's Garden," a man hollers on the other end. His accent reminds me of Mother's heinous Chinese impersonation. "What's your address?" After I give my address, he pauses, then chirps, "No take your order. Sorry, I know you on diet." Click.

I am tempted to call back and berate the man, but I decide it's a waste of time. Obviously, the man is a prankster. I don't have time for such people; I have a good-bye party to throw.

"Ray's Pizza."

"Hi, I'd like to order two medium cheese pizzas and three large sides of ranch dressing."

"Address?"

I state my building number and street name before he interrupts me, calling out to someone, "Junior, get me that lady's address." A few seconds pass before he returns. "What apartment?"

"Fourteen."

"Sorry, girl, I'm under strict orders not to deliver to you," the man offers amiably.

"What? By who?" I screech with a mixture of indignation and alarm.

"Some lady hit the block about an hour ago, explained your liver can't process fat. The whole neighborhood is in on this; we're going to make sure you stick to your diet."

I slam the phone down, my vision clouding with anger. I am barely able to dial the numbers, I am so irate. As soon as the ringing ceases, I start screaming, *"My fucking liver can't process fat!!!"*

"Okay...I think you want Janice," Janice's husband, Gary, says uncomfortably.

"Sorry," I mutter between huffs of rage.

"Hello?" Janice says perkily, exacerbating my frustration.

"My *fucking liver* can't process fat?"

"Drastic times call for drastic measures," Janice replies.

"Who do you think you are? Stopping the entire neighborhood from delivering to me. It's outrageous! Inappropriate! Unethical! Creepy!" I scream.

"I've invested a lot in you, and watching you waste an entire week of healthy eating on these Friday-night binges is simply unacceptable," Janice explains flatly.

She has drawn a line. If I continue to yell, this will surely result in my firing. I sense Janice is at her limit with me, college degree or not. I stop. I look down at the black tights, A-line skirt, and ballet flats Janice bought me.

"How long have you known?" I ask, choking on embarrassment.

"Please," she says with a sigh. "The whole time. Running off every Friday afternoon like you just got a new vibrator."

"Eww."

"I'm getting you ready for the world; stop being so damn ungrateful!"

"Ungrateful? Look in the mirror—you act like I'm lucky to run errands for minimum wage! I'm an Ivy League graduate, you know. This shit is way beneath me!"

"I admit that finding someone I can stand to be around for crap pay isn't easy, but the bottom line is I am helping you, so shut up and say thank you!"

"Thank you," I say weakly before continuing, "You're the Fairy Godmother I always wanted, only a whole lot meaner."

"I take that as a compliment. Oh and Anna, I wouldn't even try walking in to get takeout. I gave them your picture."

Chapter Nine

I always imagined it as winning the lottery. First, I would crumble in shock, repeating, "I can't believe it!" over and over again. Then with a burst of adrenaline, I would spring to my feet, dancing around the room, high-fiving myself. Never in any of these fantasies did I think it would fly beneath the radar, bringing forth no response whatsoever. Yet that is exactly what happened. Walking down Broome Street at a rapid pace, I ran ChapStick over my sore lips. Something about this reminded me of the pain I endured when I first arrived, my legs swollen from rubbing against one another.

And that's when I noticed it. My legs no longer touch when I walk. They didn't touch yesterday or the day before, yet beyond that I am unsure when this blessed event actually occurred. Odd, given how preoccupied I have been with envisioning myself thin, that such a colossal accomplishment transpired without my conscious knowledge. Yet somewhere along the seven and a half months since I handed Janice my handwritten and photocopied résumé, I have lost fifty-nine pounds. I estimate that to be the body of a six-year-old girl. Mind you, *I* far exceeded that weight at six. Naked or clothed, I am now a different person. Well, not entirely. My face remains ravaged with acne, but my ass no longer falls below my knees.

Hello Fatty,
Even in the dark, the rough texture of your skin is vis-
ible. It's tough and crunchy with large red sores and small
white pustules. People focus on your brown eyes just to
stop themselves from barfing.

xoxo Anna

Even with my body on track, insecurity plagues me. My face greets me every morning with red bumps and maroon scars that even the heaviest makeup fails to conceal. Unless people agree to talk through a screen or remain five feet away from me, I cannot bear to make them continue engaging with such a face. When I was fat, people assumed my acne was because I ate pizza and fried food. Now that I am skinny(ish), people presume it's due to poor hygiene. Why does no one ascribe it to bad genetics or exposure to toxic chemicals? Tired of the quiet expressions of repulsion, I approach Janice about this sensitive matter. She pays me minimum wage and doesn't offer health benefits, which is horrendous. Conversely, she buys me clothes, feeds me, and generally improves my exterior, so I might have to call it a wash.

Standing across the island in D&D's kitchen, I watch Janice chop celery with the precision of a surgeon. There is no second-guessing or fear in her movements. She is preparing a celery root soup with horseradish crème fraîche for a women's luncheon. And even though the combination sounds peculiar to my unrefined palate, I am sure it will be scrumptious. Nervous, I inhale deeply before speaking.

"Ever wonder what you would do if you cut off a

finger?" I ask, realizing only after the fact that the words send a strange serial killer vibe.

Janice immediately stops chopping and looks at me warily. "What did you say?"

"You know, let's say you cut off the tip of your finger, thinking it was celery. What would you do?"

"I would probably scream and dial 911."

"What a luxury that must be!"

"Excuse me?"

"You know, to have health insurance," I say melodramatically.

"What is this? You rent *Sicko* last night and now you're going all Michael Moore on me?"

"Well, you have to admit, it's sad for people like me."

"If you cut off your finger while working here, I promise to take you to the hospital, or at least drop you at the Canadian border," Janice says snarkily.

"It's about more than the big stuff," I continue.

"What? What is it? You're killing me. Do you want health insurance? Is that it?"

"Well, yes, that is it. How do you expect me to go through life knowing that if I get hit by a taxi or beaten to a pulp on the subway, I will be receiving worse medical care than the guys in Attica? Plus, I have really bad acne and need to see a dermatologist."

"Finally tired of looking like a thirteen-year-old boy on the verge of getting his first boner?" Janice asks with a wry smile. "I'll help you, but if you want insurance, you're going to have to step it up. Maybe learn to cook?"

I nod in assent. I don't really care what I have to do, I just need help taking the next step here, and Janice is only too glad to provide it, offering me her dermatologist's private number within minutes of my pronouncement.

Skin care in New York is an institution with a protocol all its own. For instance, if you want to bypass the four-week-long waiting list to see a good doctor, you need either a rapidly growing mole or a referral. Janice puts in a call to her dermatologist, a man she sees once a month, allowing me to jump the list. By the look of Janice's skin, I suspect she paid for her pores to be sewn shut, but if I can look half as good, I'll be ecstatic.

Arriving at Dr. Gunda's Upper East Side office, I am decidedly nervous. I worry he will tell me that I am beyond help. My hands sweat as he enters the sanitary office. He's nearing sixty, with glasses and a bald spot.

"Hello, Anna."

"Hi," I offer meekly as he approaches.

He pulls a hanging light in my direction and begins inspecting. "Let's see what we've got here."

Not to be critical, but his skin isn't that impressive. A few feet away and I see blackheads on his nose. Isn't he supposed to be a professional?

"Anna, how long has your skin looked this way?"

"Um, you know, I'm not exactly sure."

"An estimate. Six months? A year? Two?"

"Um, more like fifteen."

"Fifteen years? Have you sought help before?"

"I bought a lot of different stuff at Rite Aid: Neutrogena, Stridex, Oxy Pads—stuff like that."

"Most of that dries out your skin with alcohol, and that won't help you since you have serious cystic acne. The only viable option is Accutane. But it is an incredibly strong drug that can cause birth defects. By law, you've got to use two forms of birth control. Is that an issue for you?"

Oh my God, Dr. Gunda thinks I am sexually active. No one has ever made that assumption before. God bless him.

"No, that won't be a problem at all, Dr. Gunda," I say happily. "When can I start?"

"We'll need to check your liver before we start. I'm going to send Martin in to draw some blood."

Martin is a male nurse dressed head to toe in white, including weird geriatric shoes with lifts. Watching him prep the needle and tying my arm off with a plastic band leaves me feeling strangely aroused. Not by the needle, but the man holding it. While not empirically attractive, he exudes confidence and authority in his white uniform. And it turns me on. Staring at him with dreamy girl eyes, my cheeks blush. The more I try to halt the blushing, the hotter I get. Martin returns my intense gaze, inserts the needle, and winks. Am I light-headed? Did that really happen? Or did I imagine it?

"Are you feeling okay?"

"Yeah," I mumble, dizzy from the wink and loss of blood.

"You probably hear this all the time, but you've got gorgeous veins," Martin says reverently.

"Really?"

"They're easy to find. Nice and big, like straws."

"Gee, thanks," I respond, thoroughly enjoying the compliment. My cheeks are now cherry red with excitement. After he removes the plastic band, I plunge into depression knowing Martin will soon depart. With dangerously low blood sugar, I whimper to express my gloom. And yes, I whimper out loud. It sounds similar to a dog in heat. Humiliated, I pretend the last minute never happened. I never whimpered in Martin's face. Rubbing my sweaty palms together, I pray that Martin will wait until I leave the office before mocking me cruelly to the staff. Worst of all, I will now need to find a new dermatologist. Martin watches me, but I refuse to turn my pockmarked face.

"Would you mind if I asked you out sometime?"

This is a small miracle.

"Oh, that would be...great."

"Excellent. I'll get your number from your file," Martin says, holding my vials of blood.

The beauty of meeting a man at the doctor's office is he already knows my condition, not that I could do much to hide the topography of my face. Martin is aware of the measures I am taking to eradicate them. If he weren't already aware of this fact, I would find it necessary to bring it up. "Hey, I know my face is covered in pimples. Don't worry, I'm seeing a doctor."

Thankfully, I don't need to explain a thing as I sit across from him in a small Nolita restaurant named after one of my favorite things, bread. He's in dark jeans and a black dress shirt.

I'm nervous, but not for the reasons one would expect from an "almost virgin" on her first date in months. I am not worried about what will happen later. I actually look forward to the physical stuff; it seems much easier than talking. Conversation magnifies my weirdness. Come to think of it, sex probably does as well.

We order, then sit in silence for almost sixteen seconds. I count to distract myself from the little voice telling me to scream.

I want to scream. I want to holler at the top of my lungs to relieve the pressure in my chest. After wiping off my sweat 'stache, I prepare to act normal.

"So what got you into medicine?" I ask quietly.

"I had bad acne—the worst—almost ruined my life. Ended my first marriage, and after that I knew I had to get involved, help those less fortunate."

Wow, I've never thought of the plight of the pimple as such a significant societal issue. Clearly, I was wrong. I knew that pimples stopped relationships from starting, but I had no idea they had the power to kill them.

"You're really beautiful. You remind me a lot of Parker Posey."

"Thanks," I say as my cheeks blush twelve shades of red.

"I really admire the fact that you don't cover up the acne with foundation, because a lot of beautiful women try to do that. It's a force greater than they are. Sometimes it's as simple as denial. They can't admit what's really happening because they don't know how to fix it. They need tools. We provide those tools. I wish I could help every woman who needs it, but it's hard. Some of them don't have insurance, and seeing a doctor, especially a dermatologist, is a luxury they can't afford."

"That happened to me. I had to beg my boss for insurance," I say animatedly, enjoying the fact that I can relate to the downtrodden. I want Martin to like me, to respect me. He is a man of morals, ethics, and civil duty.

"No one should have to beg for help. That's why I want to start a free clinic for the underprivileged."

"You're incredible," I breathe, honestly moved by his speech.

His confidence is mesmerizing, and he seduces me with his compassion for those born with overactive sebaceous glands. I follow this Gandhi-like figure through the streets of New York, listening raptly to every word, only occasionally bursting out with "Yes!" when overcome by one of his comments. We wind up on his couch, two feet apart, staring into each other's eyes.

For the first time in my life, I want to engage in sexual intercourse with the man I sit before. No need to watch Tom Paris on a rerun of *Star Trek*.

Martin leans over, placing his soft hand on my bumpy cheek.

"You're a great candidate for Accutane."

"Thank you," I awkwardly respond before he places his lips on mine. His soft lips brush against mine sensually, awakening urges I didn't know I had. I want to sleep with this man. He touches my breasts over my sweater, and I actually shiver with anticipation. This level of sexual excitement surpasses anything I have ever known. I want to scream, "Take me!" as they do on tawdry soap operas. "Have your way with me!"

Excitement without release equals pain. I am in the throes of female blue balls. I may actually die from an impacted libido. Martin has been engaging in over-the-clothes petting and dry humping for almost two hours now. Emboldened by pure horniness, I lead Martin's hand under my clothes, but he retreats. Anger builds under my sweaty clothes as he continues his dry-humping crusade. Martin's face twitches with ecstasy. I stare, anger morphing into disgust as I realize what's happened.

"Um, did you finish?" I ask clumsily.

"That was amazing."

"Wouldn't you rather, you know, do it?"

"I don't think so," Martin says with a shrug.

Admittedly, I am in uncharted waters, but what the hell does a shrug mean in this context?

"Why?"

"It's been my experience that women expect a lot if you sleep with them. This seems like a far kinder compromise. I have my needs met, and you don't get hurt," Martin says condescendingly.

I've been had by a pimple prophet on par with Jim Jones. This man is a fraud. He lured me to his apartment with talk of compassion for those with patchy skin, but really he just wanted to get off on an easy target. I feel rejected, as if I am not good enough to fuck, only pretend fuck.

I stand, fully clothed, and walk out. As if to add insult to injury, that pig's light stubble chafed my face, making me even more hideous than before.

As I enter my apartment, I feel the vibration of my cell phone ringing in my handbag. For a brief second, I wonder if it's the pimple prophet calling to apologize and offering to engage in actual sex.

"Mother, I'm—"

"Don't tell me, you're upset."

I was going to say tired, but since she guessed, "Well, kind of."

"About the Szechuan Slut and your father?"

"Um, no." I should have known this was a ruse to

complain about my father. "It's about a guy I've been seeing."

"Jesus?" Mother interrupted.

"What?"

"Are you dating Jesus?"

"I don't think you understand what I'm trying to tell you."

"No, I do, believe me. You want to be a nun and marry God. This is your courtship period. Barney's thought this was a possibility for a while now, you know, ever since you suddenly dumped Harry and ran off to New York."

"Barney is in no position to pass judgment on anyone's dating life. He lives at home with you and is a virgin."

"*Alleged* virgin."

"Mother, I have to go," I spit out with frustration.

"No, you haven't told me who you're dating. If it's not Jesus—"

"It's...Allah. I'm looking into being one of his seventy-two virgins."

"I don't understand."

"It's nothing. I went on a date with a guy who works at my dermatologist's office and, well, I don't think he liked me."

"And he wants you to join this group of virgins?"

"Yup," I say, figuring it's easier to agree than explain.

"Sounds like a real freak," Mother says, slowly digesting the information.

"Don't worry, I'll stay away from him from now on. I've got to go."

Janice has a slightly different take on it.

"That freak is dead!"

"Janice, please don't do anything rash. I have to go in

there every month for blood tests," I beg the following morning over a pan of sautéing onions.

"Oh, he will not be there this afternoon, let alone in a month. Who the fuck does he think he is not fucking you?" Janice says. "He's a fucking male nurse at a zit clinic."

"Oh, Janice, please," I say, disregarding the smoke wafting up from the frying pan.

"Please what? He didn't even have the decency to fuck you and pretend he'll call. That's what grown-ups do. None of this teenage dry-humping crap!" Janice hollers, phone in hand.

Sensing the intensity of the moment, I turn off the now-ruined onions and head for the bathroom. By the time I return, Martin has been fired for asking a patient out on a date. I feel a little guilty but extremely relieved that I don't have to find a new dermatologist. "Thanks," I mumble to Janice.

"The important thing is that you stay on track. Get rid of the acne, then we can handle the moustache."

"Um, what are you talking about? A moustache?"

"What, you thought it was a shadow?"

I slide my finger across my sweaty upper lip and sure enough, I feel some fuzz. Great, another thing to be embarrassed about.

"I don't want to have a moustache," I gripe.

"Be patient. First acne, then waxing."

Chapter Ten

The longer I wait to wax, the more obsessed I become with the thick hairs on my upper lip and, sadly, other parts of my body as well. Even so, the idea of smearing hot wax on my skin, placing a thin cotton cloth on top of it, and ripping each hair from its root seems downright masochistic. It is a necessary evil, however, if I want to improve my image, and I haven't come this far to shirk a little pain. I have chosen to use the services of a frosty Russian woman named Anyas. She breathes heavily and squints while spreading wax around my upper lip. She is a hardened woman, crushed by both communism and its aftermath. From the stern nature of her expression, one would think the iron curtain actually fell on top of her. While frightened by her face, I am more terrified that she will pull off all my skin with the cloth.

"Um, is this going to hurt?" I ask meekly.

"No. No, pain at all," Anyas says very matter-of-factly.

"Really?" I say with relief. It sounds too good to be true, but surely she learned in the gulag that liars would be punished.

She rips the cloth back, pulling my long brown hairs out at the roots.

"Ow," I whimper.

"Quiet. Whining no help," she orders.

Spoken like a true communist. Stalin would be so proud.

Anyas yanks the last hair out of my upper lip and in doing so officially ends my makeover. I am legitimately average in appearance, maybe even a little better than average. My eyelashes appear longer without the acne and moustache, and my eyes even appear—dare I say it—attractive!

However fabulous my eyes and lashes may be, they can't blind me to the pain of New York City night life. Standing freshly groomed in front of Stanton Social, I am painfully uncomfortable in my skin. I wish I smoked. At least then I would have something to do with my arms while I wait for Janice. Why did I agree to meet her at such a place? I can't bear mingling with the sophisticates and models who watch me, wondering what bridge or tunnel I had to crawl through to get here. Oh, I hate them. Die, pretty people, die. And yes, I realize that no one is technically staring at me, but I'm sure they are discreetly judging me. It's simply too much; I pull out my phone to call Janice to tell her that I am leaving.

"Anna?" a voice comes from behind me. It's Janice. I hang up the phone without saying a word.

"You weren't calling to cancel, were you?"

How does she know that?

"No," I lie, "I was calling…a friend."

"Did you call Moviefone and have a pretend conversation?"

"Jesus Janice, no!" Although that is an excellent idea, and I will definitely be using it in the future.

"Don't act so shocked. It's not like that would be out of character for you."

"Fair enough."

Admittedly, I am quite peculiar. I may have lost weight, acne, and unwanted hair, but once a weirdo, always a weirdo.

Trailing behind Janice, I mount the stairs to Stanton Social's lounge. It's a typical chic bar with rice paper panels and mirrors hanging above the low-to-the-ground couches. I am waiting for someone to open a bar whose theme is total darkness, creating an even playing field.

"Somewhere in here is a man you are going to have sex with," Janice mutters.

"What?" I screech, terrified.

"C'mon, you deserve it. We are celebrating the new you!" Janice beams like a proud mother after her daughter's cheerleading championship.

"Um, I'm not sure about that, Janice. Let's just have drinks," I say with the confidence of a snail in a saltshaker. We would have better luck finding me a companion at Blockbuster. Men who rent movies alone on a Saturday night are a totally untapped market.

"Absolutely not. You need to christen your new body. It's either some guy here, or I take you home to make Gary do the honors."

"Eww."

"What? I didn't say I wanted to watch," Janice dryly announces while scoping the room. "There are some good-looking men here tonight."

Looking away from Janice, I furtively scan the room. All the faces and bodies look the same. My eyes rest on the back of a man in jeans and an old Springsteen T-shirt. This is the best-looking man, from behind, that I have ever seen. His butt has literally taken my breath away. My best estimate is that he's over six feet tall, although it's hard to tell from my seat on the painfully low couch. I can't see his face, but watching his tan arm extend to grab a drink is almost more than I can handle. His posture and ease in this crowded venue tell me he's handsome. A man's appearance can be deciphered from his stance and mannerisms; an attractive man walks, stands, and moves differently than a man with a cleft palate. If only he could turn out to be a terrible beast, then I'd have a shot with him.

"Who are you staring at? You look like you're retarded," Janice says harshly, following my gaze, just as the man turns around.

He's gorgeous. He's sexy. He's perfect, except for the tall blonde woman leaving the bar with him.

"Sweetie, we need to have a conversation about something known as *your league*. That guy is *not* in *your league*. Understanding your league is essential for—"

"I was only window-shopping," I say defensively.

"Manageable expectations are the crucial companion to a successful makeover. Just because your ass isn't muffin-topping out of your pants doesn't mean you get to bed George Clooney."

"Okay, I get it," I moan with obvious annoyance.

Janice ignores me, inspecting the tables around us.

"We've got a live one to your left," she says in her best spy voice.

I slowly turn to my left, feigning casualness as best I can.

"Keep going...striped shirt."

I filter through the people until I arrive on...the child in the striped shirt.

"He's in junior high," I respond.

"So you'll buy the drinks. It's a one-night stand, Anna. You don't have to marry him. Give him a second; he may grow on you. I'm going to the bathroom." Janice stands and performs a conspicuous head tilt, giving Junior High the go-ahead. I raise my vodka tonic to my mouth and sip slowly.

"Hey," Junior High says with a smirk.

I want to ask if his mom forgot to give him lunch money.

"Can I sit down?"

"Um, well, my friend is coming back soon. She's quick in the bathroom. Sometimes she doesn't even wash her hands."

It's not that I think Junior High isn't good enough for me, I honestly have no idea how to interact with the opposite sex.

"I think your friend is making a hasty exit."

Janice blows me a kiss while heading for the stairs. Shitty Fairy Godmother! If I had a glass slipper, I would throw it at her head.

"Um, I guess she is," I stutter.

"Can I get you another drink?"

My fear of contributing to the delinquency of a minor evaporates after vodka number three. Alcohol is the reason there are six billion people on the planet; it allows strangers to get naked without hesitation. For the record, this child is a graduate student at Columbia University. Of course, to me he'll always be Junior High, the first guy to have sex with my new body. I'm not sure if the feeling that I am a pedophile keeps me from enjoying myself or whether I just haven't yet gotten the hang of sex without blubber. Still, it isn't the worst experience in the world, and to be honest I need the practice.

Chapter Eleven

P lease, let's take the elevator just this once," I complain in the lobby of an exclusive apartment building on Spring Street in SoHo.

Dressed in my now-obligatory head-to-toe black, I scrunch my eyebrows together pathetically, hoping to evoke sympathy from Janice.

"Absolutely not. This is maintenance. If you start taking elevators, you might as well start eating donuts again," Janice replies firmly.

"Fine, no elevator," I sigh as I place my black ballet flat on the first of several hundred stairs. The fact that Janice is right doesn't make climbing five flights of stairs any easier. However, I am thrilled to report that I can actually climb five flights of stairs without becoming winded. A little perspiration behind my kneecaps is the worst of it.

As we approach the client's door, Janice and I both perform a quick check to make sure we are presentable. We wipe invisible lint off each other, plaster huge smiles on our faces, and ring the bell. Seconds pass before the front door slowly creaks open. My eyelids flutter, unsure at first what they are looking at. I swallow a massive quantity of air and wonder if delirium is a previously unexperienced by-product of enforced stair climbing. It's statistically impossible; there are millions of people living in Manhattan. The odds must be one in two million of running into him.

But it's him. He's in the same Born in the USA shirt and he's even dreamier up close than across a crowded bar. Moreover, he's much better looking without that blonde whore on his arm. Seeing his lean six-foot-one body, hazel eyes, and thick mane of black hair up close is almost too much for me. He's absolutely dreamy. Okay fine, his nose is imperceptibly crooked, yet somehow this only adds to his overall perfection.

"Hi, I'm Janice Delviddio from D&D Catering, and this is my associate, Anna Norton."

Both Janice and Mr. Perfect turn to me, expecting me to say something resembling hello. Unfortunately, I can't speak. My trance is in full effect—mouth open and eyes glazed. I try to make myself say something, but I am physically incapable of making a sound. Maybe it's best, as I would probably grunt or scream inappropriate sexual comments about his body. I only wish I could see him from behind again.

"I'm Ben Reynolds. Please come in."

Ben Reynolds. Ben Reynolds. Ben Reynolds. Even his name has that inherent cool feeling, like "Jake Ryan" in *Sixteen Candles*. As I cross the threshold into his spacious one-bedroom apartment, my eyes lock on Ben's butt—that same wonderful butt that caught my eye a couple weeks ago. Swooning, I follow Janice and Ben into the apartment.

"You look great from behind," I mutter. Oh God, no! I said that aloud. My cheeks burn with embarrassment; never has a blush hurt quite so much. What a time for my vocal cords to kick back into action.

Janice looks at me with irritation before bursting into

laughter. Ben follows suit with the perfect laugh; yes, I am already drunk on the Ben Kool-Aid.

"That's not what I meant. I meant to say that...some people's backs don't complement the front...side of their body...as naturally as yours does. Really a good fit. And that is all I meant when I said you look...great from behind...," I trail off quietly, dying of humiliation. This is not the romantic introduction I was hoping to one day tell the *New York Times*.

"No need to explain," Ben says with a smirk. "I appreciate a woman with a sense of humor. Please sit."

He even knows how to diffuse mortifying interactions. The man is a god.

The three of us sit down at Ben's modern Swedish dining room table. I compose myself, but Ben once again unhinges me, this time in the form of a large black-and-white photo. He is shirtless on a sailboat. How can I concentrate with his chest, a rippling mass of perfection, taunting me? He has a thin layer of hair on his chest, which I find sexy in a 1970s Burt Reynolds kind of way. Ben watches me drool over his picture, wondering no doubt if he needs to alert the police to the presence of a stalker.

"That was taken last summer off the coast of Greece," Ben says smoothly to me.

"Gary and I honeymooned in Greece. It was gorgeous," Janice adds, speaking like a normal human being.

"I'm not married, so I've never been on a honeymoon. Ben, have you ever been on a honeymoon?"

It is official: I have social dyslexia. I cannot properly determine appropriate and inappropriate behavior. If God were fair, he would endow me with a special skill to compensate for my complete lack of social intelligence. Perhaps he could make me a witch like Samantha Stephens or a genie like Jeannie (do genies have last names?).

"No, I am not married," Ben says with a reassuring grin.

"Neither am I," I say dreamily. There may actually be stars floating out of my eyes or hearts swarming around my head.

"Yes, I know."

"How do you know? Oh, you looked at my hand," I offer coyly.

"Ah, no, you just mentioned it."

"Let's get down to business," Janice interrupts ferociously.

Yeah, the business of Ben and Anna smooching. Did I say that aloud? Oh thank heavens, for once it seems I didn't.

"My parents and I are strict vegetarians," Ben says. It's the last thing I hear as I start planning for my conversion to vegetarianism. I have a lot to do: join PETA, the Humane Society, and maybe invest in a cat pin. Wait, I think a cat pin says "loser" more than "vegetarian." It's incredible; I already feel healthier. I know it's only been a few seconds, but being a vegetarian works for me. If asked, I will cite both moral and health reasons for the sudden decision. I can't very well tell people the truth; I converted for an intense sexual attraction.

Having committed to vegetarianism, I'm able to focus long enough to hear that Ben is a corporate lawyer at Benson and Silverberg, a large firm in Midtown, but regrets not going into environmental law. Mental note: rent *An Inconvenient Truth* and start recycling.

I try not to stare at Ben, but I can't help it. It hurts to look away from him. His every pore, freckle, and follicle hypnotizes me as Janice discusses the importance of a good gherkin.

"Anna, you love gherkins," Janice says, leaning in closely to whisper, "You look retarded again. Stop staring."

"I love...gherkins...love them."

My heart beats irregularly, creating a shortness of breath as I avoid looking at Ben. The longer I divert my eyes, the more my chest constricts, creating an audible wheeze. I inhale slowly. I must marry him. He is definitely the one.

"Anna, do you need some water?" Janice asks irritably, clearly annoyed by my asthmatic dog imitation.

"J-j-j-just taking a few deep breaths."

"Well, now it's time to stop," Janice says with her eyebrows raised above her hairline.

"I-I-I ammm trying," I stutter.

Without any warning or provocation, Janice delivers a *Dynasty*-worthy slap across my face. I imagine there is now a red handprint on my right cheek, but at least I can breathe normally again.

"You were having a panic attack; I needed to snap you out of it." This from my boss, apparently a newly minted MD.

"I got carried away taking in the...lovely...air freshener," I lamely declare.

"I don't use air freshener," Ben interjects.

"Oh, maybe it's you, then." Clearly my brain is not

getting enough oxygen because I again said that aloud. I wish the seven-second rule for food applied to stupid comments; you have seven seconds to pull them back and pretend they never happened.

The phone rings. Ben stands. Oh, how he stands. I am mesmerized.

"You need to...how should I say this? Shut the fuck up," Janice whispers while clutching my arm. She has a unique brand of sympathy, which generally includes the *f* word.

"I'm sorry...it won't happen again...really..."

I absolutely cannot wheeze again. This is serious. A faint rasp still lingers in my chest, causing me great anxiety. Maybe I should hold my breath, suppress whatever is dying to exit my body through my throat. Sweat beads slide down my breasts, igniting an intolerable itching sensation from the areola to the armpit. Why, God? Haven't you punished me enough? Haven't you met my family? Surely they are adequate retribution for my mistakes. This is worse than the time I peed on the couch while watching *The Exorcist*. Mother believed me when I told her I fell asleep and dreamed I was sitting on the toilet. The truth is, I got so scared that I peed myself. Obviously, I suffer from strange reactions to stress.

My breasts are on fire. They throb as if doused in a mixture of poison ivy and chicken pox. I can't take it anymore; I must alleviate the itch. Maybe I can subtly rub my arms across my breasts. Oh, the relief. This is pure heaven.

Well, not exactly, since Ben is watching me engage in this peculiar behavior. So much for first impressions.

Somehow, Janice wraps up the meeting and holds my

arm firmly as she says good-bye and heads to the front door. Ben, perfect gentleman that he is, extends his hand for me to shake. I want to smother it with kisses as deranged Italian men do in movies. I yearn to press my face against his slightly hairy chest and scream, "After all I've done to be with you—vegetarianism, environmental activism—the least you could do is marry me." However, I don't do any of those things because one, I am inches away from the sanitarium as it is, and two, he's out of my league. For the first time since my overhaul, I hate being average. Forgettable, boring, average Anna isn't capable of getting Ben. Instantly, my transformation is silly and pointless, a cruel joke to verify my inability to achieve my desires. Downstairs, on the verge of a mental breakdown, I wait for Janice to rattle me with barbs and impersonations of my atrocious behavior, but she doesn't.

"Okay," Janice says, jotting something on a piece of paper, "here's your list for today...okay?"

"Yup," I say overenthusiastically, trying to quiet her worrisome glare. She clearly noticed that I have an ill-advised crush on Ben, but thankfully she isn't mentioning anything.

Walking down Mulberry Street with a single piece of paper in my left hand, I miss Ben. I want him. I need him. It's insanity. I miss everything about him, from his smell, to his eyes, to his voice. An incredibly childish and petty idea crosses my mind. I reject my own idea, embarrassed by its juvenile nature. But it returns, and this time I imagine what it would feel like to hear Ben's gravelly voice again. Logically, I know that I have surpassed my humiliation threshold for the day, yet I can't stop myself.

I plow aggressively down the street, eyes darting

around in search of a pay phone. On the corner of Broome and Mulberry, I discover a dirty, gum-covered antique of a pay phone, drop in fifty cents, and dial the number I memorized off Janice's pad while sitting at the dining room table. Crank calling used to be a favorite pastime of mine until caller ID and *69 went and ruined it. I have chosen to use a pay phone instead of using *82 on my cell to block my number because I can't take the chance of a technical glitch. What if *82 doesn't work and he sees my number? Then what? There would be no plausible explanation to give him or Janice, whose crazy psychic abilities would no doubt ferret out this indiscretion.

It's ringing.

I'm nervous, slightly worried that a case of Tourette's will come over me, prompting me to spill my guts to him, confess my undying lust for his body.

"Hello? Hello?" Ben's gorgeous voice comes through the receiver, clear as a bell.

I silently mouth hello back to Ben, as any good stalker would do. My emotional regression has occurred at an alarmingly fast rate. I went from seminormal adult to utter adolescent loser in less than two hours.

If only the world was a magical and whimsical place, a world in which Ben does not realize he is out of my league. We date, fall in love, and eventually marry. We live together in his one-bedroom apartment until we have kids and move to Westchester. Our kids are so cute. I know all parents think their kids are perfect, but Madeleine and Jacob truly are flawless. I originally chose the names for my children with Lance Bass of 'N Sync, but I think he'll understand.

Loser, my mind screams. Unless women can get pregnant over the phone, there isn't going to be a Madeleine or a Jacob. *Loser!*

Walking back to work, the proverbial black cloud hangs over my head, reminding me what a horrendous loser I am. I miss my pretend husband and children. This is proof of my dysfunctionality: only losers or people with severe mental disorders experience such emotions. There is obviously something wrong with me. I have allowed a total stranger to alter my perception of life.

Average is a place I have worked tirelessly to arrive at, and now I've deemed it worthless since I can't have Ben Reynolds. This is a man I just met who does not have any feelings for me. I am embarrassed and revolted by my thoughts. I refuse to engage in this any further and make the conscious decision not to mention my thoughts to Janice. I unlock and push open the front door, bags in hand.

Janice is in the middle of the kitchen, chopping at a frenetic speed. Ideally, I would run to her, confess my outrageous feelings, and demand she make it happen. However, even Janice, my relentless champion, knows this one is pointless. Ben is in a galaxy far, far away...from me.

"There's fresh fruit in the fridge," Janice calls out to me.

"Thanks," I say quietly.

"What is it? You look blotchy and stressed," Janice says, stopping to peruse my physical status.

"I don't know; maybe I was in the sun too long."

"You need to wear sunscreen; the sun ages you."

Great, I am already spiraling downwards. After two minutes of looking average, I'm descending into unattractiveness again. And it's not going to stop. Time is a brutal and worthy foe, cruelly punishing women as they age. Maybe I should try to find Harry on MySpace; he was the only man I've ever met who didn't care if I was revolting. In fact, I think it turned him on.

Sitting at the counter shoving fruit into my mouth, I check my cell messages, only to discover Mother has been diversifying her portfolio.

"Anna, I made a large investment and I need to discuss it with you. Best, Mother." Mother's idea of a large investment translates to wasted money on the home shopping channel, QVC. Upon her death, I am to inherit a wealth of costume jewelry, food processors, fruit dehydrators, and unused celebrity-endorsed gym equipment. Her shopping prowess is the least of her peculiarities; most notably she has taken to ending all conversations as she would a letter: Best, Mother. Like with the phony glasses, Mother believes that the "Best" salutation makes her appear more intelligent. Mother's quest to seem knowledgeable is boundless; she will stop at nothing—except, of course, reading. Picking up a book is where Mother draws the line.

Calling her back would be the mature and kindhearted thing to do, but I'm not in the mood to listen to asinine investment strategies and theories on my father's relationship with Ming. I would much prefer to muse about Ben and the alternate universe that allows us to be together. I accept that in this reality, a man of his looks and social stature cannot deign to be with someone such as myself.

But that can't stop me from imagining a world where it's possible.

PART

III

The Downside of Dating Up

Chapter Twelve

Lights. Camera. Loser.

Standing in front of a frustrated Janice, I devolve into hysterics at the mention of Ben. I can't face him after days of intricate fantasies about the two of us in wedded harmony. Seeing him and realizing the impossibility of my dreams is too heavy a burden to bear. Humiliation is all the night can bring, so why go?

"I'm not going...I can't. Hire someone else," I beg Janice with streams of mascara-colored tears running down my cheeks.

"You are going. I am not asking you, I am telling you. The party is tonight, and you will be there along with the crew, helping me as you always do. Do you understand?"

"No...no...I can't. I can't do it," I whimper. "You don't understand."

"What? What don't I understand?" she explodes back at me. "All this because you told him he has a nice ass? Big deal. A guy like that gets hit on every day. I wouldn't be surprised if his own mother hit on him. He won't even remember it."

"I can't bear to be around him. I'm some pathetic loser with a crush on him."

"Sweetie, yes he knows you think he's hot. So what? He thinks he's hot. He probably thinks everyone thinks he's hot. Men like Ben fuck too many models to remember one normal girl who said he had a cute ass. It's not a big deal. No one cared but you, okay?"

"Okay," I mutter, wiping tears from my face. "Sorry, I—"

"I know," Janice cuts me off.

A deep level of shame washes over me as I realize that the man I have spent countless hours mentally obsessing over probably doesn't even remember my name. I can't believe I have made this guy out to be such a big deal. Let's not forget he has that barely visible bump in his nose. Total freak show, not to mention egomaniac. He hung a picture of himself without a shirt in his own apartment. Who does that? A show horse.

He's probably bedded every size-four woman in the five boroughs and has the STDs to prove it. An ease returns to my face as I mentally annihilate Ben.

By 5:00 p.m., I am stationed in the kitchen adjacent to the Waldorf-Astoria's fourth-floor banquet room. With Juan and the rest of the waitstaff buzzing around me, preparing plates, I tell myself that Ben has a small penis. No one is perfect. Ben has everything else, so he must have a small penis, or maybe no penis at all. Perhaps he's really a woman, or a hermaphrodite. This is what I have been driven to by the unfairness of genetics. Why are some born with so much while others have to fight for the dregs? If only the principles of communism could be applied to genetics, giving everyone exactly the same advantages.

With the party in full swing, I work diligently to distract myself from the fact that Ben is on the other side of the kitchen door. I yearn to see him one last time, to see the face that makes my stomach churn with anxiety, fright, and a healthy dose of self-loathing. I have never felt so much for someone I knew so little.

I know I shouldn't, but I am going to peek; after all, I may never see him again. Although, he may have brought that blonde beast from the bar. Talk about utter misery, watching them suck face. Okay, he doesn't really seem like the "suck face at the Waldorf" kind of guy, but watching them hold hands will be almost as horrendous. I am staying in the kitchen, where I belong.

The only downside to this decision is that I don't get to interact with the old people attending the party. I absolutely love oldies. They don't intimidate me or make me question the fairness of genetics, since age evens the playing field. A pretty woman and an average woman aren't that different at seventy or eighty; the only real difference is in their memories. For men on the other hand, age can be a distinguishing force. I have long fancied the idea of dating a seriously older man. I am not talking about the forty-five-year-old divorcé with salt-and-pepper hair. I am referring to the sixty-four-year-old retiree with memberships to both the country club and AARP. A man in his sixties can still be debonair, but with reasonable expectations. Aware that his value is on the decline, an older man will gladly overlook my appearance for my youth.

"Anna, you are young, nubile, and—," my dashing older man proclaims.

"And beautiful?"

"And still contributing to Social Security."

"Oh, Mr. Lincoln, let's get married."

In my older man fantasy, I refer to him by his surname, which always happens to be a president's name. Don't ask me why; I have no idea. The first time I had the fantasy I chose Mr. Taft, and it snowballed from there.

With images of me dancing across ballrooms, I decide to stop acting like the redheaded stepchild relegated to the kitchen. Hiding out here, I am passing up the opportunity to meet an older man, to become a kept woman. It's not such a bad life—dinner by five and widow by forty.

Pushing Ben to the furthest, most inaccessible part of my brain, I press open the door to the Waldorf-Astoria ballroom. Dark, perfectly cut suits and chic dresses swarm the servers as they meander through the crowd. It's a well-kept horde with money and a liberal flair. I hear smatterings of Bill Clinton nostalgia, with more than a few people mentioning how different things would be if McGovern had won in 1972. These people don't wear fur, watch Bill O'Reilly, or vote for anyone with the last name Bush.

Slithering through the Democrats, I look for both Janice and my geriatric husband-to-be. Janice will force me back into the kitchen, afraid that I will cry again. I continue to scan the room for my grandfather/boyfriend when I spot Ben talking with a petite older woman. My stomach hurts. Ben. My throat constricts. Ben. My heart stops. Ben. The mere sight of him makes me uncomfortable in my skin. Every cell in my body begs to look away. Ben must emit some incredibly powerful pheromone, because I simply cannot take my eyes off him.

A tall, slender woman passes in front of him; his eyes follow her well-toned derriere. The small woman grabs his face and scolds him for his naughty behavior. He smiles politely but continues to watch the woman's ass cut through the crowd. The old woman, maybe an aunt or neighbor, pulls Ben by the arm. I head left, following them as they nod and wave at other guests. The old woman stops in front of a stocky young woman. To be blunt, the young lass is all ass. She is not fat, but she is definitely chubby. I feel bad thinking it, but it's true. Ben shakes hands with the young woman with blonde hair to her shoulders and bangs that remind me of second grade.

Craning my neck to decipher the body language, I inch closer to the area of interest. The old woman watches the two chat with an excited, almost crazed expression on her face. Oh my dear lord; that old bat is trying to set them up. I recognize the smug look from the night Janice arranged for the Junior High field trip in my pants.

I laugh. Oh, I laugh hard, by myself in the middle of a party. This is the most ridiculous scene I have ever witnessed. Ben's eyes roam the room searching for an out as the old woman attempts to ignite a spark with the plump girl. The old woman must not know about the other blonde in his life, the one with legs that span the length of this girl's body. It's almost painful to watch. Even I am better looking than this one. Did I just think that? I've never considered myself better looking than another woman, but it's about time.

After many a strained expression, Ben breaks free from the triangle of matchmaking. Headed straight for the bar, I duck through conversations, bump into people, and do what's necessary not to lose sight of him.

With Ben firmly planted at the bar with a beer in his hand, I slink behind a nearby potted plant. My behavior is alarmingly reminiscent of a character's in a bad sitcom, yet I continue. Seated at a crappy table, hidden by a decorative tree, I notice the puffy top of the old woman's hair making its way through the crowd, headed straight for Ben.

"Benny, that was very rude of you," the woman scolds.

"Leslie Haggens? She's a lovely girl, but there is no way I'm dating her," Ben responds.

"She is a fabulous girl. A wonderful personality and a successful lawyer. This is what you need—someone with real emotions, someone who actually has feelings. A nice girl, not like that—"

"Please stop. I am never going to date Leslie—never—and as for . . . I don't want to talk about her."

And with that, Ben walks away. The old woman orders a martini, and I excavate myself from the tree, avoiding the stares of my tablemates.

"Hello!" A tall older man with glasses and a thick gray mane yells from the stage, tapping the microphone with his fingers. "Is this thing on?" The old woman who was harassing Ben joins the tall man onstage. Suddenly, it all makes sense. These are Ben's parents. To my great surprise, they are not Zeus and Aphrodite, but a normal-looking couple. How did they create him? Ben looks like the love child of Elvis and Brigitte Bardot, not this pair.

Ben's father is attractive in a dentist or accountant kind of way, while his mother resembles a Madame Alexander doll, at five feet tall with mounds of puffed-up hair. Standing on stage, both dressed in navy blue, they enthusiastically beam at the crowd. My catering experience has taught me that for regular folk, having a party thrown in your honor is akin to winning an Academy Award; it demands a moving speech.

"As some of you know, I met Milly at camp. She was thirteen and small for her age. It wasn't love at first sight for me, thankfully, since I was a counselor. To be honest, I thought Milly was annoying. She was a vegetarian in the fifties, and back then, no one was a vegetarian. No one liked her, from the janitor to the head counselor, but she didn't care. She had integrity. When the boys went deer hunting, she held a one-woman protest. Ten years later, I was a law clerk to Judge Marvin Smithson, and in walked his irrepressible daughter Milly. It was love at second sight. She made me question everything. I gained compassion for other life forms. She changed me for the better. Even in the depth of our most miserable fight—some of you may remember the Gore versus Nader debacle of 2000—I couldn't imagine life without her. What else can I say about a woman who gave me not only a soul but a son? She's magnificent."

Damn Mr. Reynolds! The poster child for marriage made me cry. Tears roll down my cheeks, washing away so-called waterproof mascara. My father would never have spoken about Mother in such a way. I wonder if he toasts Ming with such passion. My nose drips, and I wipe it on my hand like a derelict child. I look up and notice not only Ben but also his mother watching me. My face, awash in emotion, cannot hide what I am feeling. I offer an honest smile, one that few people have seen. There is no hiding who I am in this moment. I am a woman in black slacks, a white dress shirt, and an apron crying over the love of a couple I have never met. While his mother pulls at his sleeve, Ben lifts his arms slowly.

Dear God, no! Ben pays homage to my prior breast-rubbing incident by reenacting it. Mortified, I turn around and storm into the kitchen.

In the kitchen, Janice waits for me with a paper towel and a wry expression.

"What is with all this crying? It's madness. You must wipe your face."

"I was touched by their love," I explain a tad defensively.

"Anna, it was a toast. No one tells the truth in toasts. He's probably porking his paralegal."

"Jesus, Janice, how do you hear that and respond with porking?"

From behind us comes, "Personally, I prefer screwing. It's to the point without being crass."

"Fuck me," Janice mutters.

I turn around slowly to see who has joined our debate. *Oh my God,* it's Ben. I wipe my face at warp speed. Janice, momentarily paralyzed, has lost the power of speech.

"I wanted to thank you ladies for a wonderful evening."

Janice and I both nod, unsure what to do in this awkward scenario. I avoid eye contact with Ben, still reeling from his breast-rubbing gesture.

"And ask Anna if she would join me in the last dance."

It's the "No one puts Baby in the corner" moment I have wanted my whole life.

Chapter Thirteen

In the middle of a room packed with elderly couples dancing, Ben Reynolds holds me in his arms.

Well, sort of. Technically, his hands are on my hips, but this induces a feeling of faintness in me so strong that I lean into his arms. No matter the cause, the result is fantastic.

I notice both Milly and Janice watching us from separate corners of the room, each smiling in genuine appreciation of her own creation. I squeeze Ben tightly to reinforce his presence in my arms. It's clichéd, but I never want this moment to end. It simply isn't fair that the song was already playing when we got on the dance floor. I deserve more time. Like Cinderella, I sense the clock approach midnight. I embrace Ben a little tighter, storing all sensory details in my memory.

Ben laughs.

This can't be good. Oh, no. Was this all some elaborate ruse to humiliate me on the dance floor? I pull back as the music ends.

"What? Am I a bad dancer?" I ask defensively, prepared to scream at him if he says something nasty. I may have the mind of a junior high student, but I will not allow someone to debase me like one.

"No, not at all. It's just... I'm not used to being around such an emotional woman."

"Emotional?" Is that code for repulsive?

"Not in a bad way, in a charming way. The tears at the speech and the way you held on tightly as you danced."

I don't entirely trust my ears, but I believe he said that without any sarcasm. It sounded like a legitimate compliment.

"Thank you."

"So, the party is pretty much over."

"Oh yeah, I have a lot of cleaning up to do."

I knew this time would come, but it is devastating to feel my beautiful carriage turn back into a pumpkin. Ben looks to his left, raises an imaginary glass to his mother, then turns back to me. I am not an idiot; I know that his mother is prodding him to give me a chance. I suppose most mothers are suggestive and interfering when it comes to their son's dates. Still, it's a shock and an enormous compliment that she likes me. Well, maybe not that enormous a compliment, seeing as she pushed that blonde tub earlier.

"Do you think Janice would let you slip out for a drink if I promised her my parents' anniversaries until death?"

"Yes," I blurt out quickly. "I think so . . . it seems like a possibility," I add, trying to play it cool.

Whatever the reason we are thrust together, I deserve to enjoy it. After a lifetime of jeering insults, I rejoice in the feeling of butterflies in my stomach and palpitations in my heart, regardless of the circumstances. Admittedly, being prodded onto a date by his mother is not ideal, but it's not as if I am paying her. Or him. Though I would. And he did accept the nudge from his mother, which he didn't do with poor Leslie. That counts for something in my book.

★   ★   ★

We chat awkwardly as we walk a few blocks down Lexington, stopping at an unmarked door next to a Duane Reade. Downstairs is a jazz bar reminiscent of a bygone era; a place where Humphrey Bogart would have drank. The black and white checkered floor complements the red patent leather booths, which are private enough for a man to get to second base. I can only dream of testing this observation.

The floor-level stage is barely able to accommodate the three men playing the saxophone, bass, and piano. As I watch the men play, annoyance nibbles away at me. Why did I waste my youth listening to Celine Dion and 'N Sync? If I had only known this moment was coming, I would have educated myself on jazz, wowing him with an intelligent and thought-provoking review. Oh no, the music is winding down. Why didn't Janice drill me on normal human interaction? I'm not going to survive ten minutes, let alone an entire date.

"Can I get you another drink?" Ben asks, miraculously bypassing the music-review segment of the evening.

"I'm all right. Thanks."

Ben smiles and begins to drain his bourbon. Damn, he is sexy. Everything from his hands to the velvet locks of hair on his head make my libido stand and salute.

"So did your parents enjoy the party?" I ask shyly, desperate to ignite a rapport.

"Yes, I think they did, thank you. You pulled off an incredible feat with the food. It's not easy to make vegetarian gourmet. Mom was very impressed."

"Oh, good."

Silence. Why won't the band play another song? More silence. Exchange awkward smiles. Please someone have a heart attack, throw up, or start a fistfight. We need the energy to get a dialogue going.

"Where did you say you were from?"

"Ohio. You?"

"Born and raised in New York. Do you like it here?"

"Oh, yes...I like it a lot...," I stutter stupidly. I sound as if I am talking about vanilla ice cream. "It's different than Ohio in all the right ways."

"I'm sure," Ben says with a nod, signaling the waiter for another bourbon. "Are you sure you don't want another glass?"

"Oh, no. I'm fine, thanks," I say meekly. Fear stops me from drinking more. I worry what I would do if intoxicated around Ben. As we start to do the strained smile thing again, the waiter approaches with Ben's bourbon.

"Anything else?" the waiter asks politely.

"Just the check," Ben says.

The butterflies and heart palpitations have given way to a sickening sense of doom. I thought basking in his presence, regardless of what got him here, would be delightful, but it's not. It's horrendously painful to see total apathy on a man's face, to watch him drink to numb the misery of the situation. His desperation to get the check and leave is disturbingly apparent. This was a one-off pity drink to get his mother off his back. I am an idiot for believing that it could be more.

"Your father's speech was very touching."

"I wasn't sure you enjoyed it, with all the tears," Ben says with a slight lift of the eyebrows.

He's smiling, but it feels like he's laughing at me. He

may not even be consciously aware of it, but he's definitely mocking my sincerity. Part of me wants to stand up and tell him to fuck off and to save his charity for the homeless. Another part of me wants to sob, showing him the pain he triggered inside me. What can I say? Former nerds are a fragile lot.

"I was moved by the honesty of their relationship. By your mother's determination to do what she thought was right, and how it inspired your father to be a better man," I say with all the dignity I can muster. "She seems like a woman of great character—always looking out for those with less. A mother who probably made you invite everyone to your birthday parties, even the ones you weren't friends with, the ones you would never be friends with, but you invited them because she told you it was the right thing to do. And maybe it was in fourth grade, but the lesson has stayed with you...," I peter off, sneaking a peek at my date. I am surprised that Ben's expression is one of discomfort. His face is contorted in a manner I've never seen from someone so beautiful.

My face, in contrast, is clear, calm, and resigned. I will not cry here. I have frozen all sentiment, with the plan of thawing it safely in the confines of my own apartment, on the pages of Hello Fatty. Ben remains silent, swishing his bourbon around his glass, avoiding eye contact.

"Well, I have a busy day tomorrow. Thank you for the drink."

"I'll hail you a cab," Ben says, preparing to stand.

"That's not necessary," I say genuinely, without a trace of malice, before walking away from the table.

I am not mad at him. I am not mad at his mother. I am mad at me. I believed in something ludicrous and in doing so placed myself in front of a firing squad. Maybe it was intense lust or the onset of schizophrenia, but I thought I saw something in him, something that was supposed to be mine. Now I realize that I projected onto him a world of feelings I have long wanted to experience. He was merely a vessel, albeit a seriously handsome and utterly shallow one. And I was a tool he used to satisfy his mother's wish, never worrying how it could affect me.

I need to get home as fast as possible. I step off the curb and raise my arm. The headlights make me squint. Surprisingly, I am not fighting off tears; instead, I am rather numb, with a twinge of budding pride. I walked off. I didn't wait for him to holler last call on the pathetic excuse for a date. I saw his intense disinterest and ulterior motives and I walked out. I may not be very attractive. I may not have a powerful job. I may not have the best social skills. But I just discovered a small, miniature, tiny little badass inside of me.

"Anna!"

Great, just when I found the silver lining in this godforsaken night, the schmuck returns. A cab pulls up just as Ben reaches me.

"I . . . um . . . wanted to say," Ben babbles, looking less self-assured than I would have guessed he could, "thank you for a lovely night." He reaches across and lightly pecks me on my lips.

I am shocked beyond belief, but somewhere within me, I manage to summon words, "You're welcome."

I get in the cab. I tell the driver to take me to Brooklyn, sit back, and laugh. I think that kiss may have fucked with Ben's head even more than mine.

Chapter Fourteen

From beneath my 1970s flower-laden sheets, which Mother "entrusted" to me, I mull over the events of the evening. I conclude that a slight, imperceptible shift in the tectonic plates or the alignment of stars prompted Ben to kiss me. Either that or FG splashed Ben with a heavy dose of magic.

Oddly, I'm not sure if I'm pleased he kissed me or annoyed. Was that a pity kiss at the end of a pity date? Was that a genuine moment that neither one of us will ever be able to explain? Will I hear from him? Is it asinine to want to hear from him after the night I had?

I was fine when I left, even proud of the manner in which I handled his behavior, but then he had to go and brush those soft, perfectly symmetrical lips against mine. It's as if he infected me with a chemical, recharging my attraction to him. I am deeply grateful he didn't use tongue, or I'd be irrevocably in love with the guy.

"Ahh," I yelp, startled by the intercom buzzing.

No one ever buzzes me, except when I've ordered take-out. It's only happened once before, and that was by accident. They were looking for Mrs. Bester a floor below me.

"Hello?"

"Delivery for Anna Norton."

"What did you say?" I ask incredulously.

"Delivery for Anna Norton."

"That's A-n-n-a N-o-r-t-o-n, right?"

"Yeah, lady. Anna fucking Norton, are you coming down or what?"

"I'm coming down," I squeal as if Bob Barker just invited me down to contestant's row on the *Price Is Right*.

I throw open my front door clad in only a robe and slippers. The flannel robe is from the Gap, circa 1990s. The slippers grossly predate the robe. I hurdle down the stairs to the building's main entrance, curiosity speeding my every step.

I fling open the door half expecting to find Janice ready for a full debriefing. But it's not Janice; it's something far more bizarre: flowers. Yellow roses, to be exact. Who would send me roses? No, I tell myself. It's not possible. On the other hand, he did kiss me last night. They are definitely not from Janice. She would never deign to send flowers in a plastic vase with a color-coordinated satin ribbon. It's a little surprising from Ben as well. I thought he was more sophisticated than that.

"Lady, are you gonna sign this or what?"

"Oh, of course," I blurt out, realizing that I have been debating the identity of the flowers' sender for at least a minute.

My heart pounds as I start back up the stairs. Could Ben really have sent me flowers? And if so, what do they mean? Yellow roses traditionally mean friendship, and a man as sophisticated as Ben surely knows his way around a flower shop. This was clearly a deliberate act.

Hello Fatty,
Don't get too excited. I kissed you because we're only friends.

Warm regards,
Ben

Or perhaps he just likes the color yellow? Is it possible that he wrote something romantic? The mere thought of a man writing me a note makes my body tingle. I plunge my nose deep into the bouquet to inhale the fragrance before pulling out the small white card. Pressure mounts, setting off a spasm in my lower back and a dull thud in my left temple.

Squinting and limping, I manage to get back to my apartment with the roses. Safely back on my futon, I pull out the card and read:

"Your father and Ming are having a bastard won ton. Hope these flowers buffer the blow. Best, Mother."

Ming is pregnant. I choke back the visual image of Dad having sex with anyone but Mother—or really the image of Dad having sex with anyone at all. I realize all children have difficulty accepting their parents' sexuality, but I have trouble thinking of them with anything other than Barbie- and Ken-type bodies under their clothes. Why would Dad procreate while still living in the same town as Mother? Or more accurately, why would Dad procreate *period*? The only idea more revolting than Dad having sex is Mother following his lead, but I am quite sure she's been celibate since the divorce. Barney lives with Mother, so he would know if anything happened. According to Barney, she sleeps with her bedroom door open in case he needs something, which means she's not even having a good time by herself.

For fairness' sake, Dad should not be having sex if Mother isn't even masturbating. Moreover, a man with two grown children does not need another child. The child buffet is closed. He has had enough. Why would he even want another child? He was never particularly interested in his paternal role with Barney and me. He may have remained in the house until we finished school, but he never participated in any child-rearing activities. His only role was that of silent observer.

Inevitably, Dad will be a better father to Bastard Won Ton than to Barney and me. The absence of Mother alone will improve his parenting skills threefold. A part of me is jealous that Bastard Won Ton will get a better version of Dad than I did. Growing up, my disappointment in Dad was eclipsed by my immense pity for him. He was in a suburban jail with the harshest warden east of the Mississippi River. He could have spared Barney and me years of madness if he had stood up to Mother, but he didn't. Instead, he remained Mother's hand puppet until joining Ming and the traveling infidelity circus.

If I am this out of sorts, I can only imagine Mother's state. It's possible the flowers were sent from a hospital bed, where she's recovering from a mental breakdown.

Clearly, the flowers are Mother's way of making me call her; reaching Mother with a lithium drip in her arm would be a stroke of luck. I can feel her telepathically guilting me right now. I force myself to pick up the phone and dial. It rings. Is it too late to hang up? Mother has caller ID. Damn. She believes that calling and failing to leave a message is the equivalent of walking by someone you know on the street and not saying hello. Mother punishes such an act with a series of late-night hang-ups. She blocks her number, then spaces out the calls so that each time the phone rings, the person will have just fallen back to sleep. I cannot endure that type of torture right now.

"Hello?"

"Mother, it's Anna."

"You must be proud; your father learned to ride the fortune cookie."

Is there an appropriate response for such a remark? I don't think so.

"Why didn't Dad call me himself?"

"He's too busy snapping up baby kimonos and learning how to bow to remember his only daughter."

"I find that hard to believe."

"As hard to believe as your father having a baby with his mistress?"

"Ming is his girlfriend now. You guys are divorced."

"They both have big old *A*s on their chests for life."

"No one uses the word *adulterer* anymore. Jesus, Mother, this isn't the *Scarlet Letter*."

"Assholes, my dear. Your father is an asshole, and Ming is an asshole with a side of plum sauce."

"She's not Chinese."

"She was a part of that Tiananmen Square thing. She drove the tank. You realize that your brother Bastard Won Ton will have a war criminal for a mother. Makes you appreciate me."

"How do you know it's a boy?"

"The hospital performs amniocentesis on all bastard children to make sure there aren't any deformities."

"I have to go."

"Why?"

"I need to call Amnesty International to look into this war crimes thing."

"I am available if they have any questions."

"I'm not serious."

"I am. Best, Mother."

Standing shell-shocked in my apartment, I wonder

how Mother found out. I can't imagine Dad would call her and not me. However, Dad would call Barney. I pick up the phone and hit redial.

"Hello?"

"Mother, Amnesty is calling me back later. Can I have Barney, please?"

"Your brother is taking one of his naps."

"Wake him up."

"This is not China. I don't take orders," Mother snaps dramatically.

"I'm sorry. Will you please wake up Barney?" I say softly, desperate to appease her madness.

"His door is locked, and I don't want him walking out here and grabbing the phone without washing his hands."

"Fine. Have him call me back."

Certain things ruin sexuality and all the fun that comes with it. One such thing is Mother informing me of my brother's masturbation habits. Barney's "naps" single-handedly (no pun intended) support the Internet porn industry. My need for a normal male distraction has never been quite so profound.

I still can't believe Ben kissed me. With the ground-work for a childish crush already in place, I decide to take advantage of the new technology for stalking. Google is far superior to driving by someone's house. I type Ben's name into the box in eager anticipation of information; the mere notion of reading about Ben makes me want to leap out of my skin.

Who knew Ben Reynolds was such a popular name? There are nine thousand Ben Reynoldses in the United States alone. I remain undeterred; a few hours of research can't stop me. In Boston, Massachusetts, a cute nine-year-old named Ben Reynolds was recently appointed captain of his soccer team. Ben Reynolds of Hampstead, North Dakota, is a sad man with a face of broken capillaries. Lay off the drink, Ben. Moving on, I find a link to a Brown University student on the crew team. Brown University's newspaper includes a photo of my Ben and his crew team after rowing their way to victory. He is shirtless again. Modesty is not one of Ben's defining characteristics. Not that I am complaining; his body is porn for me. I could stare all day, mesmerized by each indentation.

Logic crushes my lust abruptly. I will never see him again. Although that may be a good thing, since I could easily descend into inappropriate licking. That's right; I want to lick his chest. I am gross. I must look away. No more smut!

The phone rings, saving me from my impure thoughts.

"Hello?"

"Mingster's preggers," Barney announces casually.

"Mother told me. How come Dad didn't call us?"

"He called me last week, asked to meet at the food court."

"Why didn't he call me?"

"He wanted me to tell you since we're so close."

There is a pause, a very long pause. I decide to let this one go.

"And you waited a week to call me?"

"It takes nine months to have a baby. What's five days?"

"Okay, Barney," I mutter. "How do you feel about the baby?"

"I'm holding off on forming an opinion until the thing can talk. Most likely won't have a verdict for at least two years."

Long pause.

"I think Mother is heading for a breakdown."

"Most accurate, but I can't discuss now. Mother and I have reservations at Le Jardin d'Olive."

"You looked up how to say that on the Internet, didn't you."

"10-4, Anna." Click.

Barney is clearly my parents' child. I recognize his inability to connect emotionally as a family trait. As kids, Barney and I used to play the most mundane of imaginary professions. While other children played doctor, lawyer, or vague rich person, we had no such aspirations and were content to play The Wherehouse (the Blockbuster of its time) or post office. We spent hours pretending to check out videos or deliver mail to each other. The mail consisted of old birthday cards from our grandparents and junk mail our parents threw away. In the case of videos, since we didn't actually own any VHS tapes, we used books. It wasn't conscious, but in retrospect, I recognize a desire to keep our expectations manageable. In the Norton house, no one dared dream big for fear that we would bottom out at below average. Well, at least I've hit my mark.

I decide to call Janice to fill her in on the rest of the evening's events and, right after I hang up, the phone rings again. I ignore it and crash onto my bed. I don't have the energy to listen to the details of Mother and Barney's meal at Olive Garden.

Chapter Fifteen

Brushing my teeth is especially important after dreaming that they crumbled to dust upon biting into an apple. I am embarrassed by how often I fall asleep without brushing. This is a by-product of never sharing a bed with anyone. It's easy to let the plaque and halitosis build up when alone. Who cares if my breath stinks? It's not as if anyone kisses me goodnight. To compensate, in the morning I perform an exceedingly thorough job of brushing and flossing.

This morning I thrust my toothbrush forcefully along the ridges of my tongue. While gagging myself, I punch in my voicemail password, prepared to learn how many breadsticks Barney hid in Mother's purse.

"Anna, it's Ben Reynolds."

"Holy," I say, accidentally releasing frothy toothpaste water from my mouth. "He called!"

"Are you free for dinner tomorrow? It's last minute, but I thought I would check. Let me know."

What is going on? I think with a mouth full of toothpaste. Unable to brush and concentrate on the events at hand, I spit my foamy liquid into an old coffee cup. Should I call Janice to get her advice? Should I erase the message? I can't. I want to believe in him again. I shouldn't, but I do. I want to believe that I did see something in him the first time I spotted him across the bar. Dialing Ben, my heartbeat echoes in my eardrum.

"Hello?"

"Ben, it's Anna."

There is a long pause.

"Um, Anna Norton."

There is another pause.

"You called me last night."

Total radio silence.

"Sorry, I just got this phone and I keep muting myself by accident."

"Oh, how funny," I say maniacally. "Gee, that is really, really...funny."

"How are you?"

"Um, I would say I'm...good." Okay, keep it short. I need to wrap this up as soon as possible to decrease my odds of humiliation. "I'm running out to meet friends, but I would love to grab dinner tonight."

"I thought I would cook for you."

Silence. Why does he want to cook for me? Is he embarrassed to take me out in public?

"It was pretty loud the other night, so we didn't really get a chance to talk."

"Oh, of course," I say, thinking *what a load of crap*. Our lack of conversation had very little to do with the band.

"How about 7:30 at my place?"

"Sounds like a plan."

"Sounds like a plan" is such a nerdy response. It is something Barney would say. I must learn to speak like a grown woman before tonight. I hang up and immediately dial Janice.

"Janice, it's Anna," I say in a voice so calm it's almost catatonic.

"What happened? What's the matter?"

I'm silent not because I want to torture Janice but because I am tongue-tied with shock. "Is it your mother? Did she hurt your father? Or the Chinese girlfriend who's not really Chinese? I had a feeling this was coming. She didn't sound right in the head."

"Mother is still working up to physical violence. This is about Ben."

"Oh, no! You didn't do anything violent, did you?"

"He called."

"He called?" Janice repeats. This is clearly not an outcome she had prepared for.

"And asked me to dinner...at his apartment."

"Will you be offended if I say I am surprised?"

"Not at all," I respond truthfully.

"I thought that peck on the lips may have been a 'sorry I hurt your feelings but I am a good-looking asshole' kiss. I love that I am wrong. The man is insanely sexy!"

"I know. That's what makes me so nervous. Ben is the first handsome man I've ever had dinner with—ever—in my whole life, including friends and relatives."

"Don't worry, we'll do a dry run at my place. I'll be Ben. I do great impressions."

"That would be helpful but, see, the date is tonight."

"What? Did he get a last-minute cancellation?"

"Janice," I yelp in frustration.

"Sorry. Let me think. The best advice I can give you is to look him in the eye and try not to talk much. The less you say, the less you'll have to regret tomorrow."

Having digested Janice's advice, I indulge my fantasies of the impossible. Could Ben actually want to be with me?

Hello Fatty,
Don't be a slut. Sex on the second date does not a couple make.

—Anna

Regardless of what isn't happening in my pants, it's vital for my mental state that my body be properly maintained. I don't care if all the hard work stays hidden beneath my clothes.

Tonight's ensemble consists of a simple low-cut black cardigan over a black tank with pencil jeans and ballet flats. I toyed with putting my hair up but decided having it "flip-ready" would be better. As a child in the 1990s, I envied popular girls from across the room as they flipped their hair from side to side. This unfortunately etched hair flipping onto my psyche as a sign of cool.

As I try to concentrate on my makeup application, noting with pleasure the smoothness of the skin beneath my custom-blended foundation, a nagging voice remains in the back of my mind.

Hello Fatty,
You are making a terrible mistake. The man is going to use you like a Kleenex, then toss you in the gutter. Whatever odd nerd fetish he has will inevitably pass. Then what? A long, slow dive off a high-rise in Midtown? Or you will remain an emotional wreck who spends the next forty years talking about the man who

*broke her heart on the second date. Good luck with all
your endeavors.*

—Anna

Even with knowledge of a possibly negative outcome,
I simply cannot say no to Ben.

I exit the L train at Sixth Avenue and walk down to
Spring Street in an effort to calm my nerves. By the time
I ascend the stairs to Ben's building, I am slightly less anx-
ious. I perform a quick breath test and armpit sniff before
heading toward Ben's door. Funky nervous-girl breath
and malodorous pits can derail even the greatest of dates.
Luckily, I pass both tests. Standing in front of Ben's door,
I put on an exaggerated smile and raise my hand to knock.
Before I can make contact, the door flies open.

"I thought I heard you out here," Ben says with a
warm smile.

"You must have 20/20 hearing or whatever the equivalent is," I say meekly.

"Something like that."

He kisses my cheek politely, making me wonder if this
is just a friend thing. Is he trying to apologize for the other
night? Confusion and teenage hormones overwhelm my
body as I enter his apartment.

"Can I get you a glass of wine?"

"Yes, please," I say as if I were an English child visiting her grandmother.

I follow Ben to the kitchen, where he reaches for wine-
glasses. I suck in my breath as his shirt rides up, exposing
the crevice that separates his abdomen and legs. I make a
mental note to find the technical term for this area so I
can accurately refer to it while speaking with Janice.

"Red or white?"

"White, please."

"So what did you do with your friends?"

I forgot about my outing with friends. What would a normal girl do with her girlfriends? "We did some... shopping and...grabbed a bite. Pretty regular girlfriend stuff."

"What did you buy?"

"Um, you know...things...like makeup. Girls love makeup, or so I've heard. No, I mean, I haven't heard, I know. Girls love makeup...and we are no exception," I babble.

"What are their names?"

"Who?"

"Your friends?"

"Um, well, you know Janice, and the other two are...Donny and Marie."

"You can't be serious."

"Why? Do you know them?" I ask him, panicked.

"Donny and Marie? The brother and sister with the variety act?"

Oh my God! No wonder that rolled right off my tongue. *Donny and Marie!* Where the hell did that come from—I never even watched their show!

"I always forget about them. These are two random, unrelated women. Donny is actually a nickname for Donna."

Silence. Great, here we go again. Another weird freaking evening of stilted conversation.

"You know, about the other night," Ben says solemnly, "I shouldn't have kissed you."

Here we go, the "sorry I kissed you, let's be friends"

speech. He brought me all the way over here to ease his conscience over some nerd he pity-kissed.

"I should have asked you first. I got a little carried away."

Is he serious? I don't have a clue how to read him. Where is the damn periodic table of male/female conversation? I missed it in all my years of studying. I've never been so profoundly confused.

"Don't be silly, it was...lovely," I say with slight embarrassment.

"Yeah, it was," Ben agrees sweetly before pulling my hand toward the living room. There are appetizers on the table. I would forgive him grand theft auto, burglary, or a variety of other misdemeanors for being considerate enough to put out olives and cheese.

"I thought a lot about what you said, about my mother making my father want to be a better man...inspiring him to want more for himself, from his life."

"You're blessed to be the product of that kind of love. Most people aren't inspired when they listen to their parents discuss their relationships. They're depressed, or at least I am."

"But that's the thing. I've never really been inspired by their relationship. In fact, I've hardly ever thought about it. It wasn't until you said that the other night that I started thinking about it."

Ben presents dinner on his modern table, clearly illustrating how he maintains his physique. The meal is a nutritionist's wet dream: tofu, steamed vegetables, and brown rice. I thought people only ate like this at ashrams and fat camps. I hide my shock so Ben will think I also eat healthy.

"I hope you like tofu."

"I love tofu! I eat tofu pretty much any time someone else would eat meat. I actually sent that to the board of tofu to use as a slogan—Eat tofu when others eat meat!"

The board of tofu? I have completely lost my mind.

Ben smiles at me as I stand.

"I'm going to wash my hands before I eat…the tofu."

The tofu? I've forgotten how to speak English properly.

Standing in front of the bathroom mirror, I am face to face with the woman whom Ben Reynolds has cooked dinner for. How the hell did I get here?

I lean over to turn off the faucets when something in the wastebasket catches my eye. It's a crumpled photograph. I grab it and unfold it quickly. It's her—the blonde from the Stanton Social. She's even more beautiful than I remember. Apparently, curiosity killed not only the cat but the nerd. Looking at this woman's features reminds me what a second-class citizen I am in relation to Ben. The only good news is that if her picture is in the trash, they're probably over.

I return to the table with a forced smile, and Ben picks up right where we left off—tofu.

"How long have you been a vegetarian?"

"It's been a while. I can't even remember. You?"

This isn't technically a lie, since I don't remember if I last ate bacon the day before I met Ben or two days prior.

"My parents are strict vegetarians, so I was raised with it. I had a rebellious period in my teens. Big Macs and Whoppers. The whole fast food thing. Then we took a family vacation to a slaughterhouse, and that put an end to it," Ben says morosely. "Now my mom asks all the girls I date if they're vegetarians. I think she wants to make sure I'm not tempted off the path of the righteous."

"That's okay," I say, feeling oddly protective of Ben's mother.

"And if they say no, she describes a chicken's last hours of life in excruciating detail. She even has pictures. Gela, my ex, barfed right at the table."

Anna destroys Gela in my imaginary name contest.

"I don't think she will ever show her face at Cipriani again," Ben says seriously.

Think of your father naked, I tell myself. Don't laugh. He's being serious. Unfortunately, nothing can stop the roar of laughter within me. I explode, giggling hysterically the way kids do when teachers tell them to stop. The more I try to stop, the more I laugh.

"I guess it is kind of funny," Ben says with a laugh.

I finally manage to get myself under control, wiping away the tears from my eyes. "Sorry...I...um...I'm just happy I'm a vegetarian."

"Me, too."

Our eyes lock. Am I in a Hallmark movie? This is remarkable. Well, except for the mention of his ex-girlfriend *Gela*.

"That story really doesn't make my family sound too normal," Ben says with a hint of self-consciousness.

"Oh, please! My family belongs under a circus tent compared to yours. My older brother, Barney, is a chronic masturbator who lives at home with Mother. He claims to have some sort of Internet job, but I've yet to see a pay stub or any proof whatsoever. Mother doesn't mind because she's retired and now spends all her free time shopping off QVC or bad-mouthing my father and his girlfriend, Ming, who used to be his secretary until he left Mother for her. Oh, and now Ming's having his baby, and Mother has named it Bastard Won Ton."

"Bastard is a hard name to pull off," Ben muses.

"I don't know. Bastard Won Ton Norton has a certain ring to it," I reply.

He places his hand on mine and laughs. His hand electrifies my body, sending a tingling sensation to my feet.

"Let's have coffee in the living room."

My legs wobble, but I manage to place one foot in front of the other, keeping my eyes firmly trained on Ben's back. I lower myself onto the cream-colored, modern, and unquestionably expensive couch. It fits Ben's sophisticated image, but this isn't the hemp couch I expect from a vegetarian. Having grown up in Ohio, I imagine vegetarians as hippies with tie-dyed shirts, VW buses, and carob chip cookies. I never dreamed they could come in the package of a wealthy, stylish New York lawyer.

Bruce Springsteen's "Dancing in the Dark" plays in the background. Up until this moment, I never paid much notice to Springsteen. Now his voice will be a quintessential reminder of the dawn of happiness in my life.

"I don't think I'll ever be able to call anyone a bastard again. Not without thinking of some cute little baby, and that kind of ruins the whole thing."

Ben delicately puts his coffee cup down on the table, then runs to the stereo. The music reverberates off every piece of furniture in the apartment.

"Um, are your neighbors...," I mumble to myself.

Ben, oblivious to my internal debate on noise control,

rocks out on air guitar. I am both pleased and horrified to note that he looks silly, even ridiculous. After all, he is a grown man in a very fashionable apartment playing air guitar as if it were his parents' garage in 1986.

"Do you like Springsteen?" Ben yells over the music.

"Oh, yeah. He's the Boss," I say without any irony whatsoever.

Mistaking my lameness for a sardonic sense of humor, he laughs before trying to pull me off the couch. My arms go limp. I don't know how to dance or play any air instruments. I was actually thrown out of band for allegedly molesting a clarinet. It's a long story. Ben leans over me, bringing his mouth dangerously close to mine. I blush. Without breaking eye contact, he takes hold of my hips, raising me to a standing position.

"Remember the video," he says, moving behind me, his hands still on my hips. "He pulls Courteney Cox on stage."

I snap my fingers, doing my best imitation of her bouncy dance.

This is the single most romantic moment of my life, beyond any fantasy, because this is happening. I am incapable of acknowledging that life existed before or will exist after; it's right now that matters.

"I bet this is how you got all the girls at Brown," I say with a laugh that quickly sours. Ben didn't tell me he went to Brown, and he knows it. As if trapped in an episode of *Three's Company,* the music abruptly stops. The tension mounts. Sweat beads form on my upper lip. Within seconds, I will have a full sweat 'stache, or worse, another breast-rubbing incident. I should have listened to Janice and kept my mouth shut. Now it's too late. I must say something.

"I Googled you. But not in a stalker-ish way, more of a friendly research manner."

Total silence. I am Kathy Bates to his James Caan in *Misery.*

"That's okay, I Googled you, too."

He leans toward me, then stops inches from my lips. The anticipation kills me. Ben closes the three-inch gap and softly kisses me. Unable to control myself, I open my mouth wider than Mick Jagger at the dentist. My arms and legs tingle with passion. My heart beats loudly as my stomach turns with butterflies. This truly is the greatest kiss in the history of nerds. I half expect streamers and confetti to hail down on me from the Board of Nerdy Women. I am the poster child for nerd redemption, and Ben is my sweet reward.

The power of the kiss increases exponentially with each second, dissolving my sexual apprehensions. Ben's hand slowly caresses my waist, his fingers sneaking beneath my shirt. He kisses my neck while his hand passes over my bra-covered breasts. My nipples immediately react, joining the rest of my body in a state of extreme arousal.

Within minutes, I am topless on his white high-thread-count sheets. Ben removes his shirt. Gulp. Don't lick him. He'll think it's weird. It will ruin the moment. I purse my lips and caress his chest, lightly running my fingers over his nipples. My nipples meanwhile are still pointing fervently to space.

Ben unbuttons my pants. Suddenly, I'm nervous. Cool people probably have sex differently than nerds, complete with a distinct vocabulary of moaning and acrobatic positions. I will pale in comparison to the thousands of seasoned lovers Ben's experienced. My body tightens with stress, withdrawing into itself like a turtle under its shell.

"Are you okay?"

"Um, I guess you could say that...I am a little...nerdous...I mean, *nervous*."

"We don't have to do anything," Ben says in a soothing voice.

He pulls me into his arms, placing my head on his slightly hairy chest. His hand glides over my hair.

"It's been a long time since a woman has been nervous with me."

Why did I tell him that? He's going to throw a Valium into the hallway and tell me to fetch it.

"I feel so special," he says in a silly tone of voice.

"Shut up, bastard," I say, raising my head and looking directly into his eyes.

My trepidation disappears. He wants me as I am. I let him pull off my jeans with one hand as his other hand caresses my thigh. Dressed only in underwear, I watch Ben take off his jeans and underwear. He is gorgeous naked, as I knew he would be. Ben kisses my feet, slowly making his way up my legs. He arrives at my black cotton underwear, then aggressively pulls them down my legs.

Ben lowers his body on top of mine. My hand wanders down his chest. Ben watches me, waiting for me to make the obvious discovery. It's like Pandora's box. I have no idea what I will be unleashing. Ben senses my hesitation and places his hand atop mine, guiding it the rest of the way, the perfect mixture of tenderness and passion.

While I know this is extremely uncouth, I would like to get today's date tattooed on my derriere as a day that will live in infamy for nerds everywhere. I had sex with Ben Reynolds. Yes, *the* Ben Reynolds. I'm naked, having intimately shown every part of myself to the most attractive man in the five boroughs, yet I'm peaceful. While it sounds like the makings of a Danielle Steel novel, we fit together perfectly.

I playfully hit Ben's well-toned arm and say, "I can't believe you Googled me!"

"I was going to put a note in your locker, but I didn't want to scare you off."

I lean in and kiss him. I am almost comfortable enough to lick his chest. Seriously.

"It's pretty amusing because there is a picture of an Anna Norton online. Only it's this fat teenager in front of the Washington Monument. Definitely not my Anna Norton," he says with a kiss to my forehead.

Ben means this as a compliment, but in reality, it feels like a cruel joke. The fat teenager *is* me. I was on my senior trip to the capital five years ago. Part of me is relieved that he can't recognize the ugliness of my past, that he wouldn't even think that person could be me. Yet I cannot deny that Ben's delivery of the word *fat* is on par with *burglar, robber,* or *convict;* there's an association of blame or guilt for the person's predicament. The *f* word repeats at inaudible levels in my mind. I am no longer the fat teenager on the outside, but I am clearly the same girl on the inside.

Chapter Sixteen

J anice! I had sex!" I boom into the phone.

I haven't even showered yet. There is something strangely erotic about knowing I have the residue of sex with Ben Reynolds on me.

"I hope you used a condom, 'cause a guy that good looking—"

"Yes, I used a condom."

"And?"

"It was amazing, I didn't even think about—"

"All the women that came before you?"

"Um, no," I say with attitude. Why does she have to say things like that?

"Or will come after you."

"Jesus, Janice! *No!*" I roar. "I was trying to say that I didn't even think about my performance."

"Exactly, and your performance would be in relation to Ben's past and future conquests."

"Janice, stop saying that. He will never sleep with anyone again!"

"Okay..."

"I mean I hope he doesn't sleep with anyone else. Damn it, I have no chance here, do I?"

"I'm sorry. I think you and Ben are both great, and I am sure you will have sex again."

"We are both great. Equally great. Right?" I say to reassure myself.

"Sure, sweetie," Janice offers patronizingly. "And to prove how great you are, why don't you stop by Peter Produce and get eggplants for the ratatouille?"

Janice always calls our produce man "Peter Produce" even though his name is Stan. I guess Stan doesn't go as well with the surname Produce.

Dejected, I trudge past the brass mailboxes in the lobby of my building en route to buying eggplants. A dark manila envelope catches my eye. I turn for a closer inspection and see both my name and address printed on it. This is not a good sign; the last delivery I received was from Mother announcing the conception of Bastard Won Ton. She's probably stolen the sonogram from Dad and Ming and drawn horns on poor Bastard Won Ton's soft skull. I rip open the envelope, fully expecting to amass another year's worth of material for therapy. I discover a CD, a small envelope, and a sheet of letterhead with instructions.

1. Listen to CD.
2. Read note.

It's not signed, but it's from Ben. The letterhead has his law firm, Benson and Silverberg, on it. I smell the small envelope, hoping to discern a trace of Ben's scent. Like an overeager child on Christmas, I want to open the note immediately. Wait, this could be bad. Am I getting excited prematurely? Technically, this could be a well-planned parting gift. Is this Ben's sophisticated manner of dumping me? Unsure what to do, I pause and write a mental Hello Fatty entry to prepare me for whatever comes and to ward off bad luck.

Hello Fatty,
It's not you, it's me. I am a shell of a human, but still the best-looking man you've ever been with sexually. Here are a few songs to remember me.

                                        Lovingly,
The man who dismantled your ego in less than forty-eight hours.

                                        P.S. No hard feelings.

Back in my apartment, I put the CD in my 1990s boom box and sprawl out on the floor. In the words of Pat Benatar, "hit me with your best shot." I push play and shut my eyes. I half expect some break-up anthem, but instead the distinctive opening bars of "My Girl" by the Temptations peal out; even I know this is definitely not a break-up song. This is not my worst fear, but rather one of my oldest dreams, a mix tape. In junior high, a mix tape was the ultimate sign of affection, and while it's been twenty-odd years since it was at the height of its popularity, I believe the gesture's significance remains intact. *"He likes me!!"*

I quickly open the off-white envelope. The navy blue ink stands out against the expensive paper, as does the question "Will you go steady with me? Circle one—yes or no—and put it back in my locker. Ben."

There is a slight chance I fainted. As I am already lying on the floor, I can't tell for sure. All I know is that I am out of breath and woozy. This is it. It is happening. I have confirmed proof in my hand. This is not a fantasy or a delusion, but an actual occurrence. Ben likes me and not in the platonic manner. He wants to be my boyfriend. It's more than elation and euphoria that keeps me pinned to the ground, it's shock. After a quarter of a century, I have finally gotten what I want.

An hour of prep later, having completely forgotten the eggplants, I run to catch the L train with freshly blown out locks, lip gloss, and brown eyeliner that works hard to make my eyes pop. Happiness clouds all rational thought. Once in SoHo, I dial Mother, for reasons mostly unknown to me.

"Yellow?" Barney answers.

"Barn...I have a boyfriend...and I'm not talking about Jesus," I say jubilantly.

"You didn't even notice I said *yellow,* not *hello.*"

"Barn...a boyfriend...a tall and sexy boyfriend...a man that women faint at the sight of," I say, ignoring his previous comment.

I am too happy to be annoyed or irritated by my brother's weird ways, so I just hang up. I needed to tell someone from back home, someone who knows what horribly unattractive beginnings I come from. And yes, Barney may not have responded like a normal human being, but I don't care. All I care is that I am en route to tell Ben yes! I bolt up the stairs to his apartment, arriving out of breath and sweating with anticipation. I pause to reapply lip gloss before ringing the doorbell.

Please be home. I ring the doorbell. Nothing. I bang my fist against the door and, able to restrain myself no longer, yell.

"Ben! Beeeennnnnnn! Bbbbbbeeeeeeeennn!" My inner drama queen arrives with guns blazing and eyes misting. Not since I cried over the death of my college roommate and *friend* Jane Zelisky have I been so theatrical. Do I lower myself to the floor mumbling Ben's name? Or pound on the door one last time?

"Ben, please open up," I plead, pumping my fists against the door.

"I'll take that as a yes," says a voice from behind me.

I don't answer. I run. I grab. I kiss.

Chapter Seventeen

In the middle of Central Park, I watch beautiful, slender women smile seductively at my boyfriend. I hold Ben's arm proprietarily, but it does little to deter these women. Ben is neither amazed nor shocked by the attention. This is his reality, gorgeous women check him out. They smile at him and he smiles back, not in a lecherous manner, but as an acknowledgment. Or is that merely wishful thinking on my part? Men pass without batting an eye in my direction. Actually quite a few grin at Ben as well. Open-minded flirt that he is, Ben grins back. Every time. He places a blanket on the grass on this unusually sunny fall Saturday, pulls out the *New York Times* and I rest my head in his lap. I happily forget the women as Ben reads articles aloud. I never read the paper. Any paper. I know it sounds ignorant, but world affairs depress me. "Babe, can you believe that?" Ben says emotionally.

"It's terrible," I say shaking my head. I have taken to saying everything is terrible when Ben reads the paper to me. It is a safe bet that whatever he read was indeed quite terrible. I honestly want to expand my scope of knowledge, but there is an insurmountable problem. Close proximity to Ben negates all intellectual capabilities. Instead, my mind wanders to thoroughly embarrassing fantasies like Ben and me in matrimonial bliss. Mr. and Mrs. Perfect Reynolds. With my face nuzzled in his warm charcoal gray Patagonia, I am safe. Staring up at Ben, I find it hard to fathom that he's my boyfriend. I feel like he's on loan to me from a museum, he's that beautiful.

On the way back to Ben's apartment, we take a detour down West Houston to stop at Jones Bakery. He is obsessed with their apricot and chocolate rugalach. It's a tiny, unkempt shop that clearly hasn't been remodeled since the late 1960s, a true hole in the wall kept in business by stoned NYU students with the munchies. Behind the counter is a twentysomething sprite with chipped black nail polish and cheap gold jewelry. She doesn't compare to the well-groomed ladies that prowl the streets of Manhattan. However, she is young, she is cute, and she knows it. Women aware of their assets have an edge I envy. Even if their assets are limited, the mere act of acknowledging them doubles their appeal.

Ben peruses the rugalach while I internally debate buying some for my neighbor, Mrs. Bester. An expression of gratitude from the old deaf woman would warm me. Moreover, I can tell Ben about it and let him praise my generous nature. While I am busy debating whether the sketchy motivations behind my act of charity would be too obvious to pull it off, Bakery Bitch attempts to *hand-feed* Ben a piece of rugalach. I snap to attention, grab the morsel out of her hand, and feed *my boyfriend* the tiny pastry myself. Yes, Ben's hands are full, but that is no excuse for the Bakery Bitch to feed him as if he were a trained monkey. More important, why does he lean in with his lips slightly parted as if being fed by strangers is a common occurrence?

"May I try a piece as well?" I ask Bakery Bitch with the nastiest stare seen outside of female incarceration.

I bend forward to see if she will hand-feed me. Her hand hangs in the air. I didn't think so. I grab the pastry, stuff it in my mouth, and savor the buttery contents. Ben is completely oblivious to the girl-to-girl subtext. I touch his arm sweetly as I chew. Bakery Bitch's open mouth conveys her disbelief that he is *my* boyfriend. I stare a message to her: "I am the only one who hand-feeds him." It is a complicated stare, but I manage to get the meaning across. Outsiders may misinterpret the look as one of intense food poisoning or nearsightedness, but believe me, Bakery Bitch understands.

"Babe, what do you think? Apricot or chocolate?"

"Apricot," I respond robotically.

"Okay, we'll take a pound. What's your name again?"

"Gwendolyn, but my friends call me Gwen. Ben, right?"

"Good memory, Gwen."

Why is he calling her Gwen? She said her friends call her Gwen. Is this a pathetic attempt to be her friend? Plus, you can't be friends with people with rhyming names! Gwen and Ben...disgusting!

"I had no idea you were such a regular here, Ben," I interject in my best pseudo-casual tone.

"I love pastries."

As if channeling Mother, I want to scream, "You better not want any pussy pastry!"

"I'll get a pound for Mrs. Bester downstairs."

"Babe, that's so thoughtful of you."

As I predicted, he is touched by my charitable act. I am deeply disturbed by my dubious attitude toward charity, but pleased that I can give Bakery Bitch a look of

benevolent superiority. Ben tips Bakery Bitch two dollars
and leaves with a sexy smirk.

"See you next week, Gwen."

Is this a standing date? What is she like when I am not
here? Does she hand-feed him naked?

Two days pass before I finally stop thinking about
Bakery Bitch. I hardly have time today to fret over Ben
as Janice and I work a party for two PR girls, Jo Allen
and Fiona Worthington. In a small boutique on Little
West Twelfth Street in the Meatpacking district, we celebrate Jo and Fiona's book on how to throw the perfect
party, which apparently requires that everything be violet, including the food. Jo is a beautiful, tall woman with
the kind of cascading blonde locks that inspire normally
rational women to get hair extensions. Fiona, on the
other hand, is a short redhead with glasses and a nose as
overbearing as her personality. I savor the idea that Fiona
secretly envies Jo's beauty as much as I do. It comforts me
to know that I am not alone in my insecurities.

PR girls are a strange breed of insecure bitches that
exude the type of cruelty most often seen in high school
cheerleaders. They are fake in every sense of the word.
They are judgmental. They are mean. They are elitist.
They are also our clients, so I nod and smile when they
make snarky remarks about "the help." I know that every
finger in the room will be tickling their tonsils creating a
wall of violet vomit in the sewer and frankly, I find that
disrespectful. They are literally flushing our work down
the toilet. Still I forge on stacking violet meringues and
macaroons in the corner of the bustling party. With my
back to the guests, I unprofessionally sneak a coconut

macaroon. Bitchy women set off the defensive eating mechanism of my youth.

"You can't get fat if you want to be Mrs. Ben Reynolds," Janice announces a little too loudly.

My mouth is too full to retort, so I roll my eyes.

"Did you just say Ben Reynolds?" Jo asks from behind us.

"Yes, I did. Why?" Janice asks. Every muscle in my body tenses as I wait for the response.

"Ben Reynolds, the lawyer at Benson and Silverberg?"

I don't feel so well. My throat burns as I swallow the violet mass.

"He's a lawyer. Anna, is that where he works?"

"Yes. That's him. Ben Reynolds, son of Milly and Arthur," I exclaim gaily, trying to sound unconcerned.

This conversation scares me. Is New York the size of Mayberry? How could she know Ben?

"How do *you* know him?" Jo asks me with an astonishing emphasis on the word *you*.

"He's *her* boyfriend. Now, what can we do for you?" Janice interjects protectively.

"We need more cupcakes," Jo answers before turning her crystal blue eyes on me.

"Tell Ben hello from me. I dated Ben before Gela. Not an easy gig. Good luck with it." Jo smirks as she walks off.

"Fuck her. She's the kind of Waspy bitch who agrees to anal sex so she can be a virgin for her husband. Pay her no mind."

"What did she mean by 'good luck'? And are you implying that Ben did her in the ass?" I ask with mounting hysteria.

"Don't be naïve. All good-looking men have done it. It's the dorky ones that never manage to get their girlfriends drunk enough to try."

"Do you think he wants to do that with me?"

"I don't know. Has he tried?"

"No, is that a bad sign?"

"You have got to be kidding me," Janice guffaws.

The knowledge that Ben dated Jo shouldn't come as a surprise. She is tall, gorgeous, and sophisticated with attitude to spare. I loathe him for being so superficial. Jo has the personality of burnt plastic, but she is undeniably seductive. With violet frosting wedged beneath my nails and a thoroughly dented ego, I head home. The subway, filled with regular-looking people, comforts me. It's important to remember that the Jos and Bens of the world are the freaks of nature. Most people do not look like them and couldn't even with the help of a sharp scalpel. A suffocating sense of inferiority chokes me as I remember Jo's hypnotic presence. I want to binge. The rugalach I purchased for Mrs. Bester come to mind. They are probably stale by now, but that's nothing a little half-and-half couldn't fix. I should have delivered the rugalach days ago, but I didn't. Maybe I am destined to relapse. A dull pain twists in my stomach as I ascend the stairs in my building. Dating Ben is a terrible strain on my confidence. I am so far out of my league that I cannot afford to deteriorate in any way. I've already had a macaroon today, the rugalach must go! I throw my purse onto the bed and grab the rugalach from the top of my minifridge. Knocking loudly on Mrs. Bester's door I battle a deep fear. What if the old bat isn't home? I'm not sure I can control myself.

"Mrs. Bester, it's Anna from upstairs," I shout loudly,

slapping my open hand against the door. "Hello? Mrs. Bester?" I shriek.

Finally, the door opens. The old woman sports an annoyed look with a half-smoked cigarette hanging from her mouth.

"I brought you some rugalach, Mrs. Bester."

"What did you say?" she asks with irritation.

"I brought you some rugalach," I clearly articulate while presenting the box.

"Oh. They must be from my son."

"No, no. They are from me," I say while pointing to myself.

"What?" she asks accusingly.

"They are from me."

"No, he's married," she says with an eye roll.

And with that, she shuts the door in my face. Not only did I not get credit from the old bag for the rugalach, but she also managed to reject me on behalf of her son.

Utterly defeated by both Jo and Mrs. Bester, I jump back on the L train to see Ben. I must remember that he has chosen me, as I am. Of course, for good measure I exit the subway early and power walk. As Ben's girlfriend, I need to be in the best shape possible. Ben opens the front door with his shirt off. Damn, he's sexy. I raise my eyes from his chest to his gorgeous face. He pulls me into his arms, pressing my face against his torso. I take a deep breath and then I lick his chest. Even if I lose him, I will have done what I always wanted to do.

"Babe, are you licking my chest?" Ben asks curiously.

"Why, do you like it?"

"Yeah, but not in the hallway."

"Uh, okay. Do you want to put a shirt on and get some food?" I ask trying to make him forget my licking.

"I'd rather order in and play Monopoly with my favorite bastard…"

"You are so romantic," I say jokingly. "And to think I didn't even know you liked board games."

We eat Chinese food on top of an old blanket so as not to ruin the high thread count Frettes. Then we fall asleep without ever passing GO.

Chapter Eighteen

B abe, wake up. Stop pretending," Ben stirs me from a night of deep sleep. His voice calls me back to consciousness as if I'm a patient waking from anesthesia. I try to focus my eyes, grateful that Ben's voice is not an amalgamation of years of fantasies, but an actual man calling me to him. He rubs my arm while saying my name. My boring insignificant name takes on a beauty I never knew it had.

"Hi," I say in a groggy voice that is as sexy as I can manage at this early hour.

"You're cute in the mornings," he says with a kiss on my lips.

I turn my head to shield him from my less-than-delectable morning breath.

"You make me happy."

"You make me happy, too," I say, jumping out of bed.

"Hey, where are you going?"

"I'm brushing my teeth so I can be nice and fresh to kiss you."

He smiles. Right answer. Ben likes me nice and fresh.

Ben's bathroom, like the rest of the apartment, is clean, mostly white, and modern. The faucets are from Waterworks and the towels are fluffier than my pillows. Ben stands behind me in his white boxers brushing his teeth. I'm in a white tank top and cotton underwear. We are commercial-worthy cute, embodying a lifestyle that could easily sell toothpaste. Well, except for the gagging sound Ben makes while brushing his tongue. Following suit, I brush my tongue as Ben kisses my neck. Something rises in my throat, a huge air pocket, better known as a burp.

"Ahhh."

"Are you okay?"

"Uh, yeah. I got a little carried away with the brushing," I explain with embarrassment. I have officially spoiled my commercial-worthy morning. Ben heads into the bedroom to change for work as I stare at myself crossly in the mirror.

"Babe, tonight we're meeting John and his girlfriend at Misery."

"What's Misery?" I ask innocently, assuming it's the latest restaurant to hit Manhattan.

"Some new club."

I hate clubs. They are the adult equivalent of school dances, establishing who is popular and who is not by where you stand and how you boogie. Not to mention, clubs are stomping grounds for the New York women I strive to block from Ben's viewpoint.

"Misery? Why would they name it that?"

"It's irony, babe."

"Wouldn't it be better to stay in for another round of Monopoly, Chinese leftovers, and sex with your girlfriend?"

"Burpy Bastard, I will be delighted to have sex with you after Misery."

"How generous of you."

I can't dance in front of Ben and his friend John or worse, John's girlfriend. She's probably an outrageously sexy dancer whereas I'm more of a foot tapper. There is no doubt in my mind that I will look ridiculous next to her. My best bet is to utterly blend into the background. Ideally, John and his girlfriend will only remember a blurry girl standing near Ben. "Hey, did you see Ben's girlfriend?" John will ask his girlfriend.

"I know she was there, but I can't remember her for the life of me. Although, there was a blurry figure holding Ben's hand when he left."

In regards to my deep-seated abhorrence of nightclubs, clothing is a close second to dancing. I am most comfortable in simple and conservatively stylish black ensembles. Dressing with a premium on tits and ass is just not my forte. I try on two different breast-enhancing tops, but neither do much with what I've got. Tears of stress form in my eyes. I'm still the fat kid desperate for clothes to miraculously turn me into a new person. I should tell Ben the truth about feeling out of place in clubs. I doubt he would even mind if I skipped the evening altogether. However, if he meets someone, I'll never forgive myself.

In front of the mirror, I role play an introduction to John and his girlfriend. They smile instantly charmed by my sharp wit. Unfortunately, even in my pretend meet and greet, I can't think of anything witty to say. The phone rings, rescuing me from this painful practice session.

"Hello?"

"Babe, I'm not going to make it home beforehand, can we meet in front of Misery?"

"Are you sure? Can't we tell John to make it a little later?" I ask desperately.

"No, I think it's easier for me to meet you there."

"I can meet you at the subway stop."

"That's too complicated. I'll probably grab a cab from the office. This isn't a problem is it?"

"No, of course not."

Standing alone while throngs of better-looking women pass me is not a problem. It is a deep immersion in the seventh circle of hell. I survey the women surrounding me. While they range from petite gamines to lanky supermodels, they are all sexy. I may finally be thin, but I am totally lacking in sex appeal. The longer I stand here, the more uncomfortable in my own body I become. I cross my arms and tuck my hands into my armpits, creating an invisible straight jacket for myself. This is too disturbing an image, so I unfold my arms and place them behind my back. This is a posture most often taken by museum docents or butlers. Annoyed with myself I drop my arms, in all their awkward glory, by my side. Short of sitting on them or cutting them off, I have no other options. I am ready to take my proportion-challenged arms home when I see a cowboy on the horizon, coming to save me. In a navy suit and pinstriped shirt, Ben is nothing short of perfect. His lips are cold and incredibly satisfying against my face. I want to devour him, here on the street for everyone to see.

"Who's Benny kissing?"

The voice is shrill, the East Coast equivalent of a Los Angeles Valley girl. She didn't actually say, "Like, who is Benny, like, kissing?" but she may as well have. I immediately give up hope of her having an IQ above her bra size. I haven't met John's girlfriend, Lisette, before, but I am able to assess a great deal from her appearance. She was born into money, attitude, and apparently a lot of makeup. I would not be surprised if her mother applied a little gloss on Lisette before cutting the umbilical cord.

Lisette's natural expression is one of beautiful disgust, as in "I'm beautiful, and you're disgusting." Or perhaps that expression is unique to me.

"This is Anna, Ben's girlfriend. Remember I told you about her, she's a caterer," John says delicately as if speaking to a child.

"Hi, nice to meet you," I offer with a warm, albeit phony smile.

"Hey," Lisette says coldly before turning to Ben. "Benny," she squeals throwing her thin alabaster arms around my boyfriend.

I hate Lisette. And this is not just because she was mean to me. I have far loftier and nobler reasons; she's a lady loather. The type who claims all women are jealous of her, making it impossible for her to be friends with anyone except men who want to bang her. In a testament to his stupidity, John enjoys thinking that everyone wants to sleep with his girlfriend. John is one of Ben's colleagues at Benson and Silverberg as well as a true sycophant. He expresses his love for Ben through strange side-by-side man hugs where he throws an arm around his shoulders and whispers in his ear. He tends to say cheesy things like, "You and me man. We're in it for life." Ben loves the attention too much to correct John's assumption that they are best friends and most likely will not be "in it for life."

As irritating as I find John, Lisette far surpasses him. Seated between her date and me at a small table, Lisette insists John order a bottle of Cristal. He agrees as a means of impressing both Lisette and Ben with his generosity. I, on the other hand, am not even on his radar. Ben talks to John while Lisette and I ignore each other. We may as well be at different tables since we both refuse to make eye contact with each other. Clearly, our rocky introduction extinguished any possibility of friendship. Ben watches me while listening to John. Every couple of seconds he steals a quick glance in my direction. At first, I think this is because he is enamored of me, but soon I realize he is trying to communicate a message. I already know what he's going to say so I avoid locking eyes. Ben pauses his conversation with John and whispers in my ear, "Talk to her."

I assume he means Barbie's less intelligent twin. I nod, knowing that short of running out of Misery I have no choice. I swallow what's left of my happiness and turn toward Lisette, who is actually twirling her hair like bimbos do on television.

"So, what do you do, Lisette?" I ask in a forced tone.

"PR," she responds flatly.

"Public relations fascinates me," I say with an impressively straight face. This is a total and utter fabrication for the sake of conversation.

"PR also stands for personal retail," Lisette responds snarkily.

"Good to know. What exactly is personal retail?"

"I am hired to sort through clothes for my clients so that they don't have to waste their time with all the crap."

"Oh! A personal shopper. I've always wanted one."

"I don't think they have them at the Gap. And, so you know, *shopper* isn't really a cool term. That's why we call it PR, personal retail."

"Wow, learn something new every day. Shopper is derogatory. I had no idea that you guys were so politically motivated. Impressive."

I take a second and jot down a quick mental entry in Hello Fatty:

Dear Lisette,
I was so sorry to hear of you contracting the first case of
flesh-eating herpes.

Warm regards,
Anna

"Now is personal retail, as you call it, a new major at
universities? Something you studied?"

"What?"

"Did you study," I say bitchily, "you know go to classes
for personal retail?"

"No..."

"What did you study at college?"

"I didn't finish..."

"*You* didn't get a degree?" I say with thick sarcasm.

Lisette shakes her head while rolling her eyes.

"Well that is surprising," I say insincerely. "I went to
Penn, that's the University of Pennsylvania," I continue
without any modesty. "It's part of the Ivy League."

"You major in home ec?"

"I majored in molecular biology. My abilities in
the kitchen are an added bonus," I screech inches from
Lisette's face.

I cannot believe I said that. I sound like a pompous
idiot.

"Yeah, sure."

"Excuse me?" I ask in amazement.

"Whatever."

"Was *whatever* one of your vocabulary words on the
GED?"

"You know what I heard? Girls who study too much
don't know how to dance. Is that true, Hannah?"

"It's Anna," I say harshly, stopping before I fib regarding my dancing abilities.

Lisette smirks at me, stands, rubbing her hands down over her small waist and tight ass before heading onto the dance floor.

Apparently, Lisette's theme song is Tina Turner's "Private Dancer." There really isn't any other explanation for her behavior in front of the table. If she wasn't attractive this would be a pitiable display of sexuality, but since she is, every man in a thirty foot radius watches. Ben tracks her gyrating body with his eyes and I quietly detest him for it. Of course, I stare, but as a matter of disgust, not excitement. If that's what Ben wants in a girlfriend, I should relinquish my title and point him in the direction of the nearest strip club. Lisette strokes every inch of her body while miming ecstatic facial expressions. Oh, please. This woman isn't turned on by her own touch; it's the audience that's getting her off. Ben continues to watch as I seethe with rage. It's disrespectful and cruel to subject me to such a blatant display of interest in another woman. I am confident that he has an erection, which I assume is part of Lisette's perverted mandate for the evening. My boyfriend imprudently salivates over this illiterate whore and he has the nerve to hold my hand. Driven by hormones, fear, and anger, I release his hand and seize his crotch. I am prepared to snap his penis in half! Except, it's limp. He may not have an erection, but I am still displeased with him for allowing the night to descend into a peep show, so I swat at his penis in punishment. Ben laughs. John stares at us.

"John, what is Benny laughing at?" Lisette asks, standing in front of the table like a disappointed schoolchild.

"I don't know. Ben, why are you laughing?" John

inquires quietly as his face contorts with angst. Watching them squirm is pathetically satisfying.

"Anna...I am laughing at Anna. She is sharp witted this one."

How Ben turned my crotch check into a litmus test for wittiness is beyond me, but I am pleased nonetheless. His eyes communicate that he understands me without saying a word. He watches me, conveying something much more important. This is something I never thought would happen. Ben Reynolds is in love with me. Yes! He really is! He smiles bright, amused by me, brimming with a pride I have never seen before.

"I love you, Ben."

"I love you, too."

Chapter Nineteen

Standing in D&D's kitchen, Janice marinates chicken breasts for a publisher's lunch while I chop fresh rosemary. My conversion to vegetarianism has made the tasting aspect of cooking poultry, meats, and fish difficult, but luckily Janice has picked up the slack. Holding a pale pink breast in her left hand, Janice pauses before responding to my big news.

"He loves you?"

"Don't act so surprised!"

"I didn't mean it like that. It's just that I have Chia Pets older than this relationship."

"It's been four months. That is a very, very long time for some insects...and me."

"I'm happy for you. How did he tell you?"

"Um, well, actually, I told him first."

"Jesus Christ, you told him first?"

"So? He said it back," I respond defensively.

"Did he have a choice?"

"Of course, he could have said..." What could he have said? Sorry, Anna, I like you a lot but....

"I'm sure he loves you, but for future reference, wait for the guy."

"Thanks for ruining my moment yet again," I whine.

"With a guy like Ben—you know, someone with a lot

of…options—it's important not to crowd him. Let him make those first big steps."

"I didn't realize love was so political."

Love is not only political but extremely physically taxing. And I'm not talking about sex.

I am referring to the elliptical machine, weight training, and Pilates. Ben is the impetus for the maddening physical punishment I endure daily.

Maybe love has this effect on everyone, pushing them to be the best they possibly can be. Or more likely, exercise obsession merely affects women whose boyfriends are exponentially better looking than them. Whatever the reason, ever since Ben and I exchanged the *love* word, a profound need for fitness has taken hold. When I stay at my place in Brooklyn, I usually do a combination run/walk/Jazzercise around the neighborhood with my iPod playing at a deafening level. Remarkably, I am not embarrassed to exercise in my Brooklyn 'hood. The way I see it, everyone there already thinks I'm a weirdo. Janice's restaurant ban put me at the top of the local wack-job list.

This morning, buzzing with energy, I run through my neighborhood to the soundtrack from *Fame*. I turn the corner, excited to finish, when I see smoke.

My building is on fire.

I stop and stare, mouth open, watching the building burn before my eyes. Then I realize I should do something. Should I scream? Does the fire department have a direct line, or should I call 911? I am appallingly bad under pressure. I dial 911 with *Fame* still blaring in my ear. Someone else must have called because I hear sirens in the distance. Elderly residents hobble out of the building. My mind immediately goes to Mrs. Bester. Did someone knock on her door? Could she hear them? Should I go in and rescue the old broad? I can't move. I'm scared. Running into a burning building, having seen *Backdraft* on cable, feels like a bad idea. Oh, thank heavens the firefighters are here. Mrs. Bester is their responsibility. Almost on cue, I spot Mrs. Bester stumbling out of the building. I dial Ben's number, desperate to share my harrowing tale with someone.

"Ben, my building is on fire," I cry into the phone as the firefighters begin to douse the flames.

"Are you still in it?" he shrieks. "Get out!"

"No," I laugh at his emotional response. "No, I'm on the street, but it's still really scary."

"Jesus, Anna, you almost gave me a heart attack!"

"Babe, I promise to always leave a burning building before calling you, but will you come out here? I'm not sure what's going to happen."

"I'll leave now. And don't go near the building."

"Okay," I say, thrilled with the knowledge that if I perished today, a sexy man would cry at my funeral.

Seven hours later, Ben holds my hand as we climb the stairs of my building. Nearing the fifth floor, I notice smoke damage on the walls. Mrs. Bester's door is charred beyond recognition, which makes sense, since she started the fire. Turns out the grumpy woman was smoking cigarettes in bed. I thought everyone knew that mattresses were highly flammable. I'm not even a smoker, and I know that. A floor above the old woman, extensive smoke damage continues down the hallway, my front door black with soot. Ben unlocks the door, holding me at arm's length while he makes sure it's safe.

"It's not good," Ben mumbles from inside.

I inch closer, afraid of what I will find.

"Oh my God . . . it's ruined," I say tearfully.

Black swaths of soot cover the walls. My formerly white futon is gray and dirty. My personal effects—my one framed photo, computer, and clothing—are all intact, albeit covered with a very thick residue of smoke. Thank goodness all my clothes are black.

"The important thing is you are okay," Ben says as if he were my mother.

"Thank God I have such crappy stuff."

"Where's your suitcase? Let's get you packed up."

"What do you mean?"

"You can't stay here; this place is going to have to be gutted."

"Really?" I ask, surprised.

"What, you thought a little paint and potpourri, and you'd be back in by the end of the week?"

"I don't know what I thought, but I hate moving," I moan.

"You'll stay with me until we can find you a new place, preferably one with your own bathroom. Honestly Anna, I can't believe you lived like this."

"What can I say? I love the dorm life."

"It's time for you to get a grown-up place. Something like mine."

It's strange to unpack at Ben's place, even if it's only temporary. I feel awkward putting the one framed photo of my family next to the bed. The portrait is in a cheesy butterscotch frame with the word *Family* carved into it. I loathe the frame more than the picture of Mother, Dad, Barney, and me at my sixth-grade graduation, but I can't bring myself to change it. Mother gave me the framed photo the day I left for Penn. It was a rite of passage—leaving my family behind, taking only a small reminder with me. It doesn't make any sense, as my parents were always unhappy, but I'm nostalgic for the time when they were still together. Ben leans over me as I stare at the photo.

"Who are they?"

"Um, that…these people…are related to me. My uncle and his family."

I can't bring myself to admit that the large ball dressed in a ruffled pink dress is me.

"Speaking of family, I've been meaning to tell you, my parents want to do a lunch and officially meet you."

"Why?" I ask with a shocked expression.

"They are curious about you. It's not every day I take in a boarder."

"Very funny. This is temporary. I am going to be out of your hair shortly."

"Babe, I love you. There's no rush."

Ideally, I would have liked more than a day's warning about meeting Ben's parents. At least I have my own private bathroom in which to prepare myself. A whole new world with no toilet seat covers or slippers in the shower. As I stand in front of the bathroom mirror applying a respectable amount of makeup with the lights dimmed and the door locked, I decide to cultivate a relationship with God. Meeting Ben's parents is too significant an event to go without checking in with the unverified man or woman upstairs.

Growing up, I never gave much thought to God. I passed churches, synagogues, and televangelists without batting an eye. I was solely focused on FG. "Dear God, please let today go well. I am still unsure if you exist, but if you do, please don't be offended that I doubted you. If you don't, I'm talking to myself in the mirror."

Vegetarian Glory is the most expensive vegetarian restaurant in Manhattan, Mecca for tofu lovers. Sitting at the four-top table, Ben and I look at each other with blank expressions. I can't tell if he's nervous, too, or if in my panicked state, I am simply projecting.

"Babe, stop stressing out."

"I'm not stressing out at all," I say, obsessively rubbing my damp palms against the white linen napkin.

"It's lunch. No reason to sweat it."

"Sweat? I'm not sweating. Do I look like I'm sweating? Is that what you're trying to tell me?"

"You're cute when you're nervous. It makes me want to take care of you."

"You didn't answer my question. Do I look sweaty? I don't want your mom and dad to think I have a glandular problem."

"They're here."

Across the room, I spot Mr. and Mrs. Reynolds heading our way. Milly has her hair done in the same puffy monstrosity as at the anniversary party. It adds at least six inches to her diminutive height. I wipe my hands at a feverish speed, but it turns out my hands are entirely composed of water. They are leaky breast implants, and I am on the verge of being felt up by the most important people in the world. I must avoid skin-to-skin contact at any cost. I will leave the napkin in my hand while greeting them. Or is that more peculiar than having damp hands?

They are fast approaching. I smile maniacally. Ben steps out from the table to hug his parents. I stand behind him, playing the part of the smiling damp troll. Milly offers me a huge grin and starts to put out her hand for a formal handshake. I lunge at her with my arms open, embracing her in a mammoth hug. I wipe my hands on the back of her jacket discreetly during the hug.

"I told you this one had a lot of emotion," Milly exclaims proudly to Ben.

"I feel as if I know you already and, well, I hug people I know," I stammer lamely. I cling to her small body, rubbing my hands in a circular drying motion on her back.

"Why don't you give Arthur a hug now?"

I guess my hug has gone on a little too long.

"Oh, right."

I give Arthur more of a pat–pat hug in an attempt to appear normal.

"Anna, we loved the quiches. They were delicious, right?" Milly prods her husband affectionately at the table.

"Anna, the quiches were delectable," Arthur says sincerely.

"Of course, you must hear that a lot. Right?" Milly says with a smile.

All of Milly's sentences end in ambiguous rhetorical questions. Unsure what to do, answer or ignore her, I decide to go with the nod and am obliged to do so continuously throughout the meal.

"Now Anna, let's get down to business," Milly says sternly. "Are you a vegetarian? Or do you celebrate the mass slaughter of our friends by ordering them in restaurants?"

"Jesus, Mom," Ben offers quietly.

"I am a vegetarian," I say with a smile.

Milly stares at me. Is vegetarian not enough? Should I add more to my résumé?

"I am also a registered Democrat."

Milly continues to stare at me.

"And I recycle...and I give money to PETA. And I...usually wear a cat pin."

"Arthur, I may cry," Milly says with a heartfelt look to her husband. "Anna, I knew the second I saw your beautiful display of emotion at our party that you were the right girl for my Benny. Call it mother's intuition, but I knew."

"Oh, how sweet. Thank you."

"After Carcass dumped him, I knew I needed to intervene, help him out with the selection process a little," Milly says with a wink.

"Her name is Gela, and I think we've all heard enough about that...whole...thing," Ben says politely but with anger simmering visibly beneath the surface.

"Don't get fussy, Benny," Arthur says politely. "It comes with dating a rancher's daughter. All those nice outfits were paid for with blood money."

"Cow blood," Milly chimes in emphatically.

"Enough about Gela. It's making Anna uncomfortable."

"Me? No, I'm fine talking about Carcass or...um... Gela."

"No, he's right. No more...Gela. Thank heavens Ben listened to me. I knew he needed someone with compassion. So when I saw all those tears, I just knew you would be right for him. Not like all the impossibly gorgeous and superficial women he normally chooses. I knew he needed a nice, regular girl. And clearly, I was right, wasn't I?" Milly says, beaming with pride.

"Oh," I say, unsure what to make of her comments. I knew she pushed him to have drinks with me, but hearing her explain it feels downright dreadful.

"Anna, if you ever have a son, you must make sure he gives all the girls a chance. It's the only way they find the right ones. Trust me on that," she says, studying the menu.

While my mediocrity makes Milly happy, it certainly doesn't have the same effect on me. My stomach turns painfully as I listen attentively as Milly reveals all the charming habits Ben had as a child. Finally, the afternoon draws to a close.

Milly stands next to me at the coat check, inspecting my profile. I am uneasy but do my best to hide it.

"I like you, Anna, you know?"

"Thanks, Milly. I like you, too," I say with fake cheerleader enthusiasm.

"You're not like the other girls Ben brings home. You've got substance."

Is *substance* a euphemism for fat?

"Oh, thank you," I say with a strained smile.

In the back of a yellow cab, Ben holds my hand. I stare out the window, mulling over lunch. For the first time since I met Ben, I wish he wasn't with me. I wish he were anywhere but here. The confusion would be easier to digest away from him.

"They really liked you."

"Good," I barely mange to respond.

I am the crying average girl his mother instructed him to date after the beautiful Gela dumped him.

"I'm sorry about all the Gela talk."

"Don't be silly. It was fine. I just didn't realize she dumped you right before we met."

"She didn't dump me," Ben says defensively. "It was mutual."

"That's not what your mom said," I offer warily.

"Fine. She dumped me. Happy?"

"Yes, I am very happy that your gorgeous girlfriend dumped you so cruelly that your mom intervened and made you give us regulars a try."

"Anna, it wasn't like that."

"Oh really? I have two words for you: Leslie Haggens."

"How in the hell do you know Leslie?"

"I overheard you at the bar, telling your Mom you would never date someone like her. Then two hours later, you asked me out…to make your mom happy."

"But Anna, if you already knew all this, why are you so mad?"

"I don't know. I guess I just don't like thinking that you had to be pushed into going out with me."

"Mom didn't push, she merely suggested. And maybe I wouldn't have asked if she hadn't, but thank God she did. I love you."

"Am I just a consolation prize? A rebound helping you get over Gela so you can move on to your next model?"

"I don't want a model, I want you."

"Gee, thanks, Ben."

"I didn't mean it like that. Mom pointed you out to me because she wanted me to be with someone a bit more grounded and compassionate. But I fell in love with you on my own. All of you—your big brown eyes with long black eyelashes, the way you light up when you laugh, the way you spoke about being inspired by my parents made me see something completely different in them. And isn't that what my father was talking about? Being with some-one who opens up the way you see life, who you never want to be separated from. I've never had this with any-one. You've got to see that. You are the first woman I've ever lived with."

"It's temporary; that doesn't count."

"Not anymore. I want you with me...always."

The reality of our differences weighs heavily on me now that my heart is invested. But I can't let him stop lov-ing me over a stupid fight.

"I'm sorry. I love you." I smile bravely and stroke his back the way I know he loves.

There is no man on earth I could love the way I love Ben. I want to believe that there is no other woman he could love the way he loves me, but I'm not sure.

Chapter Twenty

The world is a scary place when you're dating a handsome man. Women constantly take in his physical appeal. Sexual excitement sparks in their eyes, then travels down to their lips, which crack into seductive smiles. Then they glance at me and stifle a laugh. The suppressed laugh conveys their disbelief that I am Ben's girlfriend. I am not a troll or a repulsive-looking woman, but I am far from the model or pageant winner one expects to find on Ben's arm. He doesn't help the situation with his need to smile at every person who smiles at him. He laps up attention like a neglected dog. He is not secretly insecure and seeking validation wherever possible; he merely takes pleasure in being the man in the spotlight.

Ben joins me in bed to watch the *E! True Hollywood Story* on *Full House*. His interest in the trashy program exponentially increases with the Olsen twins' screen time.

"I'm not sure why the whole twin thing is so enticing, since sisters don't do threesomes . . . but it is," he confides.

"Yeah, sisters usually aren't so into each other sexually," I respond, wondering if all handsome men are this loathsome when it comes to women. Swallowing protests—and my integrity—I remain silent, not wanting to rock the boat. I think of my parents and their dysfunctional marriage. While there is nothing I logically want to emulate, I can't help but remember that Father's silence bought them decades of marriage. So if I can keep my mouth shut, maybe I will get decades of Ben.

As the Tanner family drama unfolds, Ben begins to rub my arm. His hand creeps closer and closer to my breasts with each brush. Houston, we have contact. Ben massages my left breast, keeping his eyes trained on the *Full House* spectacle of underage sirens. If he thinks he can use my body to fantasize about tabloid twins, he is sadly mistaken. Animal Planet, here we come.

"Babe, why'd you change it?" Ben moans.

"What? I thought you loved animals?"

"I do, but we were watching twins..."

"Listen, McPervy, now we're watching San Francisco's K-9 unit!"

So much for not rocking the boat.

"McPervy? Where is all this hostility coming from?"

"Hostility? I am *not* hostile! I am simply exercising my right to change the channel."

"Well, you better be careful, or I will exercise my right to a new girlfriend."

He's kidding, right? I am not laughing. Tears. All down my face. Tears. Why am I crying over a joke?

"Babe, c'mon, I was kidding. I love you."

I cannot think of an explanation suitable for the situation. Instead of even attempting to rationalize my behavior, I bury my splotchy face in his arms. Insecurities echo through my mind as I reflect on my growing fear of losing Ben. Sure, I am safe from the Olsen twins luring Ben away, but what about the masses of sexy women in Manhattan? They all seem to salivate at the thought of relaying an important message to Ben—that he can do better. It doesn't help that Ben's general demeanor is funny and charming. I want him to turn off the charm and stop flaunting himself all over town. His friendliness is an invitation for women to engage with him.

A few days later, Ben and I partake in some quick precaffeine sex before hitting our local Spring Street Starbucks. A woman with a pixie haircut and green doelike eyes approaches, focusing harder on Ben with each passing step. She presents a coy smile, which Ben happily reciprocates. Bitch. And I mean that about both of them. By the time we reach Starbucks, I am literally relieved to get him off the street.

"I'm going to wash my hands. Get me a triple-shot venti latte with skim milk."

"You got it, babe."

Five minutes is barely enough time for me to wash and dry my hands, let alone make a new friend. But not for Ben. I return to find him chatting with Coffee Slut #1 behind the counter. She appears to be around twenty-two, with porcelain skin, a size-four body, and golden locks to her shoulders. Even with a green apron and visor, she looks good. Her smile says, "I'm fun. Screw me." As I approach, I hear her say, "Thanks, I will definitely e-mail you." My heart pounds. I am on the verge of total organ failure. How can I live a normal life when the man of my dreams isn't safe in Starbucks? Two feet from Ben, I breathe heavily to garner his attention. Ben winks at me, then continues talking to Coffee Slut #1. My boyfriend is leaving me for the girl with coffee grinds under her nails. My breathing intensifies. I must end their conversation. Now. I will feign fainting. It is a cheap move, but I am desperate. I close my eyes and collapse onto the floor without breaking any vital bones.

"Anna! Anna!"

I "awake" to Ben hovering over me saying my name with such concern that I feel guilty.

"Anna? Anna, are you okay?"

I am speechless with guilt.

Coffee Slut #1 approaches with a cup of water; as she hands it to me, she says the words that send the last rational thought out of my head.

"Is your sister okay?"

Of course. She assumes I am his sister. Ben was openly flirting with her in front of me. The rage of my youth returns with a thud, fully condensed and focused on Coffee Slut #1.

"I am *not* his sister. I am his girlfriend. And if you had been doing your job, maybe I wouldn't have slipped on this...slippery floor."

Suddenly, falling due to her incompetence is far superior to fainting.

"Anna, honey, I don't think you fell. I think you fainted."

"Ben, you are a lawyer, not a doctor!"

"I know, but your eyes were shut."

"Yes, that's how I fall. Do you or the barista have a problem with the way I fall?"

It takes every ounce of willpower to say *barista* instead of *Coffee Slut #1,* as she deserves to be known.

"Let's get you home."

"Fine."

I give my version of the evil eye to Coffee Slut #1 and vow to learn voodoo to undetectably inflict primitive pain on this young thorn in my side. We definitely need a new coffee shop, preferably an all-male one.

As we walk home in silence, I admit to myself that I am a complete lunatic. The most unfortunate part is that Ben knows it. I can see it in his eyes. He's questioning who I am as a person. He is conjuring up images of Glenn Close in *Fatal Attraction*. I could not have handled the situation worse if I tried. In blaming Coffee Slut #1, I showed mental instability. I reach my hand out like a frightened child, unsure whether my parent will accept me. Ben takes my hand and continues to walk in silence.

"I'm sorry. Seeing you flirt with the barista, giving her your e-mail, and falling so abruptly got me a bit out of sorts."

"Come on. Don't be that girl. She's only a law student looking for a summer internship."

Yeah, right. The only internship she wants is the one under his desk. My face must betray my thought, because he shakes his head with irritation.

"Seriously. I was not flirting with her. She's a child. You're being ridiculous."

"She's not a child. She's actually older than a lot of your *Full House* crushes. Can you understand how I could interpret the situation as upsetting?"

I embrace honesty. Not full disclosure, but partial honesty.

"What's upsetting is your being so easily threatened by me talking to another woman. Are you going to stop me from talking to women at work?"

"Let's just drop it."

"Fine."

I call Ben an asshole in my mind. He cannot hear it, but it makes me feel better. I want to rip my hand from his, but that will trigger a bigger fight. A cute brown-haired girl approaches us. Ben smiles at her. Screw him; I take my hand back.

"What is with you?" Ben asks with a heavy helping of bitchiness.

"Why do you smile at every woman who walks past you?"

"Are you kidding me?"

"Am I kidding you? No, Ben, I'm not! Why do you do that? We have been out of the house ten minutes and you have ogled two women, and that doesn't even include the Coffee Slut!"

"*Ogled?* What are you talking about? I can't smile at people? And Coffee Slut? Anna, this is such an ugly side of you. You know, I don't mind if people smile at you."

"Ben, when have you ever seen anyone smile at me?"

"Ever think that's because you look unfriendly? I know you don't have a lot of relationship experience, Anna, but trust me, men are allowed to smile at other people, including women. Ask your friends. I'm sure Janice or Donny and Marie let their guys smile at women."

I seriously regret making up Donny and Marie as friends.

"Don't patronize me, Ben."

We walk home, lattes in hand, in total, angry silence.

Men have an innate lack of understanding when it comes to jealousy.

Don't be *that girl*. What Ben doesn't realize is that we are all *that girl*. Every woman who has ever uttered the words "I like you," "I love you," "I give a shit about you" is *that girl*. In essence, *that girl* is a girl who cares enough to protect her emotional investment. The smart ones hide that part of their feelings and deal with it in a passive–aggressive manner. Men think they know women better than other women do. Women understand each other's behavior on a level that men don't even know exists; it's the emotional equivalent of canine hearing.

Upon entering the apartment, I walk directly to the bathroom. Having a one bedroom sucks when we fight. The only place I can be alone is the bathroom. I turn on the shower, letting it run. I sit on the toilet, drinking my latte. My love for Ben and his love for attention appear to have crashed into one another, frustrating me to tears in the process. Everything is about to evaporate; Ben could simply disappear from my life.

I pull off my clothes and lug my body into the steamy shower. As I lather my hair, the bathroom door creaks open. My eyes are covered in Suave suds, so I mumble "Ben?" Nothing. I move my hair under the hot stream of water. Ben is behind me. I can't see him or hear him, but I know he's there. He kisses my neck softly.

Engaging in foreplay while temporarily blind is outrageously erotic. He holds me from behind as I rinse away the veil of suds. I turn to kiss him and notice that his eyes are closed. Why are his eyes shut? Is he Photoshopping in Coffee Slut #1? Gela? One of the thousands of gorgeous women he's bedded?

"Oh Ben," I moan in hopes of eliciting an "Oh Anna."

"Babe."

I am not satisfied; Ben calls total strangers "babe." I moan even louder and throw in an orgasmic gurgle with his name.

"Ahhhhhh B-b-b-e-e-e-e-e-n-n-n."

"Oh," he moans loudly.

I'm going to have to step it up, an a cappella rendition of the name Ben with a chorus of heavy breathing. Not surprisingly, he adores the attention. This is personalized porn for him. Sexually, I should be beyond euphoria, but instead my mind races with one word, *Anna*. Say my damn name. But alas, he doesn't. The climax comes without mention of my name. We rinse off and retire to the bedroom without speaking a word to each other. We slept with strangers; the tension of the fight remains with us.

"I'm sorry we fought."

This is Ben's passive-aggressive way of avoiding responsibility for the fight while trying to end it.

"I am sorry that we fought, too, but Ben, do you understand what I'm saying about the other women?"

"Anna, I love you. I live with you. I have validated you in every way other than matrimony. Why are you making yourself crazy by being so jealous?"

"You admitted that you only started dating me because your mother made you, and you smile at every gorgeous woman who passes you. Can you really not see where I am coming from?"

"Anna, I think you're gorgeous. It doesn't matter what initially drew us together because we fit," Ben says with a kiss to my lips before getting serious. "But you need to understand, I hate jealousy. It's a real turnoff."

Oh, really? I want to destroy Ben cell by cell.

"I didn't realize I was being jealous. I thought I was expressing my feelings."

"Babe, I've been down this road with other women I've dated, and it doesn't work. If you keep acting like this, I don't know what the future holds."

"Did it occur to you that maybe there is something to it since other women have expressed similar sentiments? Or is it a big coincidence?"

Jo Allen, the PR bitch whose violet party we catered, comes to mind. I remember her smugly wishing me "good luck" when she heard I was with Ben. Now I understand.

"Anna, this is who I am. I'm not changing. Do you understand what I'm saying?"

He's saying that I cannot be mad at him for his questionable behavior, or he will leave. This is an ultimatum. Part of me wants to scream profanities in his face and walk off, but I don't. As much as I loathe him in this moment, I love him more. I cannot walk away from him.

"Yeah, I think I understand."

I have no course of action to take in this moment other than agreeing with him. Ben presented a clear ultimatum: stop expressing my concerns or the relationship will end. I heard it. I saw it in his eyes. If this was a movie and I was a better character, I would tell him to kiss my ass. But I'm not that person. I love Ben. I'm afraid to lose him. I must find a way for his ego and my insecurities to become compatible. As I lay on his chest with his arms around me, I am further from him emotionally than ever before. Fear seeps into my brain, unlocking crazy facets of my personality.

The fight remains with me throughout the weekend and into Monday morning. I am eager to get to work and ask Janice's advice. She's my only friend, but more important, she's brutally honest. I enter the kitchen expecting Janice to guide me out of the emotional quagmire known as Ben.

"Hi," Janice says without even looking up from sautéing onions.

"Do I look ridiculous with Ben?" I ask without any lead-in.

"What a silly thing to say. No!"

"Janice, as my friend, you must tell me the truth."

"You do not look ridiculous with him," she says without raising her head.

"How come the whole damn city looks surprised when I hold his hand?"

"I'm not going to lie. Ben is better looking than you are. Let me explain something to you. In every relationship, there is a Ginger and a Mary Ann. Mary Ann is pretty, but Ginger is prettier. In your relationship with Ben, you are the Mary Ann and Ben is the Ginger. You're still pretty, just not as pretty, you see? But so what? Congrats on landing him. The other ladies are just jealous."

"Congrats on landing him? Screw landing him. Can I keep him? How does Mary Ann keep all the Gingers away from Ben?"

"You could lock him in the apartment."

"I'm serious," I say glumly. "This is a nightmare. I hate how pretty he is."

"Don't act like his looks had nothing to do with you falling for him. You're telling me that if he looked like Juan, you would have fallen for him?"

"Juan the dishwasher?"

"I promoted him to waiter. Do you not pay any attention around here?"

"Fine, it may have helped a little at the beginning, but I would love Ben no matter what he looked like."

"Please! Enjoy the view and accept the dangers. Women are going to look, flirt, and do what they do. But all of that is out of your hands."

"That's it?" I say grouchily.

"What the hell does that mean?"

"Enjoy the view? What kind of lame-ass advice is that? What if I told you that about Gary?"

"Gary doesn't get many opportunities. He doesn't have the same overt lure that Ben does."

"So all I can do is—"

"Enjoy the view."

There it is then; I know my relationship will end in tears. Some barriers are simply too hard to overcome; an average woman cannot keep an extraordinary man.

PART

IV

The Makedown

Chapter Twenty-one

Tonight, I prepare a scrumptious dinner of risotto and pan-seared asparagus for my devastatingly handsome boyfriend. This dinner is meant to ground my insecurities. While I may not look like Ben's past girlfriends, I have other talents. This meal will highlight what an exquisite chef I have become. Yes, I said chef. I am no longer a mere caterer; I have promoted myself to chef. Risotto is Ben's favorite dish and in order to make it delicious, I embrace excess. I use an abundance of butter, heavy cream, and cheese. When Ben lifts his fork for the first bite, I see four cheese bridges extending from the plate.

"Babe, this...is...phenomenal," Ben says between bites. "The most delicious risotto I have ever had...even better than in Italy."

"Oh, go on," I say while pretending to blush.

"Why don't you always cook like this?"

"I didn't know you liked my cooking," I respond coyly.

"You're a genius in the kitchen, honestly. Janice is lucky to have you."

"Oh, stop it. Here, have some more," I say, lifting a large serving spoon toward his plate.

"No, one serving's enough. There's a lot of cheese in this."

Hello Fatty,
Lie! Just lie! He needs to eat more! This is the opportunity of a lifetime. Dull Ben's veneer with a few extra pounds. Nothing drastic, merely create a buffer zone between Ben and perfection.

—Anna

"Well, the thing is," I stutter, "the cheese is low fat, so two servings... actually equals one."

"Who knew they made low-fat Gruyère?"

"The innovations in ingredients these days are spectacular. I'll make some of my other low-fat discoveries this week."

Self-preservation is kicking in. I have reached my best physically, and still my desirability is painfully capped at a little above average. While yes, I have lovely brown eyes with long lashes and I'm thin, that still only gives me "cute" at best. Is cute enough to keep Ben from being lured away by one of the many sirens patrolling the city? Maybe I'm okay today, but eventually I will lose him; it's inevitable. I can't be with him every day, shielding him from offers of greater T & A. It's impossible. The only variable in this equation is Ben. Underneath his perfect façade is a man with some extra weight, a man with dimmed popularity. I need to find that man and bring him to the surface. It's the only chance I have of maintaining our union.

I don't have to be at the kitchen until 10:00, but I wake fully energized at 6:30. This never happens. I love to sleep. However, today the anticipation of making Ben chubby propels me right out of bed. Soon he will be a little round, a little plump, a little less perfect. However, he'll still be much better looking than me. I have an actual spring in my step as I grate "low-fat" Gruyère for an omelet. I use large dollops of whipped butter to brown the eggs to perfection. The short stack is excessive, but I can't contain my fervor. This is an immensely satisfying endeavor to take on. I creep into the bedroom with a tray full of pancakes, eggs, and orange juice (I added sugar).

"Good morning, Ben."

"Babe, oh my God, what is all this?" Ben asks with surprise.

"Breakfast. It's the most important meal of the day," I offer casually.

"Ah, that's really sweet, but I can't possibly eat such heavy food for breakfast."

"The pancakes are whole grain. I ground up flaxseeds for them. And the eggs, well, they're Egg Beaters with the low fat Gruyère."

"Babe, it looks delicious, but I can't. You have it."

Why is he making this difficult? Men usually don't need convincing to eat breakfast in bed.

"Oh," I sigh, "won't you even taste a little?"

"Babe..."

"How about the pancakes?" I say with a long, drawn-out sigh and a pouty expression that feels totally unnatural.

"Babe, really, I can't."

"Not even one? I got up at 6:30 to make all this."

"Okay, I'll have one pancake," Ben relents.

"Oh, goodie!"

I watch Ben chew every last bite of the pancake with an intense satisfaction. For the first time in weeks, there is hope for our mismatched relationship.

Breakfast over, Ben throws on a navy suit and yellow tie. I stare longingly at his stomach, dreaming of the day his paunch hangs over his belt.

"What? You don't like the suit?"

"Oh no, not at all. You look wonderful. Do you have lunch with anyone special today?"

"Nope. I'm going to hit the gym; I need to burn off that pancake."

"No you don't," I squeak. "It's whole wheat and flaxseed. It's good for you. You don't need to go to the gym at all."

"Babe, I gotta run," Ben says, leaning down for a kiss.

"Don't forget, the pancake was healthy. No need to hit the gym," I call out as the front door slams.

My butter-soaked omelet taunts me as I drop it into the disposal. It requires every ounce of my willpower not to drown my gym concerns in the egg delicacy and super-sweetened orange juice. However unjust, I cannot afford any extra calories. I must be the best possible me for Ben. It's disconcerting that all my work to get Ben to eat the pancake will evaporate after forty-five minutes on the treadmill. I throw away the remaining food and pick up the phone to dial Janice.

"D&D Catering."

"I'm going to be late today."

"Why?"

"I just need some time. I'm taking on a new endeavor. Something very important...close to my heart."

"I can't believe it! You're quitting on me!" Janice huffs.

"Um...no. It's a little bit more complicated than that. And it has nothing to do with you."

"I don't believe you. Do you have a job interview? Because let me tell you—"

"Janice! This has nothing to do with you! If you must know, it's about Ben! I'm trying to fatten him up, not a massive amount, but enough so women stop staring at him."

"You have got to be kidding me. You land this insanely hot guy and you want to make him fat?"

"You have no idea how difficult it is to date a man this good looking—the pressure. There are women at every corner—winking, whistling, smiling, bending over, occasionally making pornographic gestures—it's too much! You have no idea how lucky you are that Gary isn't hot!"

"He will be thrilled to hear that," Janice says with a laugh.

"Oh, Janice. I didn't mean it like that."

"I assume you aren't telling Ben about this plan."

"Well, I don't think it would work if I did," I answer seriously. "I think he'd get mad."

"I say start with donuts. Everyone loves donuts."

"He'll just do more time at the gym. He's addicted to burning calories. Why did I choose a fitness freak?"

"Cancel the membership and call it a day. And get in here by eleven. I need help frosting these damn cupcakes."

Canceling his gym membership is a Band-Aid, not a solution, but I need to start somewhere. It's a slow build to twenty pounds.

I realize my behavior falls in the morally questionable category, but Ben is simply too handsome. It's unfair to expect anyone, let alone someone with my history, to survive on his arm without a few adjustments. It sounds much worse than it is because twenty pounds will do very little to Ben. Even with the added weight, he will still be almost perfect. And that's more than most people can dream of being. If I could distribute his riches to the ugly and average people of the world, I would be a regular Robin Hood. Until then I will settle for "concerned girl-friend," nobly protecting my man. Okay, maybe "slightly selfish girlfriend" is more accurate.

"Hello, I'd like to cancel my gym membership please," I say in my best male impersonation.

"Name?"

"Ben Reynolds."

"May I ask why? Our records show that your last check-in was yesterday. Was there a problem, Mr. Reynolds?"

"It has come to my attention that a drugged-out dere-lict has been using my membership for the last few months while I was in China. This man has been . . . well, pleasur-ing himself in the locker room, or so I have been told. Needless to say, I don't feel comfortable returning to the gym."

I feel guilty, mainly because I know how annoying it is to deal with small tasks like reinstating gym member-ships. However, this is a necessary annoyance. Really, it is. This is a justified course of action for a man so striking in appearance. This is not, as I fear, a sign of following in Mother's disturbed footsteps. I am not starting down a path that ends in madness and spewing racial indignities. I am absolutely nothing like Mother . . . not a thing.

At 10:45, I roll into work with a sense of deranged accomplishment. Janice hovers over a steaming pot, her hair perfectly pulled back in a ponytail. Small beads of perspiration decorate her face, yet she still looks chic.

"Well, if it isn't Lucy Ricardo," Janice says without looking up.

"Excuse me?"

"The queen of harebrained schemes."

Lucy Ricardo is the highest of praise compared to what I was thinking about myself. Nothing is more insulting than believing that I am continuing Mother's legacy of lunacy.

"Oh, Ethel. I wouldn't be so judgmental. You were the one who called every restaurant on my block and threatened them not to deliver to me."

"Yes, but that was for your own good."

"This is for Ben's own good as well. I make him happy, and this way I will be able to keep him."

"Isn't it easier to let him just dump you?"

"I love him, Janice; it's too late to get out. I can't start over after being with Ben. Besides, he really could use some help empathizing with the average mortal."

"Well, I guess he is rather confident about his looks."

"What's that supposed to mean?" I shoot back, suddenly protective of my Ben.

"He knows he's hot. It's not his fault; he is damn attractive. A few extra pounds actually may help him understand how the rest of us live."

"Exactly," I exclaim, relieved.

"This is a cultural experience for him," Janice giggles. "I'm sure it's all very anthropological. May I ask how you plan on doing this?"

"So far I'm lying about low-fat cheese and stuff."

"He's got good genes; you're going to have to get more creative if you want results. It's not as easy as you think to get an active guy like Ben to gain weight."

"What's the best way to gain weight?"

"I can't believe you of all people are asking this. What was your favorite thing when you were fat?"

"I liked anything with sugar in it."

"There you go. But Anna, be careful. If you get caught, there will be no explaining this away."

Janice is right; I need to step it up if Ben is to gain weight. Pancakes and risotto are too filling for him; his food must be light yet packed with calories. I need . . . candy bars. They may be billed as snacks, but they have more calories than a proper meal. A few of my favorites growing up were Milky Way, Snickers, Skor, and Twix. Of all the bars, I think Skor was the most delicious and addictive. I must create a scenario in which Ben eats multiple bars a day. Perhaps I can find a way to disguise it as a healthy alternative. I can't say for sure, but I believe Nature's Way grains and honey bars are approximately the same size as a Skor bar. The prospect of dismantling my fear of losing Ben excites me, yet I can't seem to shake this feeling of profound lameness. Switching candy bars and granola bars in an effort to make Ben gain weight really is something that Lucy Ricardo would do. The only difference is that Ricky wouldn't leave her if he found out.

I employ extreme vigilance when switching the Skor and Nature's Way wrappers. I begin by sharpening the tip of a needle against the bathroom tile grout. Then, I slice a nearly imperceptible opening into the crease of the Nature's Way wrapper. I attempt to place the Skor in the wrapper, only to realize it's slightly larger than Nature's Way. Damn it! I do not want to go back to the store and start again. I grab my most precise kitchen knife and slice a little off each end of the Skor. After lightly gluing the wrapper back together, I inspect the final product. The craftsmanship is extremely impressive.

After laboriously shaving and repackaging all twenty Skor bars, I am exhausted. I lick up the chocolate shavings from the counter as a treat. The chocolate. The toffee. It's mind-blowing. I want more. Who cares about being fat? I must eat Skor bars every day, all day long. I must move away from the counter. I need more. No! I grab the sponge and wipe up the chocolate shavings before my tongue does. I can't be a casual user of candy bars. As much as I would like to, it's not possible for me. I fan out the Nature's Way bars on the counter, salivating at the notion of devouring them all.

"What are you doing? Babe? Babe? Anna, I'm talking to you."

"What?" I say, coming out of my chocolate-induced fog, having completely missed hearing Ben enter the apartment.

"What are you doing?" Ben asks seriously.

"What do you mean? I'm...standing here...in the kitchen."

"You're drooling. There's drool all down your chin."

"Oh really? How strange. Maybe it's an allergic reaction?"

"To what?"

"To these delicious bars I bought today. I guess you'll have to eat them then. *All of them.*"

"I don't want to eat them if they make you drool."

"No, they won't. It's just me. I'm allergic to the... nature...that's in them."

"The nature?"

"Yeah, you know they're called Nature's Way bars because they're so healthy."

"Okay, but nature isn't an ingredient, Anna."

"Oh, yeah. I know. I was kidding. What I meant was I am allergic to"—I pause, picking up the bar and examining the wrapper—"barley, which comes from nature. These are really good for you, so eat them all."

Yet again, I have proven to be an appalling liar. Ben rips open a bar and takes a small bite. I watch nervously, wondering if he will recognize the Skor bar.

"Wow, this doesn't taste like"—Ben pauses while picking up the wrapper—"oat bran. It's really good."

"It's crazy the things they are coming up with these days," I say with relief.

"Yeah, I'm going to take some of these to the office. Thanks, babe."

"No, thank you," and I truly mean that.

"Babe, you want to go see the new Jessica Biel movie?"

"You actually want to see that? It looks like shit."

"Who cares? She's hot."

"Here, have another Nature's Way."

Chapter Twenty-two

"D on't forget, we have dinner with Maria tonight," Ben says seconds after dropping his briefcase by the front door after work.

"Who?" I ask, lounging across the cream-colored couch.

"I told you about Maria. We went to Brown together. She's from Argentina."

"Um, no. You didn't mention this at all. No notice whatsoever. Look at my hair, Ben. Does this look like hair that is date-ready?" I screech while frantically sitting up.

"Calm down. It's not a date; it's dinner with an old friend."

Old friend? Yeah right.

"Can't we reschedule?" I ask, hoping this can be pushed to after Ben's weight gain.

"She lives in L.A.; she's only here for two nights. We should leave here in an hour."

An hour? That is barely enough time for a beautiful woman to prepare to meet an old friend, let alone an average one.

"What does Maria do?" Please say welder, professional wrestler, or fish gutter.

"She's a philanthropist."

"Is that a job?"

"It is when you have as much money as she does."

"Is she married?"

Please say yes.

"She was single last we spoke. Her ex was a real bitch."

"He was a bitch?" I repeat back to Ben with confusion.

"She. Maria's a lesbian, babe. I'm sure I've told you about her."

Knowing she's not on the team that is trying to steal Ben from me calms me down immensely, and I quickly slip into something more appropriate to meet an old college friend of Ben's: black top, black pants, black shoes. Good to go.

Maria is Penelope Cruz with a masculine flair. Her black pantsuit is perfectly tailored to fit her slim five-foot-nine-inch frame. And her black ballerina flats have that distinctive Christian Louboutin red sole. Maria is a woman cut from the same monochromatic cloth as me; we are both dressed in head-to-toe black, although she probably hasn't cut Gap labels out of her outfit. She speaks English fluently, albeit with a thick, sexy accent. Her emotive facial expressions and wild hand gestures make her feel more like a caricature on a sitcom than an actual person; for example, her incessant use of the word *darling*. She's the Argentinean Zsa Zsa Gabor.

"Anna, darling, do you prefer red or white?" Maria asks me across the table at Babbo, located in a beautiful blue townhouse on Waverly Place.

"White, please," I say shyly, feeling like a child at the grown-ups' table.

"Ben, darling, order white because that's what we girls want!" Maria touches his arm and throws back her head to laugh. If she were straight, my heart would be in my throat and my stomach on the floor. But she's gay, so I love her!

A young blonde waitress approaches and immediately locks on to Ben.

"We would like a bottle of the Friesen 1996," Ben tells the waitress with a smile.

As the waitress leaves, Maria leans into Ben. "I see you still have the same effect on women, Ben darling."

Thank God for Maria. Finally, someone acknowledges the torture I endure daily.

"What are you talking about?"

"Darling, the waitress was trying to fuck [pronounced *fohk*] you with her eyes."

"Stop it. She was just taking our order."

"Anna, he's a naughty boy. You must watch him with both eyes." Again, she throws her head back to laugh.

"Naughty? What do you mean? He's adorable!" I respond with a nervous laugh.

"Don't fill her head with nonsense, Maria. I'm reformed."

"Okay, darling," Maria says with a dubious wink in my direction.

What does Maria mean by naughty? Is naughty a euphemism for Ben's incessant need to flirt? Or does naughty mean unfaithful? My stomach sours as my brain depletes itself of serotonin.

"Excuse me, I'm going to run to the restroom."

I scan the restroom floor, looking for other patrons' feet. Luckily, no one is there. I immediately whip out my cell phone and dial Janice.

"Hello?"

"What does *naughty* mean?"

"It's called dictionary.com, you lazy—"

"No! What does it mean when a woman calls a man naughty?"

"It can go either way—fucking a prostitute or flirting with his best friend's wife."

"Shit."

"Who said it?"

"Ben's Argentinean friend Maria." I say her name with a thick Spanish accent.

"Oh, that is not good."

"What? Do you know her?"

"Well, South American women are pretty lenient as it is. I would definitely invest—"

"Okay, thanks," I interrupt Janice, unable to hear any more.

Two hours later, my mind still obsesses over the word *naughty*. So when Ben excuses himself to go to the bathroom, I decide it's time for some reconnaissance.

"Has Ben changed much since Brown?"

"He was exactly the same at Brown, except with a flock around him at all times."

"A flock of women? A flock of men?" I ask a little too curiously.

"Both, darling!" Maria laughs.

"Were you a part of the flock?"

"For a bit, right after we slept together, but I tired of the crowd," she says nonchalantly.

Did she say she slept with my boyfriend?

"Oh, I thought you were gay," I say, unable to hide my disappointment.

"I am, but for Ben, I made an exception." Again, she winks at me. The Ben situation is far more dire than I originally thought. He can turn lesbians straight.

Ben approaches, unaware of the bomb Maria dropped.

"Babe, did you get me a coffee?"

"Oh, I forgot…totally slipped my mind." It takes every ounce of willpower not to ask if there is anything he has forgotten to tell me. Perhaps screwing Eva Perón simply slipped his mind.

Back at the apartment, in my plain white tank and matching shorts, I scratch Ben's back, neurotically thinking of Maria's exception for Ben. I want to say something, but I don't want to appear possessive.

"Did you and Maria ever date?" I finally ask casually.

"Babe, I told you she's gay."

"Well, a lot of people experiment in college."

"Not her. She's a ladies-only kind of woman."

Why is he lying? Is this what she meant by naughty? He's a liar. Who is this man? Is his name even Ben?

"She's fantastic, sexy, and quite funny. I love the way she calls you na-na-naughty!" The word *naughty* lodges on my tongue, causing me to stutter uncomfortably.

"Oh, you do?"

"Yes, it's very sexy."

"How sexy?"

Ben is eager enough to have sex that I can slip in a question without setting off his jealousy detector.

"What exactly did she mean by naughty?"

"Well, I didn't excel at fidelity in college."

On that seductive note, he kisses me. I pull back.

"How about now?"

"I'm a good boy now."

"Are you willing to take a polygraph to that effect?" I ask seriously.

Ben laughs uproariously, leans in for a kiss, and whispers, "I love you, Anna."

"I love you, Ben." Or whoever you are.

Chapter Twenty-three

I have been naïve. What's a few pounds going to do to a guy who is sexy enough to turn lesbians straight? Not much. It's going to take far more to deter the ladies than some chunk. I need to go deeper. This is no longer a pet project; this is a mission. Ben may have won the genetic lottery, but that doesn't mean he has a free pass for questionable behavior. The guy clearly needs to see how the other 95 percent live. Furthermore, our relationship needs a security system to keep out intruders. This is, after all, a city with as many models as Jackson Hole, Wyoming, has people. I can't continue to send him into this city of easy women looking like he does. It's too dangerous.

Thinking back on my nerdy youth, four distinct factors come to mind: clothes, hair, weight, and acne. I omit acne from my mission. It grosses me out to kiss someone with sores on their face. I am a hypocrite, but it's the truth. Plus, crappy sebaceous glands are hormonally based and, therefore, impossible to cultivate. Hair, clothes, and weight, on the other hand, I can easily corrupt. In my youth, my imagination muted the reality of my physical form, from weight to matted rats' nests to filthy garments. Stretch pants were a favorite; in fact, anything with an elastic waistband was beloved.

With my own history in mind, I launch a plan to protect Ben while exposing him to another way of life. A different culture, if you will. I christen this project The Makedown. My train of thought is simple: makeup is applied to bring out the beauty that Mother Nature forgot to give us; makedowns are applied to lessen the excessive beauty that Mother Nature accidentally dumped on certain people.

The Makedown's three formal areas of concentration will be weight, hair, and clothes. Starting with weight, I will step up his caloric intake while slowing his exercise regimen. This requires a bit of careful planning, but step two of my plan, clothes, will help. Most people estimate weight gain or loss based on how their clothes fit. It's much easier to indulge when there's a little extra room in the waistband. Therefore, before I downgrade his wardrobe, I'll need to replace a few choice pairs of slacks with a larger size. This is tricky, but doable.

Hair is more complex. It's not easy to get a hygienic man with short hair to avoid bathing and develop matted clumps. I ponder this a while. Maybe grime isn't the way to go with Ben. It sounds dreadful, but thinning may be far more effective. Men take balding seriously; it's as important to them as weight is to women. If I lessen Ben's luscious mahogany hair, it will help him tap into a common experience, insecurity. I don't want to destroy his foundation, merely shake it slightly. Weathering the emotional impact of a little balding will undoubtedly increase Ben's compassion for the struggles of regular folks.

Hello Fatty,
You have crossed a line. You are long past moral ambiguity.
But then again, isn't all fair in love and makedowns?
                                                    —Anna

I thumb through Ben's side of the closet, inspecting slacks and shirts, cataloging which pieces are best to replace, based on the frequency of use. Obviously, replacing his tuxedo would do little, as he hasn't worn that since I met him. I need to focus on Ben's staples, black slacks. I lift the perfectly pressed, soft lambswool slacks and scrutinize the label. God damn it, it's Prada. I was naïvely hoping to find a Banana Republic label. Prada is expensive; even I know that. I rub my index finger against the fabric. It's itch-free and soft enough to sleep on. As Ben is a connoisseur of fine dining, fine women, and fine furnishings, designer clothing should hardly come as a surprise. I cover the slacks in old dry-cleaning plastic and don my finest Gap outfit. Prada, here I come.

I call Janice to ask her about her experiences shopping at Prada, but when I mention my three-tiered plan, I am unable to get another word in edgewise.

"No. No. This is too much. Do you understand me, Anna? Too much. Switching labels in pants, formulating a three-part plan—this reeks of insanity. You are acting like your mother! You need a reality check. You are a caterer; you should be here chopping vegetables, not masquerading as some sort of crazed evil girlfriend!"

"You don't understand. Gary isn't this good-looking. You have no idea the pressure I'm under!"

"What about me? I'm prepping for a luncheon alone and running a psych ward! Perhaps you forgot, but we are serving forty people lunch tomorrow."

"I didn't forget. I called Juan. He's on his way in to help you."

"You called Juan, the man you didn't even know existed, and now you have his phone number?"

"Well, after you made such a big deal out of me not knowing who he was, I felt like I had to make some kind of effort to at least get to know him."

"Have you ever heard the AA slogan 'Let go and let God'? What do you think of trying that before this three-tiered plan of yours?"

"You obviously cannot relate to what I am going through."

"Don't get huffy; it was just a suggestion."

"I gotta go. Prada's waiting."

"Well, Juan just got here—but you should be here, too."

"Bye."

I am annoyed that Janice had such a negative reaction to my plan. If she understood the agony of dating a man who looks like Ben when looking like me, she wouldn't be so judgmental. Feeling insecure and in need of someone else's insanity, I dial Mother.

"Hello."

"Mother, it's Anna."

"Anna, it's Mother."

"Yeah, I know. I called you."

"Well, you sounded so formal, I thought it best I adhere to the same protocol. I thought maybe someone had kidnapped you and—"

"Mother," I interrupt, "I wanted to ask your opinion on something. Have you ever heard the saying 'Let go and let God'?"

"Yes."

"Well, what do you think of it? Should I give it a try?"

"That is a pretty risky approach for you. God has

shown even less interest in you than your own father has. That's all I'm going to say."

"Thanks, Mother," I say and hang up before the call can get any worse.

The Prada store is located near our apartment, on Prince and Broadway in SoHo. I walk past the entrance three times, unable to summon the confidence to enter. The immaculate and ultramodern store intimidates me. Will they assess my middle-class clothing and roll their eyes at me? I can't spend all day pacing in front of the store like an expectant father at the hospital. I need to get this over with before I drop dead from anticipation. Who cares if they stare at me or scream *Gap* from the rafters? I will merely scream back, "Yes, I'm middle class and proud, bitches!" Well, maybe not the bitch part; screaming profanities in public is out of character for me. Instead, I'll probably lie and tell them I am an undercover shopper, assessing the treatment of an average consumer in their store.

"Can I help you?" a tall, brown-haired woman asks with a hideously large smile. It's been two seconds since I entered the store. These people are on it.

"Um, I am looking for some pants."

"Excellent. The women's section is upstairs. Right this way."

"No!" I blurt out loudly. "I am looking for a specific pair of pants for my boyfriend."

"No problem, we'll find what you're looking for, and if we don't have the right size in stock, I can have it sent over from another store." This woman is nice; I won't even need my undercover shopper story. She brings me a few samples before I settle on the right pair.

"Um, there's something else."

"Of course. What else are you looking for?"

"I need to switch the thirty-six size tag with a thirty-four."

"No problem, we have an in-house tailor," she responds without raising a perfectly groomed eyebrow.

"Do you get this request a lot?"

"Of course. The men in New York are vainer than the women."

I spent $1,275 on three pairs of slacks for Ben. This is a major expense for me; I have never charged so much money at once. After the interest accrues on my credit card, these extra-soft but still overpriced slacks will have cost me $1,400. My chest hurts. My throat narrows. How could I spend that much money? I don't make enough to spend $1,400 on slacks, especially when they're not even for me. I need to sit down, but I don't want the Prada bag to touch the ground. Even the bag is nicer than anything I own. This is yet another example of the different worlds Ben and I inhabit. What am I doing? I should be with a substitute teacher in a studio in Brooklyn, not with a rich lawyer with a big one bedroom in SoHo.

Sitting heavily on a nearby bus bench, I have a panic attack. Dating Ben has single-handedly been both the worst and the best thing to happen to me. It's ignited every insecurity I have while simultaneously showing me love for the first time. Contrary to my adolescent fantasies, love isn't the antidote to life's problems. It's just the beginning.

Chapter Twenty-four

Three weeks later, a slightly rounder Ben trails behind me after a Saturday-morning Starbucks run. As he sips his venti latte, he makes an odd face.

"Babe, I think they made my latte with half-and-half again. This is the fourth time this week."

Luckily, he hasn't connected me to the breve latte mistakes.

"Here, let me taste it," I offer politely. I lift his latte to my lips and savor the unbelievably rich cream.

"Tastes like milk to me."

"Really?"

"I think you've been eating too healthy, so everything tastes fattening," I lamely declare while opening the mailbox in the lobby of our building.

"I don't think so. I'm gaining weight."

"Are you insane? You look like a stick."

Before he answers, I nonchalantly hand him three catalogs, all addressed to Ben Reynolds. My father's love of ill-fitting catalog clothes inspired me. I'm hoping Ben gives this unflattering shopping mode a try.

"Someone stole my identity," Ben says seriously.

"What?"

"I didn't tell you, but I was suspended from the gym while they verified my identity. Apparently, some man called up claiming to be me, canceled my membership, and accused me of pleasuring myself in the locker room. And I just got three catalogs for cheap clothes. I've never shopped at any of these places."

"What about your credit cards and ATM card. Any strange charges?"

"No, nothing."

"Ben, it seems odd that someone would steal your identity and only cancel your gym membership and send you some catalogs."

"I know, it's really messed up. I don't even want to go to the gym; everyone thinks I've been wanking off in the locker room," Ben responds morosely, igniting a pang of guilt within me.

"Maybe this is a sign from the universe that you should start shopping from home. Let's see what they have to offer," I suggest enthusiastically.

"Anna, I'm not shopping from some cheap catalog. I'm an attorney at Benson and Silverberg, for God's sake," Ben says with frustration.

"Wow, I never knew you were such a snob."

"I am not a snob. I'm a vegetarian," Ben adds defensively.

"Wait, because you don't eat animals you can't be a snob?"

"Yeah, well."

"I take it back. You're a self-righteous snob."

"I resent that. If my income dictated that I shop through catalogs, then I would, but it doesn't, so I don't. That doesn't make me a snob."

I actually agree with him, but I want him to buy something from the catalog, so I continue. "Whatever you say...snob."

"Big words from a girl who cuts the Gap labels out of her clothes. What? Are you ashamed to shop there?"

"How do you know about that?" I demand, trying to hide my embarrassment.

"I got suspicious when none of your clothes had labels and the trash was filled with Gap bags."

"I am not ashamed of the Gap. I cut out the label because I believe all labels are ridiculous. I don't care where my clothes come from. I'm not as shallow as you are."

"Good, let's order you a new wardrobe from the catalog. How do you feel about polyester?"

"Shut up!"

"Here is a lovely orange pantsuit made from a polyester blend. Oh, and look at those buttons—gold leaf."

"Fine! You're right. I won't shop from a catalog," I relent. "However, shopping at the Gap exclusively is different from shopping at Hermès, Prada, and Gucci exclusively."

"Don't try to make me feel guilty, Anna. I recycle, don't eat animals, vote Democrat, and donate ten percent to charity. I deserve to shop wherever I want!" Ben yells at me as he opens the front door.

"Fine, so do I," I scream back.

"And stop getting plastic bags at the Gap! They take a thousand years to biodegrade!" Ben shouts.

"I suppose you bring your own canvas sack when shopping at Gucci!" I retort, flopping onto the couch. Ben slams the bedroom door.

Facedown in the couch, something wells up in me. It's not tears or anger, it's laughter. I laugh uncontrollably. What a ridiculous fight! Who is the bigger snob? Who will shop from a catalog? Who recycles? Who the hell fights about such idiotic stuff? I gasp for air as my eyes water. Ben opens the bedroom door with a similar expression. He collapses next to me as we shake with hilarity. Ben chokes out the words "orange pantsuit" before descending into paroxysms of laughter. We playfully hit one another, wheezing for air, astonished by the stupidity of our fight.

Cheap clothing, whether from a catalog or not, is out. Clearly, Ben takes pleasure in labels. I find a solution in a more obscure brand of luxury clothing, Façonnable. While flipping through *Home and Garden,* I saw an ad for their line of high-end flannel shirts. Wasps predominantly wear these shirts while shooting birds or other defenseless animals outside their country estates. Of course, getting Ben to wear these plaid specialties will require a well-thought-out presentation. That or a stun gun.

Chapter Twenty-five

"How do you watch this shit? Every episode is exactly the same," I complain to Ben.

"You just don't understand the show, babe. And for the record, there are three *Law & Order*s, so obviously I'm not the only one who thinks there's something to it."

"But you're a lawyer. Why do you want to waste your leisure time watching a show about your work? It seems kind of boring."

"Anna, I practice corporate law. I don't get to cross-examine child molesters and murderers," Ben says seriously. "Hey, can you get me a Nature's Way? I'd get up, but it's about to start."

"Fine," I mumble, secretly satisfied that the Nature's Ways have become such a hit. I knew Skors were the way to go. So damn addictive. I hand him the bar, then lay my face against his chest. Onscreen, some hairy-faced perp lies to two hardened detectives with hearts of gold.

"That guy's kind of hot."

"Who, Stabler?" Ben asks excitedly.

"No, the bad guy."

"That guy? He's disgusting."

"It's the facial hair. It's so rugged and sexy."

"You told me you hate beards."

This is true; I have said that on more than one occasion.

"Um, I was referring to the women who date gay men—beards. I don't like those ladies, but men with beards, yeah I'm into it."

"Okay," Ben says, distracted by the television.

"I have a recurring fantasy of being taken by a poorly groomed man with a beard. Really wild hair, 'cause that's how it makes me feel, wild."

"What are you talking about?" Ben asks, now focusing fully on me.

"Well, just like this show offers excitement that your job doesn't have, sometimes I want a man with a rough, wild beard." I'm not sure how much sense I'm making, but I see Ben study the actor with an air of calculating appraisal.

"I think I'd look good with one."

Yeah, right. I smile, knowing the seed has been successfully planted. The phone rings as Ben shoves the Nature's Way into his mouth. I head for the living room, not wanting to disturb Ben during his precious *Law & Order*.

"Hello?"

"*Start spreading the news, I'm coming today.*"

Oh my God. I cannot allow this to happen.

"No, you aren't."

"*I'm trying to be a part of it. New York. New York!*"

"Mother, I forbid you to enter the state, do you hear me?"

"Your brother has a girlfriend."

"What? How is that possible? And what does that have to do with anything?"

"She hustles Raisinets down at the cineplex."

"She works at the concession stand? That's perfect. But as to the relevance—"

"Anyway, I'm lonely. Thought I'd come stay with you.

Meet this boyfriend of yours, see your new body, the Big Apple."

"No."

"No? You can't say no to me. I'm your mother."

"Yes, I can. You said no to me my entire life."

"That wasn't me."

"Who was it then?"

"God."

"God said no to me?"

"Unfortunately, yes. I didn't want to agree, but he strong-armed me."

"Mother, you can't stay with me—ever. You are not allowed to enter the state of New York without my permission. Am I clear?"

"Wow, after all these years of defending you to the big guy, you go and prove me wrong."

"Mother, you're not even religious."

"I'll have you know I bought a limited edition Bible in Ebonics."

"What?"

"If black kids break into the house and see that I have a Bible in Ebonics, they will walk right out the door on account of me understanding their plight."

Ignoring Mother's asinine security theory and her trademark racism, I simply ask, "They sell Bibles written in Ebonics?"

"QVC cares about race relations."

"Mother, listen to me. Stay in Ohio. No one in New York will accept you. Absolutely no one!"

I can't handle Mother on a good day, let alone when I am knee deep in securing Ben a place in the less-than-perfect category.

★   ★   ★

While I wait for the stubble to develop properly into facial hair, I attend to my own hair needs. I can't let myself go just because Ben drops a few notches. If anything, it's time to increase my butt clenches, gym visits, and bikini area maintenance. I am a huge fan of Nair's extra-strength hair removal cream, in large part because it doesn't require me to lay spread-eagle with an angry Russian between my legs. Not that I am prudish, but Anyas, the waxing communist, goes places my gynecologist has only heard of. A little cream, even with the strange chemical smell, is much easier. I flip through celeb magazines while the cream sets for ten minutes. I never let Ben see me during this process, because it would shatter his image of me as effortlessly average. Nair shrinks your hair, slowly thinning entire patches until there is nothing left. From the look of the hair shrinkage, I have another three minutes until rinse-off. Any sooner and some hair will remain.

Wait. I just had a true eureka moment. I am so impressed with myself that I have half a mind to share my brilliant idea with Ben. A few drops of Nair in Ben's moderately priced shampoo will subtly thin his full-bodied mane. My goal is to dull the locks while lightly weeding out some follicles. However cruel it may sound, it could do wonders for Ben's confidence to find a few extra hairs in his hand when shampooing.

My mixing complete, I sniff the bottle. A few drops of Nair smell surprisingly strong. My eyes tear up, and not just from the smell. Oh, the guilt. What have I done? Is Nair over the line? I didn't put that much in the shampoo. I wouldn't be surprised if there was no effect at all.

After all, Ben doesn't shampoo his hair for ten minutes, the amount of time needed to see serious results. And if by some chance Ben experiences a little thinning, it will be good for him. He should weather a crisis of confidence about something silly and superficial. It's part of the human condition, and he has missed it. This is an anthropological mission, right? I decide to text Janice, ask her opinion on the matter.

"Is the loss of hair important to a man's character?"

She wisely texts back, "Fuck off, it's 2:00 a.m."

By the time I leave the bathroom, Ben has fallen asleep with the television on and a half-eaten Nature's Way on his chest. I switch off the television and climb into bed next to Ben. After removing the Nature's Way bar from his chest hair as best I can, I rest my head on the pillow. I'm exhausted, yet I can't sleep. I am perplexed by what I have done, yet simultaneously scared I haven't done enough. I could still easily lose him. More than anything, I want The Makedown complete so I can erase it from my memory. A slightly downgraded Ben will be a more appropriate boyfriend for me—attractive but not gorgeous. I can handle attractive; it's gorgeous that kills me.

I still can't sleep. Should I throw away the shampoo? Is it too much? No, this is the best thing for us as a couple. I am bringing us closer together. We will be more in harmony, right?

I yank the sheet off me, feeling claustrophobic from its touch. I need to do this to stay with Ben, but it's undoubtedly wrong to deceive the man I love. Frustrated, I head for my old stomping grounds, the kitchen. I wrench open the stainless steel refrigerator, allowing the cold air to calm my nerves. If I were still the old me, I would devour the vanilla fudge ice cream until suitably numb. For a few seconds, I flirt with a relapse before remembering that I must remain strong. I am a soldier on a mission, and as such, I must remain focused on the task at hand—Ben.

By the soft light of the fridge, I undress. Standing naked in my kitchen, I check my gear: spoon (check), ice cream (check), naked body (check). It is now or never. I cross the threshold of the bedroom with the concentration of a front-line commando. I lay the spoon and perspiring ice cream on the nightstand before lifting the sheet slowly off Ben's naked body. The humility-challenged Ben insists on sleeping in the nude. I stand above him, mindlessly debating the statistical likelihood of a fire hitting the building while both of us are naked. His face distracts me. It's slightly rounder than usual, but still devastatingly handsome. I am ready to seduce him, then stuff him full of ice cream. Like a frightened private on the eve of my first mission, I shut my eyes and will myself to jump. I land on top of Ben's naked body.

"Ahhh!!!!!!" Ben wails in pain.

I didn't mean to land with such force, but the whole military theme riled me up.

"What in the hell are you doing?" Ben screams.

Man down, abort operation.

"What's happening?" I scream back, good soldier that I am.

The lights flick on. A livid Ben stares at me. The clock ticks. The pressure mounts. He wants an answer. Is there an appropriate answer? I dig deep into my *People* magazine vault. Since moving in with Ben, I have embraced the celeb rags in the bathroom, often rereading issues while handling location-appropriate business.

"Why are you yelling at me?"

"You jumped on my dick at 2:30 in the morning! Is this some kind of joke? Does this amuse you?" Ben asks angrily.

It's a fair assumption, based on his pained expression, that I did serious damage to his equipment.

"I don't know; the last thing I remember is taking an Ambien."

Is he going to buy this?

"You don't remember anything else?"

"Nothing. Although I do remember reading somewhere that women were waking up in the middle of the night and eating without any recollection after taking Ambien."

"But you're not eating anything."

"Well, I'm assuming that ice cream isn't yours," I say, pointing to the pint on the nightstand.

To my great relief, he laughs.

"You're naked with a pint of ice cream."

"It appears that way. I'm sorry if I hurt you. I didn't mean to."

"I'll survive."

"Do you want some ice cream?"

"Sure."

The next morning, I wake to the sound of both the shower running and the phone ringing. Annoyed, I pull the pillow over my head and wait for voicemail to pick up. After five seconds of silence, the ringing begins again. It continues until the voicemail picks up. Two seconds of silence follows before the phone starts ringing again. Gritting my teeth in frustration, I emerge from beneath my pillow and pick up the phone.

Before I can even say hello, I hear it. It's an irritating but familiar sound. It is my overweight brother smothering the receiver, as he has done since he was a child.

"Barney?"

"I've been made aware of some mighty disturbing information."

"What?"

"You banned Mother and me from the state of New York."

"I didn't ban you, just Mother, although please don't come. This isn't a good time."

"Anna, we miss you."

"No you don't."

"How can you say that after all the postcards we've written?"

"What postcards?"

"Those cheap sons of—"

"Barney?" I interrupt.

"I thought if I mailed them without a stamp, they would have to send them to you to get the postage, since there's no return address."

"What the fuck happened to my hair?" Ben screams from the bathroom.

Shit.

"Barney, I have to go," I say, slamming the phone on the receiver.

Ben stands teary-eyed in front of the bathroom mirror. There are five clearly visible hairless patches on his head. It's undeniable, yet I try to deny it.

"What?" I ask stupidly.

"Do you not see this huge bald patch on my head?"

Ben asks with intense frustration. Evidently, he hasn't noticed the other four.

Hello Fatty,
You are definitely going to hell.

—Anna

"Oh that," I say nonchalantly.

"Yes, *'oh that.'* What is it?" Ben screams hysterically.

I never thought Ben could remind me of Mother, but he does now. Ben's dramatic expression in the mirror along with an exaggerated sense of disaster reeks of Mother.

"Looks like run-of-the-mill male-pattern baldness," I explain in a soothing tone.

"It appeared overnight. Baldness doesn't appear overnight, Anna!"

"Calm down. Maybe it's an allergic reaction. Now that I look a little closer, you seem to have some other spots around your head."

"*What?* Oh God, no!"

"Don't worry, no one will notice."

"Anna, my head is half bald! My life is over. Do you hear me? Over! I'm not going to work."

"Babe, I'm sure whatever it is will go away, and your hair will grow back."

"Or it will continue and I will be completely bald by the weekend! I'm losing it. God, why me? How can you do this to me?" Ben wails while looking at the ceiling.

"Ben, you need to calm down. It's hair. It will grow back."

"What if it doesn't? I'll be...ugly! Women hate bald men. They make fun of them, they call them bowling balls." Ben theatrically stutters as if he's lost his penis or some other close relative.

"Trust me, it will take a lot more than a few bald patches to make you ugly."

"That's what I used to think, but obviously I was wrong."

"Ben, you're still gorgeous. Look at that face."

"Are you sure?"

"Yes."

"I'm making a doctor's appointment immediately. Maybe he can give me Rogaine or something."

"If that's what you need to do."

"Are you sure I'm not ugly?"

"I promise."

"Cancel dinner with Janice and Gary."

"What? Over a little hair? You can wear a hat."

"Anna, look at me. I am in no condition to be in public. I'm ordering a pizza and watching the *Law & Order* marathon."

"Whatever you say," I say sweetly as a pang of guilt stabs at my stomach. "You know, Ben, I'm sure it will grow back."

"I hope so. Thank God I'm growing the beard. It will be a good distraction."

While Ben is at Dr. Hardin's office on Amsterdam and Broadway, I decide to implement the flannel. Ben has gained twenty pounds, started growing a beard, and developed bald patches, and soon he will be dressed in flannel. I think that is more than enough to keep the über-elite women away from him. The beard will take a couple weeks to hit its stride, but if I get him to wear flannel by that time, mission accomplished.

Façonnable is appropriately located on Fifth Avenue. At $125 per flannel shirt, I can't help but think that Kurt Cobain is rolling over in his grave. Post-Prada, I am markedly more comfortable in upper-class stores. Not that it matters, since this is the last step. As soon as I find a way to convince Ben to wear flannel, I am free to enjoy Ben in his less-than-perfect form.

As I turn the doorknob to the apartment, I hear the television blasting, signaling Ben's presence.

"Hey babe, how was the doctor?" I call out, dropping my bags on the floor. Ben stands naked in front of me with a glass of wine in his left hand.

"What happened? Why are you naked?"

"I'm trying to relax. Being naked relaxes me."

"What did the doctor say?"

"He thinks it could be an allergic reaction or stress-induced hair loss."

"Really?"

"He gave me this special shampoo to use and told me to take it easy and stay as calm as possible."

"I knew you were fine," I beam reassuringly at him.

"I would hardly call me fine, Anna. I have mange," Ben says like a bitchy transvestite.

"I'm sorry; I got you something to cheer you up."

"A toupee?"

"Ha ha. I bought you these shirts. Aren't they great?" I say, pulling out red, green, and blue flannel shirts. His already dour face contorts painfully, expressing his extreme dislike of my clothing selection.

"Babe, those are awful," Ben declares with a scowl.

"Honey, you wear them with a black suit. I saw it in . . . *Vogue,* yes, Italian *Vogue.* It's sexy. Very cutting-edge."

"Anna, this isn't my look. Plus, with the bald patches, I don't want to draw any additional attention to myself."

"Will you at least try them on?"

He takes the green shirt reluctantly. "Oh, it's Façon-nable."

Label whore. As Ben buttons the front of his shirt, his face continues to twist miserably as if biting into something horribly acidic.

"No. No way, I would never wear this."

"Well, not without any pants on, of course not."

"Babe, no."

"Ben, I spent a lot of money one these shirts. Will you at least try it on with a black suit? The sales clerk said it's all the rage in Italy, France . . . and Albania, which are big fashion places. Please try it with a suit—for me."

"Fine, but this isn't good for my stress level, Anna," Ben says, turning toward the bedroom. He returns, tucking the shirt into his now-tight "34-inch" black slacks.

He looks like Paul Bunyan at a funeral.

"You look hot," I say with a straight face.

"Are you serious? This looks like shit!"

"I think you look sexy. You're kind of turning me on."

"You're sick."

I couldn't agree more.

"There's something very masculine and . . . dangerous about you in that top."

"Are you serious?" The compliment penetrates his wounded ego.

"Uh-huh. You seem strong and virile, like you could knock someone out for looking at me the wrong way."

"Really?"

"Ohhh," I shiver orgasmically, "I don't want you to wear these out of the house. It's only for me."

Ben smiles lasciviously. I haven't seen him this happy since before I destroyed his hair, which technically was only last night. However, this morning was exceptionally stressful. Without another word, I get on my knees and perform what should really be called man's best friend. There is no better way to convey attraction and sex appeal than by giving your boyfriend an impromptu blow job in the kitchen.

"I think you're right," Ben says as I lift myself from the floor. "This suits me."

Before I can respond, the doorbell rings.

"Babe, that's the pizza. Can you get it?" Ben asks, running off to clean up. I open the door with a sense of satisfaction; mission accomplished.

"You order two double-cheese pizzas, breadsticks, ranch dressing, and a liter of Pepsi?"

"No, we ordered one pizza."

"This Ben Reynolds's place?"

"Yeah, but—"

"Then you ordered this."

"No, I'm sorry. There must be some mistake. Ben?"

"Yeah?" he calls from the bathroom.

"Did you order two pizzas and breadsticks?"

"What?" he yelps, running into the living room. "Did they forget the ranch dressing and Pepsi?"

"No, no they didn't. Never mind."

"Thank goodness. The doctor says I need to relax, and there's nothing more relaxing than this."

"Absolutely."

After one slice of pizza and half a breadstick, I pass out without even brushing my teeth. A few hours later, I roll over and find the bed empty. The clock reads 4:30 a.m. Where is Ben? I hear rustling in the kitchen. I tiptoe down the hall only to discover a naked Ben eating cold pizza from the fridge. I creep back to the bedroom in shock. The bald patches unraveled him more than I thought. Twenty minutes later, he crawls into bed reeking of cheese and ranch dressing.

Even after the 4:30 snack, Ben is up at 7:00 sharp, buttoning the Façonnable red plaid shirt. I am surprised how quickly he has taken to it.

"Thanks for the shirts. I love them."

"Oh, good. You're feeling better about your hair today?"

"I think the flannel diverts attention from the patches."

"Okay," I say quietly. I am suddenly filled with remorse over making him go to work looking like a crazed lumberjack. Ben doesn't notice my consternation as he heads into the kitchen, returning seconds later with both a piece of pizza and a Nature's Way for the road.

"Babe? Can you set the TiVo for *Law & Order*? I didn't get a chance to last night."

"Sure."

"Oh, and some more Nature's Ways would be great. They give me that kick I need in the morning."

I smile guiltily, wondering what I have started.

Chapter Twenty-six

Junk food is addictive. It is a drug, like cocaine, heroin, or crack; the junk food junkie requires an ever higher caloric intake to reach satisfaction. It's been a mere eight weeks, and Ben has devolved into an addict, ordering such fattening specialties as eggplant parmigiana, fettuccine Alfredo, vegetable tempura, french fries, and onion rings. He is on a first-name basis with most of the deliverymen in a ten-block radius, and our trash compacter looks like the Dumpster behind the food court, littered with wrappers and oily napkins.

While I was pleased with the initial weight gain, I am now concerned that Ben is on the fast track to obesity. It's time to put on the brakes.

"Babe, did you get more Nature's Way bars?"

"Yeah, I did. Here you go," I say as I toss him one from the shopping bag.

"What the hell is this?" Ben screams, staring at the real Nature's Way bar, a mass of oats stuck together with some honey.

"I heard they were changing their recipe. This must be the new bar," I say, thinking Ben must be getting wise to my dreadful lies.

"They always discontinue my favorite stuff," Ben whines as if he's a moody teenager. "I guess I'll have Doritos for dessert then."

Doritos for dessert?

"I can cut you up an apple or nectarine for dessert."

"No, I don't want that," he insists, pouting unattractively.

There has been a strange and unexpected shift within Ben the last few weeks. I would best describe it as an emotional regression. He's become withdrawn and temperamental, like a hormonally challenged eighth-grader, and a few pimples have even broken through under his messy beard. As he shoves Doritos into his mouth by the handful, I gasp in sudden realization: Ben is me, circa junior high.

I have gone too far. I must figure out how to undo the damage I have done.

After barely sleeping, I awake at 6:30 on Saturday morning, prepared to meet Janice at the kitchen to prep for a Greek party. I run from the subway station to the kitchen, busting through the door like a woman possessed.

"I can't stop him...he's descended into this fat, hairy blob watching TV and wiping food on his shirt."

"Wasn't that the plan?"

"No!" I scream. "The plan was to make him a little less attractive, not to turn him into this."

"So he's a bit chunkier than you wanted. Big deal."

"It's not just how he looks; he acts like a different person, like some—"

"Fat person? Some unhappy fat person? You should know about that."

"It's different; he behaves like a child. He needs help. It's invasion of the body snatchers."

"I warned you not do this."

"Thanks, telling me 'I told you so' is really helpful."

"You guys should come over for dinner. Get him out of the house, be around some grown-ups. He'll snap back."

Maybe Janice is right. He has spent most of his life as an Adonis and only weeks as a sloth; surely this is temporary.

After making filo dough all morning with Janice, I return home to find the television blaring from the bedroom. Not a good sign. Please, tell me he left it on by accident when he went out to do something. It's Saturday; he should be out and about. I enter the bedroom and discover Ben not only still in bed but still in his pajamas.

"You know what's amazing about *Law & Order*? It's the only show where the cast changes every season and it doesn't matter. You still watch."

Ben doesn't bother to take his eyes off the TV as I enter the room.

"Have you been watching *Law & Order* all day?" I ask, not even bothering to hide my disappointment.

"They're having a 'remembering Lennie' marathon."

"Who's Lennie?"

"He was the master of the zingers. I miss him."

"Ben, I can't help but notice you watch more TV than usual."

"TiVo has changed my life."

"It's a beautiful, sunny day, and you're cooped up inside watching TV. The beauty of TiVo is that you can watch it at any time. Why don't we make TV a nighttime-only activity?"

"Anna, this is doctor's orders. He said to relax. I don't know if you've noticed, but the more time I spend chilling at home, the faster my hair grows back."

Ha! That's because I threw out the contaminated shampoo.

"The doctor said to relax, not to be on bed rest."

Ben ignores me as I walk around the bedroom, picking up his fast food trash.

"Do you have to be so loud? I can't hear the show!"

"Ben, I'm picking up *your* trash. This room is disgusting."

"Get out of my room!"

"This is *our* room!"

"Why can't you leave me alone?"

"Fine!"

Scientists believe the chemicals in processed foods cause the premature onset of puberty. I have learned that they also cause a regression of the mature *back* to puberty.

By Tuesday night, I have come to hate *Law & Order,* especially that weird bell they ring between each scene. Even as we sit silently in the back of a yellow cab en route to Janice and Gary's for dinner, I can still hear that bell ringing in my head.

I lean forward and tap the partition, signaling the driver to stop.

"Why are we stopping here? They live another block away," Ben whines.

"I thought it would be nice for us to walk a block. Stretch our legs before dinner."

"Are you crazy? It's freezing!" Ben turns to the cab driver and insists, "Keep going."

"I don't remember you being afraid of the cold."

"I am *not* afraid, Anna. I am practical. We could get sick. My jacket isn't even lined."

"I told you to take the other coat!" I shriek with frustration.

"The other coat doesn't...fit me, okay? I had no choice in the matter."

"Why don't you buy a new one?"

"I'm on a diet. I'm not going to buy new clothes now."

"You had cheese fries and a Coke two hours ago. Must be one hell of a diet."

"I can't believe you said that."

"Please stop at the corner," I tell the cab driver with a look that conveys my deep mortification about the conversation he's overheard.

Ben exits the cab after me, then loudly slams the door. Standing on Horatio Street in the West Village, I silently debate whether my comment was justified or unnecessarily bitchy. This frustration is familiar—the sensation of wanting to lose weight while feeling incapable of sticking to a diet. The only difference is now I watch the frustration as opposed to experiencing it.

"If you think I'm fat, you should just come out and say it." Ben sneers at me.

"Ben, I don't think you're fat. I'm sorry I said that thing about the cheese fries."

Regardless of what I think, we are forty-five seconds away from walking into Janice and Gary's, and I do not have time to engage in a fight. I knock on the door as Ben does his best "let it go" smile. I kiss him on the cheek to speed things along. Seconds after I pull my lips from Ben's hairy cheek, Gary and Janice open the door and say hello in unison.

I hate happy people.

"Hi!" I exclaim a little too loudly as I reach for Janice and Gary, giving them each a kiss on the cheek.

"Hello," Janice says as Gary extends his hand to Ben.

"Ben, how are you?"

"Um, I'm okay, Gary. How are you?" Ben says in a stilted voice. I narrow my eyes at him to convey the importance of acting normal.

"Great, come in, guys," Gary says warmly. "Anna, you look fantastic."

"Oh, thank you," I say sweetly while looking over at Ben, who seems annoyed I've received a compliment. I tug at Ben's arm and make a face. He pulls his arm away and pretends to ignore me.

French music wafts from the tasteful living room, which Janice has decorated with her signature solid fabrics in gray, black, beige, and white.

"Gary, will you take their coats? I'm going to grab the wine."

Gary grabs our coats, holding one in each hand.

"Anna, is this cashmere?" Gary asks.

"Yeah, Janice got it for me as a gift."

"Nice. Not quite as nice as Ben's windbreaker," Gary says sarcastically as he exits.

Well, that certainly did little to ease the tension in the room.

Alone in the living room, neither one of us initiates conversation; instead, we listen to the music and avoid all eye contact. Loosely translated, I believe the lyrics of this song to be "This is going to be the worst, most awkward dinner of your life...dadadada...dadadada...la vie en rose." The CD case sits on the edge of the coffee table; it's Pottery Barn's *Vive la France*. Janice enters with a tray of wine and glasses. She places it next to her artfully crafted hors d'oeuvre plate. Gary returns taking the seat closest to Ben.

"What's the latest, Ben? You defending any Enrons whose stock I should be dumping?" Gary asks.

"We're transactional lawyers, not litigators," Ben responds disdainfully. He can't stand when people can't distinguish among different types of lawyers. He won't believe me when I explain that no one really cares to.

"More paper pushers than interrogators?" Gary says, further annoying Ben.

"We negotiate corporate mergers. If you consider that a paper pusher, sure."

"He's only teasing, Ben," Janice says. "Aren't you, Gary?"

"Of course," Gary says casually. "I'm more of a right-brain kind of guy: languages, arts, not very good with numbers."

"It's true, Gary couldn't figure out what to tip a waiter to save his life, but we spent a month in Paris, and he came back fluent."

"I've always wanted to learn French," I fib, desperate to ease the tension. "Ben, do you speak French?" I lamely ask my own boyfriend.

"No, I took Spanish in high school," Ben responds.

"Español es mi favorito de todos las lenguas romances," Gary says with an over-the-top accent.

"It's been fifteen years since high school."

"And?"

"And I have no idea what you're saying."

"Not everyone has an ear for languages; I guess you could say I'm lucky that way."

The room goes silent. Janice sips her wine. Ben wipes his forehead and stares off into space. Gary, being Gary, sings along to the French music playing. I cannot fathom how someone as intelligent as Janice is married to such a pretentious ass.

"I love this CD. Janice, remember we bought this at that store on the Left Bank?"

Before Janice can answer, Ben interjects, "I didn't know they had Pottery Barn in Paris."

"They don't. Have you ever been to Paris, Ben?" Gary asks with a heavy drop of condescension.

"Yes, four or five times. I only ask because I noticed the CD cover."

I just fell in love with my boyfriend all over again. I want to sit on his lap, smother him with kisses, and apologize for the cheese fries comment. I, of all people, should know the dangerous side effects of commenting on eating habits.

"That's not the CD that's playing, Ben," Gary says angrily.

"Let's eat," Janice announces.

Seated at the table, Ben and I barely look at each other while Gary engages him in a strange staring contest. Janice and I do our absolute best to pretend everything is normal.

"Ben, how are your parents?" Janice asks sweetly.

"Good. They are getting ready to go to St. Maarten for a week."

"What? You didn't tell me that," I say in a voice that cannot hide my surprise.

"I didn't know you cared. I can, however, get you an itemized menu from their trip since I know how much you love to know what people eat."

"Of course she does; she's a caterer!" Janice says lightly.

"You guys don't talk much, do you?" Gary says, gazing at Ben.

"No, mostly we sit around by candlelight, listening to music in languages we don't understand. Then we feed each other fondue. Homemade, of course," Ben shoots back.

"Would anyone care for more wine?" Janice asks uncomfortably.

"I would! And I love these Szechuan green beans. Ben, don't you like them?"

"Yes, delicious," Ben mumbles.

"You like them, Ben? Hmm. I took you more for the Snickers and potato chips type. Maybe an ice cream sundae?" Gary asks.

"Yes, I like those, too," Ben says, clearly stung by another weight barb.

I want to kill Gary with my bare hands.

"I like ice cream," I say with a reassuring glance at Ben.

"You scream, I scream, we all scream for ice cream," Janice says clumsily.

"Excuse me; I am going to the bathroom."

Ben stands and heads down the hallway. The three of us eat green beans in silence.

"Do you hear that?" Gary inquires.

Ben is talking or mumbling to himself in the other room.

"Excuse me just a second."

Walking quickly down the hall, I attempt to decipher what Ben is saying, but his voice is too muffled. I enter the bathroom behind him and listen to him whine, "Mom, he's being so mean to me."

Oh my God. My boyfriend called his mom. I grab the phone.

"What are you doing, Anna?" Ben asks.

"What are *you* doing, Ben? Calling your mom to tell on someone? I didn't know they gave law degrees straight out of preschool these days!"

I realize the phone is still on, and Milly has heard my comments.

"Milly, I apologize, but I can handle it from here. I will have him call you later."

"I want to go home. Gary's being mean to me."

"You haven't exactly been nice either. The Pottery Barn comment?"

"I can't believe you're taking his side."

"I'm on your side. But this is my boss's husband. Can you at least try?"

"Fine."

"And if you need to call your mom, do it outside so no one hears you."

Back at the table, I pretend that the entire phone call to Milly did not occur and struggle to think of a neutral topic of conversation.

Just as I clear my throat to speak, Gary breaks in with, "You know who likes Pottery Barn? My mom. Ben, does your mom like Pottery Barn?"

Gary heard. Ben turns to me with the pleading eyes of a child.

"I don't feel well. I want to go home," Ben groans.

The setting may appear to be a sophisticated dining room in the West Village, but it's actually a schoolyard during recess. Ben is the nerd and Gary is the bully. If dinner continues any longer, Gary may pants Ben. And I am positive that Ben will cry. And it will be all my fault.

Chapter Twenty-seven

D ue to a suffocating wave of guilt, I couldn't sleep at all. The horrors of the evening replayed until 7:30 a.m., when I called Janice and begged for the day off. Secretly, I think she was relieved not to have to discuss the horrendous evening we had shared. I return to bed and feel as if my head just hit the pillow when the doorbell rings. I glance at the clock; it's only 10:30. I've barely gotten three hours sleep. I stumble out of bed as the doorbell rings again. Annoyed, I peek through the peephole.

No! This must be a terrible nightmare.

Mother and Barney appear to be standing at my door. There is no way they would arrive unannounced, right? I open the door, half expecting to find that they were a figment of my imagination. Perhaps it's my conscience punishing me with cruel hallucinations for what I've done to Ben.

I open the door. Mother and Barney are still there. Someone kill me.

"What are you doing here? Why do you have suitcases?" I explode.

"I told you we were coming to visit," Mother says cheerily.

"I told you not to come. I'm afraid you're going to have to leave."

"Anna, your brother and I are extremely fatigued from the train; we need to rest."

"Mother, Barney, I am on the verge of a mental break-down and having you in a hundred-mile radius may push me over the edge. Go back to the station, get on the train to Philly, and visit Aunt Hazel. Okay? Good, see you at Christmas," I say, trying to shut the door in their faces.

"I burned down your philandering father's massage parlor and opium shack," Mother informs me with her usual pep.

"She means his garage," Barney translates.

"What are you talking about? Did I not just say that I am on the verge of a breakdown? You think this is going to help?"

"It sounds like someone needs their mother," Mother says firmly, pushing past me.

"Hey, I thought you said this guy was a lawyer."

"He is, Barney."

"Must not be a very good one judging by the size of this place."

"Barney, you may not know this since you live at home with Mother, but New York is outrageously expensive. This is a big apartment."

"Great, then you won't mind us staying with you," Barney says with a wink.

"Absolutely not."

"Anna, if my house in Ohio was an apartment in New York, how much would I get for it?" Mother asks.

"I don't understand."

"If I had an apartment in New York the size of my house, how much would it be worth?"

"Mother, I don't know."

"An estimate. Please."

"Fine. A lot."

"That's what I thought. I knew the house was a good deal."

This is one of Mother's imaginary fact-proving exercises. She creates bogus reasons to validate random aspects of her life. Today's topic is real estate.

"It was a good deal because you and dad bought it for seventy-five hundred in 1960."

"Your so-called dad is cheap."

"Mother, why are you calling him my so-called dad?"

"Real dads don't make Bastard Won Tons."

"So dad's ch-cheap?" I stutter, anxious to stay away from the Bastard Won Ton conversation. "Is that why you burned down the garage?"

"It was an accident. I suspect he has some napkin rings of mine. My lawyer refuses to file the necessary paperwork, so I had to take measures into my own hands. And my research led me to—"

"Dad's garage?" I interrupt.

"Where else would he hide something he stole from me?"

"You know what? I don't care about the napkin rings; just explain how the garage caught fire."

"Apparently, I put my cigarette out in paint thinner. It's not my fault; they should have a warning on the label."

"They have one. It says 'flammable.'"

"Well, it's not much use if it doesn't glow in the dark. I think I'll write them a letter."

"Was anyone hurt?"

"No, but your father insisted on calling the police, so Barney and I came to see you."

Barney builds a fort out of couch pillows while I stand in front of Mother in a paralyzed state of horror.

"I need to lie down," I say, walking toward the bedroom. Please, let them be gone when I wake up. I can't handle them. I can barely handle me.

A deep and phony voice awakens me. It's the QVC announcer effusing over the beauty of a lab-grown diamond. I make my way to the living room, hoping they won't be there by some miracle. Oh, dear Lord, it's worse than I thought. Barney and Ben are both in the fort. How long have I been asleep?

"Ben, what are you doing?" I inquire.

"Don't answer her, Ben. We can't hear them when we are in the fort."

"Shut up, Barney!" I snap.

"Babe, Barney's right. The fort is soundproof, so I will have to talk to you later."

"Ben, I insist that you leave the fort and speak to me in the kitchen."

"Jeez, no reason to get mad," Ben mutters under his breath as he follows me into the kitchen.

"Why are you acting like a child?" I demand.

"What are you talking about?"

"The fort. Ben, you think that is normal adult behavior?"

"Why are you freaking out? I'm relating to your brother, who by the way you didn't even tell me was coming. Stop being so uptight."

"I'm not uptight! It's just a little disconcerting that you came home from work and regressed twenty years."

"I'm getting to know your family, which by the way explains a lot about you."

"What does that mean? I barely consider us related. Distant relatives at best."

"Calm down. You should be thanking me. I got Barney to call your dad about the fire. He's dropping the charges; they're going back tomorrow."

I am stunned, but I can't figure out how to break through this brittle exchange to thank Ben, so I simply ask, "How in the world did you accomplish that?"

"Your mom has agreed to pay for the cost of rebuilding the garage, and your Dad wants the money transferred as soon as possible. Apparently, he thinks she will welch on it if given too much time. She insists on transferring the money in person at her local branch...no idea why. Your parents, they're both a little peculiar."

"I know," I sigh, shaking my head. "Mother's never trusted ATMs. She insists on going into the bank to deposit a check or withdraw money. Ben, I don't even know what to say. Thank you, you're amazing."

"You're welcome, now I got to get back to the fort."

I smile with relief and follow Ben back to the living room. I take a seat on the couch next to Mother. Barney scowls at me from the fort, which sports a "No Girls Allowed" sign.

"Barney, what does Jennifer think about your proclivity for playing in forts in your twenties?"

"Anna, stop talking. We are in the fort," Ben says humorously.

"Who do you think taught me how to build the fort, Weird Fat Bear?" Barney says to me.

"Barney, *shut up*! I told you never to call me that!"

"Anna, you need a few moments in your room," Mother says authoritatively.

"What?"

"You need a time-out."

"Are you freaking kidding me?"

"Okay, you definitely need a time-out. Stand up, young lady."

Mother pulls me by the arm into the bedroom.

"I will come and get you in thirty minutes."

"Mother, this is my apartment!"

"I am your mother. I am always in charge."

I hear Ben's voice from the living room. "Mrs. Norton, will you make us sandwiches?"

"Of course. And how about some Ovaltine, boys?"

"Yay, Ovaltine!" Ben and Barney respond.

When did my life become so surreal?

Chapter Twenty-eight

The last twenty-four hours have reinforced my decision to live several states away from my family. I wave good-bye to Mother and Barney at Penn Station after wishing them luck paying off Dad and Ming for the garage. I have accepted that there is something wrong with my family genetically—this couldn't all stem from environment. Maybe we have a rogue gene that hangs between autism and depression. There is no other explanation for our behavior.

While Mother and Barney did briefly manage to take my mind off the quickly deteriorating Ben, in their absence it rushes back to me. I ruined my boyfriend. I destroyed another human being because of my insecurities and his need to flirt. I am definitely going to hell.

Surprisingly, when I return home from the train station it's not *Law & Order* that greets me but Ben singing very sadly. It may actually be the saddest voice I've ever heard.

"*I am a rock. I am an iiiiiiiislannd.*"

"Ben?"

On the bed with his eyes shut and an iPod blaring in his ears is the man formerly known as Ben Reynolds. He doesn't know I am in the doorway, watching him sing. His voice is off key, which only exacerbates his pathetic aura. If he were singing Celine's "My Heart Will Go On," I would be confident that Barney had left us some computer-generated time machine and that Ben had literally morphed into a seventh-grade version of me.

I pat his arm, and he opens his eyes. Unaware how lame his behavior actually is, he doesn't convey any signs of embarrassment.

"Hey, what's going on?"

"Nothing," Ben flatly replies.

There it is. The word that best represents teenage depression—nothing. Nothing means everything. Nothing connotes that one is sad, confused, emotionally torn, and wallowing in a pool of shame. Nothing means there is simply too much to explain, so any attempt to do so would be futile. Nothing was the word used to answer Mother when she asked why I had such a gloomy face on my second day of high school. This is how I know nothing is definitely something. And this something is my fault. I am the kryptonite that destroyed the Man of Mass Appeal.

I lie down next to Ben and shut my eyes to block out what I have done to him. How could I be so selfish? How could I be so irrationally destructive? I have never had such a tangible reason to hate myself. In my youth, self-loathing abounded, but my moral compass was always intact. I no longer have the luxury of hating myself with the knowledge that if Saint Peter exists, he will allow me through the pearly gates. Today I admit that I am a bad person. Listening to Ben sing Simon and Garfunkel's ode to isolation poignantly reinforces what I have done. Lifting the magnifying glass to my youth, I see how my mind-set of inadequacy led me to this predicament. I feebly attempted to create an even playing field so love could be managed, patrolled, and kept in line. I should have accepted love for what it is—complicated and unpredictable.

The Makedown was morally and ethically wrong. I am profoundly sorry for it. However, I don't have time to beat myself up; Ben is sinking fast into the black hole of nerd-dom and the nothing that comes with it. I catch glimpses of the man I fell in love with, but he disappears quickly.

I created this reverse fairy tale, turning my Prince Charming into a toad, and I am responsible for rectifying it. My solution will not be some haphazard scheme containing a few mea culpas. It will be smart, multitiered, and efficient. If I weren't worried about Ben finding it, I would create a thorough PowerPoint presentation. But alas, that is too dangerous. I do, however, think a name is needed. I want something straightforward and to the point, like Rebuilding My Formerly Attractive Boyfriend. Perhaps I'll make it into an acronym, RMFAB (pronounced Rim Fab). The premise of RMFAB is simple: Ben plays the part of Cinderella, and I play his health-conscious Fairy Godmother.

As I'm afraid to commit anything to paper, I must keep the plan simple. After all, The Makedown itself wasn't terribly complicated, with its three focal points: hair, clothes, and weight. I was shocked at how quickly and easily Ben submitted to the new lifestyle. My hope is that the reinstatement of Ben's previous standard of living will be equally smooth. He will return to his gorgeous stature with nothing more than a little more compassion for the less-than-perfects.

It's frightening to contemplate returning to the stares of stunning women, but all I can do is hope that now Ben will understand how it affects me. And even if he doesn't, that's okay. I am the architect of his destruction and as such, the culpability and responsibility for his resurrection rests solely on my shoulders.

RMFAB starts immediately. If I don't combat this quickly, I will have to bring in a therapist or a trainer, or sign him up for some reality weight-loss show. RMFAB includes exercise (three-mile walks three times a week), nutrition (vegetables and tofu only), a short but meaningful conversation with his friends and coworkers about the importance of encouragement, and finally, destroying unflattering clothes. Façonnable's flannels are headed straight for Goodwill. Homeless people all over the city will be able to dress like Wasps on a weekend getaway.

Like any good plan, an organic introduction is of the utmost importance. If I move too suddenly, he will go into shock. I have personal experience in this area; I vividly remember the pain of being told to change. Whether it was Mother, our family doctor, or the school nurse informing me that my weight had become a concern, I always experienced unfathomable shame. My entire body would turn beet red, burning with dishonor, disgrace, and humiliation. I was obviously aware that I was fat, but hearing someone say it threw me into an emotional sinkhole of binge eating. It was a sad and counterproductive reaction to being told to lose weight. Many years after my last conversation with the school nurse, I still feel shame. The sooner RMFAB starts, the better. I must get Ben's formerly impenetrable confidence back.

Ben scrambles to get dressed in the bedroom as I mull over my plan in the kitchen. The sound of the phone makes me jump. I was deep in thought, focused on burning flannels and jumping jacks.

"Hello?"

"I thought I should notify you that we are now in the third trimester of Bastard Won Ton's incubation."

"Do you have a Bastard Won Ton calendar?"

"Well, recently I did purchase a Chinese calendar to know what sign Bastard Won Ton will be born under."

"And?"

"Not surprisingly, a rabbit."

"Why aren't you surprised?"

"He was conceived by a couple who clearly screwed like rabbits."

"I thought you said it only took one time."

When I was a teenager, Mother lectured her friend's daughter in front of me about the dangers of sex. She didn't bother to include me in the conversation, since it was clear to everyone that I wasn't getting any.

"At your father's age, it's quantity over quality. Especially with a China doll."

"Mother, I am too busy to discuss Bastard Won Ton," I say, slamming down the phone.

"That sounded intense," Ben says, wandering in to open the fridge. "Babe? I told you to get more Cokes. They're the only thing that wakes me up."

"I got Diet Coke instead. Same caffeine as regular Coke."

"I'll pick up a Coke on the way into the office."

"Or you could buy one of those fruit smoothies or protein shakes."

"I hate that stuff. Always gives me brain freeze."

"Then don't drink it so fast!" I say shrilly.

"I'm going to be late; I better go."

"Wait, um, I love you."

"I love you, too."

"Oh, and I am also...getting charitable today. A little spring cleaning. I may donate a few of your old shirts to Goodwill."

"Why don't you wait? I'll pick some stuff out."

"It's for the homeless, so every day you wait, they wait in the cold...freezing cold weather." I am going to hell.

"Fine. Only the old stuff. And no Armani."

"Deal."

The door slams shut, and I twirl my imaginary moustache as a reward for being so diabolically smart. In a box beneath the sink, under white rags and old *People* magazines, are three kidnapped Prada pants with thirty four-inch waists. They smell like 409 but remain in perfect condition. I hang them delicately on Ben's wooden hangers after removing the thirty six-inch-waist pants. Although I haven't yet paid off these impeccably crafted trousers, I drop them in my Goodwill bag. It is my penance, and it feels good.

Next up are the flannels by Façonnable. Ben will be angry with me for tossing them. He may even go out and buy new ones, but I must do it. He is beginning to resemble the Unabomber, with his unruly beard and proclivity toward plaid. The facial hair that has been rubbing my face raw for weeks needs to be annihilated, but I'm not sure how to approach that yet. I will see how he takes the loss of flannel and go from there.

Excited to share this step of the plan with Janice, not to mention pick her brain about Goodwill's location, I pull out my cell phone.

"Hello?"

"You are going to be so proud of me. The Makedown is over. I am donating all the flannel shirts, putting him back in his thirty four-inch slacks—"

"You went through all that and now you're putting him back together? What a waste of time!"

"No. I think Ben and I both learned a lot about ourselves in the process."

"Please, Anna, once he's back to attracting all the women, you'll freak out and start this all over again."

"No, I won't. I am now okay with his hotness. Honest."

"Uh-huh."

"I don't have time for this. I need to get rid of this stuff before he gets home. Where's there a Goodwill?"

"Third Avenue . . . at Twenty-third Street."

"Thanks."

After dropping the bag off at Goodwill, relief floods my system. Having started RMFAB, I am on my way to living a guilt-free life once again. I won't cringe when looking at my boyfriend's stomach drooping over his boxers, his bald spots, his hairy face, or his crappy clothes. He will once again be uncomfortably better looking than me. I unlock the door, my heart soaring with hope that we will soon be our mismatched selves again. Maybe a little smarter, maybe not.

"Ben?" I call out, throwing my keys on the counter.

"In here."

Ben lies on the bed watching yet another episode of *Law & Order* and drinking a Frappuccino from Starbucks. I may have to call the cable company regarding the 24/7 airing of *Law & Order*. How are addicts supposed to get anything done?

"Hey, how was work?" I say before kissing Ben on the mouth. His facial hair feels particularly prickly and rough. I pull away and notice beads of Frappuccino trickling through his beard. "Ewww," I say, revolted by the appearance of the sugary liquid in his coarse hair.

"What?"

"It's all over your beard. It looks like...semen."

"What?" Ben says in horror.

Why did I say semen? I could have said anything, but I chose semen because it was my first thought.

"The Frappuccino in all your facial hair. It's kind of gross."

"Don't forget you're the one that wanted me to have a beard in the first place," Ben shouts.

"I was wrong. I feel like I'm making out with my exfoliator every night."

"I didn't know you found me so disgusting," Ben says with a huff as he enters the closet. "Where are my damn Façonnable shirts?"

"Oh, those. I actually gave them to Goodwill."

"You gave them to Goodwill? After I specifically told you not to get rid of anything I still wear? What is wrong with you?"

"I'm sorry. I was trying to be charitable. I guess I got carried away thinking of how much the homeless people would enjoy wearing cozy flannel. I'm sorry. I'm also sorry for the semen comment. I just don't like the beard anymore. It hurts."

"The only reason I grew the stupid thing was for you," Ben says gruffly. "I'll shave it. Why don't you order some pizza while I do it?"

I want to say no more pizza! But I stop myself. It will be too much for him. I need to ease him into the plan, and today was clothing and beard. Tomorrow I start with food and exercise. Somehow, I know diet and training are going to be much harder than getting him to shave his beard and forget about some clothes donated to Goodwill.

"Oh, and get me two sides of ranch dressing so I can dip my pizza."

"Sure." I remember hiding in the bathtub shoveling Doritos into my mouth after being told to lose weight. I do not want to inflict such emotional duress on Ben. Compassion was all I wanted, so that is what I offer Ben.

"And some Cokes. Regular ones. None of that diet crap."

Why is he making this so hard? Next thing I know, he'll order a side of deep-fried lard. The diet starts tomorrow, so tonight it's judgment-free calories.

Chapter Twenty-nine

B en's whiney voice wakes me; I tuck my head under the blanket to ignore him, but he continues to talk in that annoying tone.

"What happened to these pants?" Ben moans.

"Hmm...what are you...talking about?" I mumble with my eyes shut.

"I can't believe this; it's like I gained weight overnight."

I crack open my left eye and see Ben bursting out of his thirty four-inch-waist black Prada pants.

"Maybe you've gained weight. Your other slacks have been looking tighter than usual."

"I wore these slacks last week, and they fit me great. How is this possible?"

"Babe, maybe all the pizza, and ranch dressing, and Cokes, and ice cream and stuff."

"Well, what am I supposed to wear today?"

"Wear the gray suit; it has some extra room. Why don't we start a diet? And an exercise plan? Together?"

"Where are my damn gray slacks? Did you give those away, too?"

"No Ben, I didn't. Now about what—"

"None of this would be a problem if I had my Façonnable shirts. They made everything look cool, even tight slacks."

Oh, you poor, deluded soul. I am clearly more powerful than I thought.

"Ben, babe. You know how sexy I think you are in
everything, including flannel, but it's too cutting-edge for
corporate America."

"I like being cutting-edge."

It's as if he's forcing me to come out and say it.

"People thought you looked like a lumberjack or a
miner or something very unlawyer-y."

"What people? Who said that?"

"Um, um . . . Mrs. Kranski across the hall."

"Please, she can't even see past her own nose."

"Dr. Addison in 1A mentioned something about you
being a Nirvana fan because of the flannel and all. And
that old man with the younger wife asked me whether
you're Scottish."

"Great, this whole damn building is against me, and I
have nothing to wear!"

"Babe, wear one of your Armani shirts with the gray
slacks. They're not too tight. We'll start the diet and exercise plan today. We'll do it together."

"Fine. Whatever. I got to go."

I take Ben's "Fine. Whatever" as a definitive yes. I dis-
pose of all fattening and calorie-laden foods and leftovers.
The refrigerator's drawers contain ketchup packets, sauces,
and other condiments sent along with delivery food. It's
astounding that The Makedown took on such a life of its
own. Does that mean I am not to blame for the intense
results? I long to separate what I intended from what actually occurred. I anticipated a mild adjustment, not a drastic,
personality-altering experiment. Ben regressed emotionally during the great inhalation of cheese, grease, and fried

potato products. However, that is all about to reverse itself. Ben's transition to green vegetables, tofu, and brown rice will undoubtedly affect me as well. I'm already careful about what I eat, but I have never been this strict. For snacks, I buy carrot and celery sticks, dried fruit, and plain rice cakes. As he starts to lose weight, granola bars will be given as rewards. Everyone needs a little treat, *little* being the crucial word. I cannot be careless in the eradication of Ben's problems. This must be a calculated and measured attack.

It's almost 7:30 p.m., and Ben will be home soon. I know what I have to do. I think Olivia Newton-John said it best: let's get physical! Good-bye jeans and form-fitting sweater, hello black sports bra, thin fleece shirt, and spandex running pants. I look semiridiculous, but this is the ideal outfit for power walking or running. I must prepare mentally to lure Ben into my exercise regime. I need the energy of a meth-head cheerleader after her team wins the homecoming game. This isn't as simple as concentration and psyching myself up. I need a boost. Nothing illegal or Barry Bonds-ish, just some old-school inspiration from the *Footloose* and *Flashdance* soundtracks.

I bounce from foot to foot with memories of Ren dancing in an abandoned warehouse. It was Kevin Bacon's finest hour, not to mention his car stereo's; the 1984 yellow bug blasted music throughout the entire warehouse. Pretty impressive. As I prepare to find *Flashdance* on my iPod, the front door jiggles with the familiar sound of Ben's key. I place the iPod on the table and stand with my feet a foot apart and my hands on my hips. "Give me a *B*," I shout, pumping my left arm into the air. "Give me an *E*." I pump my right arm into the air, and finally, "give me an *N*...BEN!" I scream while jumping up and down.

"What is wrong with you?"

"Nothing. I'm getting ready to take a walk. Get those endorphins going. I am so psyched about how good I am about to feel," I squeal. "Go get dressed, I'll wait here."

"Babe, stop bouncing. You're making me seasick."

"You know what will help? A nice long walk," I say with a megawatt smile to seal the deal.

"No, *Law & Order* is about to start."

"Hon, *Law & Order* is *always* about to start. Besides, we have TiVo. Come on; let's walk to the corner and back!"

"I'm not in the mood for exercise. I had a hard day at the office."

"Fine," I say, trying to hide my disappointment, "but promise me we'll walk tomorrow morning?"

Ben nods his head while yawning.

"What happened at the office?"

"Nothing."

"You seem upset. Are you having trouble with a client?"

Ben shakes his head, indicating no.

"With colleagues?"

"It's nothing."

Maybe I'm imagining it, but I have a hunch that Ben is being picked on at work. There must be some terrible bullies at his firm. I have half a mind to go down there and tell them off. Or perhaps a little conference with their wives? Although, somehow I think the kind of women who marry testosterone-heavy lawyers are not good for me to be around. They could potentially rekindle a high school–worthy bout of self-loathing with their perfect hair, tight bodies, and tennis bracelets. Ben watches me with a naughty grin as he unbuttons his shirt.

"What?" I ask innocently.

"You know, you're right. I could use some exercise."

"Great, I'll get your shoes."

"In the bedroom, that is," Ben says in his best Barry White impersonation.

"Oh, that's not a bad idea," I say, wondering how many calories sex can burn. It certainly couldn't hurt. I jump into his arms, hoping he will carry me into the bedroom, burning additional calories.

"Anna, did you hurt your ankle jumping around?"

"Uh, yeah. Can you carry me?"

"Grab my arm and hop?"

"Thanks," I sigh.

I will have to work him harder in the sack.

I kiss Ben's arms slowly while seductively stretching them, pushing them back, and holding them for ten seconds before releasing. I am simultaneously burning calories and building muscle. Does it get any better? I distract Ben from the stretching with kisses, finger licks, and cat purrs. After his arms, I kiss Ben's lumpy stomach, looking up every few seconds to hum seductively. I want to pull Ben up by the neck, forcing him to perform the dreaded sit-up. There isn't a purr loud enough to get that one under the radar. I move slowly down his torso, annoyingly bypassing the penis region in favor of his legs. I grab his left calf and slowly start to push it into a crunch. I look up in time to see Ben's face crinkle with confusion. Passing the penis region was a mistake; I overlooked the plethora of distraction the sensitive area offers. The blow job and alternating leg crunches are a package deal. No legs, no blow job.

"What are you doing to my legs?"

"Oh, um, that must be some sort of involuntary reaction."

"You've never done it before while—"

"Clearly it's a new involuntary reaction."

"A new one? I don't think—"

"Do you want to talk about this or have sex? Any more talking, and I may be over the whole intercourse thing altogether."

Ben smiles at my nonsensical rant before kissing me. Thoughts of crunches flee my mind as his hand strokes my back. He forcefully grabs my hair. I thrive on the sensation that Ben is once again in control. This is the old Ben, confident and self-assured. I am buoyed by this sensation; I want more. Bring on the fierceness and tenacity of the Ben I first saw across the room at Stanton Social. Ben lowers me to the bed, and with it, the small flame of change extinguishes.

Instead of savage thrusts, Ben offers tender waves. His soft and kind nature exacerbates my frustration. I don't deserve kindness after what I have done. With each moment, my guilt increases exponentially, suffocating any possibility of rational thought. I must take action. I cannot live under this veil of culpability. I grab his butt cheeks, forcefully plunging him into a more aggressive movement. Surely this is a better workout than his mild motions. The stronger the action, the more calories he burns. If I keep him going at this speed, it will be very beneficial to RMFAB. I am not just his lover but also his trainer and as such, I begin counting... out loud.

"One, two, three, four, five, and one, two, three—"

Ben stops.

"Come on Ben, give me two more."

"Anna, why are you counting?"

I snap back to reality.

"I . . . um, guess . . . it's time I tell you . . . I love you."

"Babe, I already know you love me. Why are you counting?"

"I was counting down to when I was going to ask . . . to go on top. Sometimes I'm a bit shy about asking."

"I'm all yours," Ben says while rolling off. "I was getting tired anyway."

For heaven's sake, he hasn't even finished two sets. I climb atop him, looking into his eyes and remembering that beyond anything I've done or he's done, I truly love him. All thoughts of RMFAB evaporate as I heed passion. I love him so much my eyes well up with tears, like a total loser. Women who cry during sex are the worst. Unless an internal organ is punctured or a limb severed, there are no tears in bed. I quickly wipe my eyes, hoping Ben doesn't notice, but no such luck.

"I love you, too," Ben says as his voice cracks with emotion and tears.

I have turned my boyfriend into a babbling, emotional pansy of a man. I might as well be in bed with Harvey Fierstein.

For Ben to cry during sex, and before his orgasm no less, means only one thing. The Makedown was far more destructive than I previously assessed. The physical deterioration lulled him into a depressed state in which he is awash in apathy. What happened to the man who made fun of the fatty in front of the Washington Monument? I

never thought I would miss that callous side of Ben's personality, but I do. I need to get him back into shape before
he gets diabetes for his fortieth birthday and a stroke for
his fiftieth. I must stop Ben's downward spiral and execute
RMFAB, by any means necessary.

Chapter Thirty

RMFAB dictates that Ben walk three times a week, and I intend to adhere to that. I brush my teeth with vigor, hardly able to contain the nervous anxiety burning within me. I lean over Ben with minty-fresh breath and shake him awake like a warden does a convict.

"Stop. What are you doing?"

"Rise and shine, sleepyhead. It's time for our walk." I grin manically in his groggy face.

"Please, stop."

"Mr. Grumpy, you will feel much better once you get those endorphins going. I've only walked to the kitchen, and already I'm buzzing!" I urge.

"Fine," Ben says, sitting up slowly.

I grab his arms and raise him to a standing position. He waddles into the closet to get dressed. I hit the kitchen, wipe down the counters, drink a small glass of room-temperature water, and finally return to the bedroom. Standing in the doorway to the bedroom, there is no sight or sound of Ben.

"Ben?"

Total silence. I walk to the closet, slowly opening the door. I am afraid of what I might find. Oh, it's worse than I thought. Ben is in the fetal position on the floor. He has compacted himself tightly with his arms around his knees.

I want to thrust my leg into his gut, forcing him awake, but instead I strongly stroke his arm.

"Wake up! No more sleeping!"

"Five more minutes."

"No Ben, you need to get up."

"Please, Anna, five more minutes. I promise I'll get up then."

"You promise?"

"Yes, five more minutes."

"Fine." I glance at my watch, noting it's 6:12.

Irritation overpowers me. Gone is the faint desire to crawl back into bed and leave my sloth of a boyfriend to sleep. I pace the living room, compulsively checking my watch while fantasizing about dropping a bucket of frigid ice water on Ben's head. This isn't merely about me; he needs this. I'm saving him. RMFAB is saving him. I look back at my watch; it's 6:14. That's long enough. Ben can't tell how long I have been gone. I lean over him, seething with frustration.

"Ben, get up!"

"Babe, I can't. My stomach hurts. I need to sleep it off."

"You need to sleep off a stomachache?"

"Sometimes when I get up too early I get a stomach-ache. Sleep is the only thing that can cure it."

"Walking can cure it better. I read that in the *New England Journal of Medicine*. Get up!"

"No," Ben whines, "I need to sleep. Please, woman, let me sleep!"

"Fine!" I relent. "I'm packing tofu stir-fry for lunch. You better eat it!"

"Okay. Can I go back to sleep now?"

I turn and leave my boyfriend in a ball on the floor of the closet. I angrily toss tofu and vegetables into Tupperware, badmouthing Ben silently the whole time. Frustration overcomes me; I want RMFAB to be over as soon as possible. Why does Ben make it so hard? I never dreamed a short walk would conjure such resistance from him. I push the Tupperware to the bottom of the brown paper sack, wishing there were a way to monitor Ben's lunches. Confirmation that he's eating them would greatly settle my nerves. My fingertips quake with aggravation as I write Ben's name in Sharpie on the bag.

It's hard to believe that I had sex last night, although I didn't have an orgasm due to the crying fiasco. Nothing quiets an impending orgasm more than your boyfriend weeping like he's a seventh-grade girl at a Justin Timberlake concert.

By the following morning, I have anxiety-induced energy to get RMFAB on track. I wait impatiently in bed, listening to the clock tick from 6:00 to 6:01. I have already changed into my spandex running ensemble, tennis shoes included. I yearn to squeeze Ben's testicles, forcing him to wake up and get into his Nikes, but I don't. After yesterday, I am determined to wait until the wholly reasonable hour of 7:00 to rouse Ben. To waste time, I switch off staring at Ben's face and the clock. At 6:47, my eyes return to Ben's face and discover he's awake.

"What are you doing up?" Ben asks groggily.

"Oh, I woke up...a few seconds ago. You ready for our walk?" I throw back the blanket enthusiastically before Ben can respond.

"You're already dressed. Let me guess. Another Ambien-induced bout of sleepwalking?"

"Hmmm? My outfit? I woke up an hour ago and thought I should get dressed . . . then get back into bed . . . to use my time efficiently."

Ben nods before sleepily wandering toward the closet. I follow close behind him to avoid yesterday's impromptu snooze on the floor. Luckily, Ben appears focused on walking this morning.

Within moments of rounding our block, I sense a problem. Ben is not interested in walking. He is interested in meandering. Small children with foot-long legs and heavy backpacks overtake us en route to school. A woman with an abnormally short left leg limps past us as Ben peruses the shop windows. He comments on everything from women's lingerie to model train sets. The people gliding past us don't register with Ben. He is too busy talking. He should be short of breath and perspiring; instead, he gabs away about nonsense.

Having tired of the window displays, Ben partakes in the thinking man's version of "what if." Most girls ask things like "what if Alan asked me out," "what if I was as popular as Pauline," or occasionally "what if I could read people's minds?"

"What do you think would have happened if JFK hadn't been assassinated?" Ben ponders aloud.

"He would have continued the march into Vietnam. Keep your knees up." Ben ignores my knee comment and continues down the tragedy-ridden Kennedy family tree.

"What about Bobby Kennedy?"

"Listen, chatty, unless you want to stay a fatty, I suggest you pick up the pace." The word *fatty* slipped out a little too easily. How could I call him fatty? Did I remember nothing of the hell I myself had endured?

"Don't call me fatty, bitchy!"

"I'm sorry, Ben, but we are currently averaging a two-hour mile."

"Don't rush me; my stomach still hurts a little."

This is the fat-person lie I know all too well. I can't let him get away with it. I may have been out of line calling him fatty, but he needs exercise.

"Can we stop at Starbucks?"

"Okay, but no Frappuccinos. They're all sugar."

"I didn't even say I wanted one. Jeez. I'm getting a mocha, drill sergeant."

I want to scream "A mocha? Why not deep-fried Snickers for breakfast?" but instead I nod.

"Ben, have you been eating the lunches I pack?"

"Yes." Ben's eyes dart around suspiciously, frantic for something to focus on.

"Remember how much you liked vegetables when we first met? I want to help get you back there."

"Thanks, babe," he says as he plants a kiss on my lips.

If he knew what I'd done, he wouldn't be thanking me.

Chapter Thirty-one

Ben is cheating. I've had my suspicions for weeks, but having confirmation is hard to swallow. Ben is a cheater, a serious cheater. This is well beyond a minor indiscretion after a few too many glasses of wine while out of town. This is a standing appointment. All those nights he awkwardly stammered when answering my questions about work lunches or dinners. How could I have been so blind? Maybe I didn't want to see the truth. I looked the other way and believed what felt good. Well, I certainly can't do that now. The proof is burning a hole in my hand. How could Ben do this to me? After what we've been through—morning walks, tofu burgers, and sit-ups. We took a vow, but clearly that means nothing to him. Ben promised over a steaming pot of vegetables that he would eat my healthy home-packed lunches. And now this! Twinkie, Twix, and Snickers wrappers are in every pocket of his slacks. He consumes copious amounts of empty calories behind my back. I assumed he would sneak a Fig Newton or two, but Twinkies? There is nothing nutritious or filling about a Twinkie; it goes straight to his spare tire. I cannot believe how painfully addicted to junk food he has become.

I have destroyed the bedroom looking for remnants of his binge eating. Under the dresser, I discover a sea of chip wrappers, mostly Doritos and Cheetos. If he eats like this at home, he must have an even larger stash at work. I imagine Ben's desk, filled with fattening contraband that he shoves into his mouth between meetings, hoping no one will notice the crumbs on his tie before plummeting into self-loathing over the empty calories and nondiet soda he consumed.

Secret eating leads to an anxiety- and guilt-filled life-style. A secret eater continually frets that someone will spot a dash of Cheetos dust, a smudge of Hershey's chocolate, or a french fry grease stain. It is a miserable existence.

In a remorseful haze, I wander toward Braham's Spice Emporium on Jane Street in the West Village. Janice is determined to have more exotic flavorings than any caterer in town. I am far too preoccupied with Ben shoving Twix bars into his mouth to be an intelligent spice buyer right now. Staring at a bag of dried Indian parsley, all I can think is how dramatically I have screwed up Ben's life. I have turned a vegetarian against vegetables.

I manage to buy the spices on Janice's list and make my way home.

The bag of spices I hold is so pungent that it takes me a second to detect the smoky odor wafting from my apartment as I unlock the door.

"Ben!" I holler as I inhale the toxic air.

The apartment is a mélange of cigarette smoke and Lysol air freshener. Ben enters the living room, doing his best impression of innocence.

"What's up?" Ben asks as if he's just turned fifteen.

"What's up? Are you serious? *What's up?*" I scream back.

"Why are you yelling?"

"Why am I yelling? The entire apartment smells like smoke and freaking air freshener!"

"Ohhh, that. John came over after work and we...burned a bagel. We sprayed Lysol to get rid of the smell."

"You have got to be kidding me. Are you really going to pull this crap on me?"

"It's true. We put a bagel in the toaster and it got stuck and caught fire. That's why it's smoky in here."

"Where is the toaster now?"

Ben inspects the kitchen counter before answering.

"Um, we threw it out."

"How old are you?"

"Thirty-th—"

"Yes, Ben, you're thirty-three, which is too old to be lying this transparently to your girlfriend. First of all, you don't like bagels."

"People change."

"Shut up and let me speak! Second of all, we never had a toaster, which makes it pretty hard to have burnt a bagel in it. And third and most important, this apartment does not stink of burnt toast. It reeks of cigarettes. Now, before I list the three million reasons why smoking is bad for you, I suggest you sit down and start talking. And this time, I want the truth!"

I am channeling every after-school special I have ever seen. It's uncontrollable. I can't stop the clichés. Of course, on TV it's usually mothers, not girlfriends screaming about the dangers of drugs, alcohol, and cigarettes.

"Fine."

"I'm listening."

"After work, John came over."

"Ben, it's 3:30 in the afternoon."

"Okay, at lunch John and I came home and—"

"What about work?"

"We said we didn't feel well."

"So you lied to your bosses."

"We were going to have a few beers and watch ESPN, but then John said he had some smokes."

"Smokes? Is that what they call them these days? Continue."

"I told John that I'd never tried a cigarette before and he laughed."

"Classic peer pressure. If he had told you to run in front of a bus, would you? Would you?"

"Jesus, why do you have to be so dramatic? I only had two cigarettes."

"Two? Already an addict!"

"I am not an addict. I just wanted to try them."

"Why? I want to know why."

"I heard they can help you lose weight!"

"Ben, Ben, Ben. I know you don't like all the vegetables and walking, but trust me, it's the only healthy way. Cigarettes will make you old, ugly, and smelly. Promise me you will never touch another one again."

"Fine. Is the after-school special over?"

Clearly, Ben watched the same shows I did growing up.

"Almost. There is something else we need to talk about. I found the wrappers."

"Anna, I don't want to talk about that."

Ben shuffles back to the bedroom, where I hear the unmistakable sounds of *Law & Order*. I sit defeated at the dining room table, processing what he told me. More than anything, I have greatly underestimated the power of Ben's friends. If John can get Ben to smoke, he can get him on track with the diet and exercise. I've always steered clear of John and all his cronies at Ben's firm, but I think it's time for a visit. In the after-school special of Ben's life, I am the annoying mom he ignores in favor of the local hoodlum, John. I must reappropriate John's influence for good, not evil. Every Thursday morning, Ben has breakfast with one of the partners, giving me a one-hour window to visit the firm and casually run into John.

The Benson and Silverberg law firm inhabits the pristinely modern twenty-fifth and twenty-sixth floors of a skyscraper in Midtown. It's the kind of heavily trafficked building that embodies modern corporate America. The building's security is akin to that at Baghdad's airport, making the hidden transport of carrot sticks and bran muffins tricky. The metal detector, pat down, and individual scanning of each food item rattles me, but I recover. I can't turn back; he is an addict. He needs help.

Ten minutes later, I chat mindlessly with Ben's assistant Mel under the pretense of having been in the neighborhood. Ben's office, like our apartment, is modern and austere, with few hiding places outside of the desk drawers. I seat myself casually at Ben's desk while pretending to care as Mel drones on about his weekend at home. I slip my fingers under the handle and silently pull out the drawer. Nothing but paper clips and Wite-Out. I smile at Mel. I pull out the second drawer—a bunch of files.

"Um, Mel, sorry to interrupt, but I should probably get going."

"Okay, I'll tell Ben you stopped by."

"Um, actually, don't bother."

"You don't want me to tell him?" Mel asks in amazement.

"He gets a little emotional when he misses me. He's very attached, like a Labrador or golden retriever with separation anxiety. Or not necessarily a dog, but a child with separation anxiety. Anyway, bye!"

I head down the hallway in search of John. I need to find him, impress upon him the importance of helping Ben, and unload the snacks. This is a straightforward mission, so I estimate fifteen minutes tops. From down the hall I hear John's obnoxious voice radiate from a small room wedged between a supply closet and the copier. It's the kitchen; this is going to be easier than I thought. John, the cigarette pusher, holds court with two younger associates at a sleek table. I smile at John and offer a sheepish wave as I enter.

"Anna, what're you doing here?"

"Um, hi, John. I just wanted to say a quick hello—"

"Ben's at breakfast with Silverberg."

"Oh, I know, Mel told me, but I have snacks for Ben."

"You brought Ben snacks? Maybe you can change his diaper while you're here?"

"Oh, John. How witty!" I retort, smiling widely. I hate John. I would like to take his face and smash it into a child's soiled diaper at this moment, but I can't. I don't have a diaper on hand, and more to the point, I need his help. "I brought some healthy snacks for Ben because I'm not sure if you've noticed, but he hasn't been eating very well lately."

The room's silence makes me question my mandate. I want to stop, make a joke, and leave. But I can't. The junk food is destroying him.

"If you guys happen to see him eat Doritos or choco-late, maybe suggest a granola bar or carrot instead?"

"Does Ben know you're here?" John asks.

"No, it was a last-minute stop by—"

"So he doesn't know you brought snacks?"

"No. Like I said, it was last minute. And the snacks are also for you guys."

"Wait, so the snacks are for us now?"

"Well, yes. I thought you guys could offer some positive peer pressure to help Ben make better food choices."

"We don't discuss food, Anna. It would be awkward to work into the conversation—"

"It doesn't have to be awkward," I say with a manic smile. "If you happen to see him go for empty calories, just stop to remind him what it does to his body. Plus, you guys can lead by example; I've included more than enough of everything," I say, pulling out various healthy snacks from my bag.

John and the other two associates gape at me. I ignore their expressions and carry on; I don't have time for mutiny.

"Excellent. Well, I should be going, but thank you. And let's keep this between us, just until Ben gets back on track, okay?"

PART

V

Good-bye Fatty

Chapter Thirty-two

The events of the last few months, namely The Make-down and RMFAB, have altered not only Ben's appearance but also my behavior. On a base level, I have desensitized myself to outrageous, bizarre, and downright insane conduct. I no longer cringe while watching strangers act out their most fundamental urges on reality television. I understand that once you cross the threshold of questionable behavior, it's a slippery slope. After putting Nair in my boyfriend's shampoo, calling him fatty, or enforcing brown-bag lunches, hardly anything registers as out of the ordinary. Whether John actually manages to persuade Ben to eat the healthy snacks is unforeseeable at this point, but at least I tried.

Asleep on the couch with a trashy celeb weekly across my chest, I open my eyes to a seething, angry, and sweaty Ben. A large vein pulsates across his forehead as he stares viciously in my direction. I am frightened of Ben at this moment.

Something about his gritted teeth and vile expression tells me to let him make the first move. I slowly sit up, sweating under the intensity of his stare. The anticipation causes my stomach to twist and turn. Part of me wants to scream, but instead I remain blank, patiently waiting for my boyfriend to explode.

"What in the hell were you thinking?" Ben yells.

"Um?"

This is all I can manage to get out. I know what this is about, but I don't know how to explain myself. I force my expression to remain blank.

"You told my colleagues that you wanted help keeping me on a diet!"

The anger of his words reverberates throughout the room. My chest tightens.

"It wasn't like that. I thought a little encouragement could help you—"

"Help me *what*?"

"Help you...lose weight."

"Why is my body your job to fix? What makes you think you are in a position to decide what needs fixing? I hate to break it to you, but you're not perfect. Actually, I think you'd look a hell of a lot better with a lighter hair color, but did I storm into your work and embarrass you in front of Janice? Did I point out your flaws publicly? No!"

"I didn't mean for it—"

"Stop! There is no 'I didn't mean.' You did it because you're shallow. I have been more patient with you than I have with any other woman I've ever dated, and I have no idea why. You certainly don't deserve it."

"I'm sorry. I wanted to help. That's the only reason."

"Anna, you treat me like a fat stepchild you're ashamed of. You monitor what I eat, when I exercise, and what I do for fun."

"Ben—"

"It's over."

"Ben, how can you say that? No! I love you! I know how you feel, but please." Tears stream down my face. My heart pounds with fear.

"You know how I feel? You know how it feels to be humiliated in front of your colleagues by someone who claims to love you? I don't think so."

"I'll change. I'll stop acting like this."

"No, this just isn't working."

"Please, let me explain. If I could explain starting from the beginning with the Washington Monument comment—"

"It's too late; we're done."

"No, please, listen!"

"I'm staying with John this weekend, but I'd like you out by early next week."

"You're kicking me out?"

"I'll give you a relocation fee. E-mail me what you think is fair."

His eyes are iced over and his voice is devoid of emotion. I cannot see one ounce of love in him. My deepest, darkest fear has been realized; he's gone. Maybe not physically yet, but emotionally.

"How can you be so cold?"

"Anna, I'm not cold. I'm done."

"You're done? It's been five minutes!"

"No, this judgmental, superficial side of your personality has been here for a lot longer than five minutes. Anyone who is so easily unglued by an issue like weight is not the right person for me."

"Please let me explain. If you will listen...it's not what you think...I'm not who you think—"

"Yeah, I know."

On that note, he walks out. He doesn't pack a bag or get his toothbrush. He leaves. The shock painfully makes its way through every pore in my body. I can't imagine a weekend without him, let alone a lifetime. My chest cripples with short, panic-stricken breaths, and my eyes blur with tears. I don't want to believe that it's true. Remembering the dark, angry expression he greeted me with only exacerbates the hurt. How is it possible that someone who loved me could come to loathe me so quickly? Ultimately, it doesn't matter. Nothing I do, think, or say can change the facts. Ben doesn't love me anymore. As I look around the living room, the beautiful furniture mocks me. This apartment, like Ben himself, is too good for me, too far out of my league. It was a cruel joke to let me have him, to experience love with him, then to rip him away, righting the universe's obvious mistake. A wave of self-loathing suffocates me.

I can't continue to lie on the floor of this apartment, which represents everything I've lost. I need a psychologically sterile environment for my breakdown. As I dial the Hudson Hotel, I wonder whether I should buck up and pay the extra two hundred dollars to die at the Mercer. I am not going to kill myself, but I am going to die. There is no way that I can continue after this; it's a complete impossibility. Breathing, eating, talking, and walking all seem grossly unfeasible without Ben.

I rip black shirts, slacks, and jackets off hangars, shoving them haphazardly into a suitcase. I don't bother folding anything. Shoes are strewn throughout the bag, along with a hair dryer, pounds of makeup and moisturizers. Between recipes and other odd papers I've accumulated, I throw in my bible of misery, Hello Fatty. Oddly, the most heartbreaking item to pack is not a picture of Ben and me but the one of my family from years ago. I let that chubby little girl down. I achieved a completely new appearance and life, only to blow it because of insecurities. I can't believe this is over, this life, this apartment, this man—all of it finished.

I call a cab, leaving my keys on the kitchen counter, dishes in the cupboard, and knife set by the sink. I want to bring as little as possible of this life with me. It's too painful.

The Hudson's cool linen is the only thing I feel. I turn to my side and crack open my eyes. The realization hits me: he left me. I am alone in a hotel without any possibility of ever being happy or even mildly content again. He will never love me again. It's been less than twenty-four hours since Ben left, and already the devastation has destroyed my soul. I am without hope, yet I wrack my brain for any possible way to go back in time, deleting my visit to Benson and Silverberg. I close my eyes, exhausted from crying. I awake almost fifteen hours later, drink some NyQuil, and go back to bed.

When I wake again, I have lost track of the day and time. I undress, finally taking off the last clothes Ben will ever see me in, leaving them in a pile by the bed. I don't bother washing my face or brushing my teeth. I dress in head-to-toe black, with large sunglasses to hide my swollen eyes. Walking through the Hudson's sleek lobby, I sense people staring at me, wondering why I'm so dirty. When life loses all meaning, personal hygiene is the first thing to go. As a smelly wreck, I yearn for comfort without judgment or expectations of improvement. This is something I don't think any rational human could offer, but I've got to find companionship somewhere.

I walk from West 58th and Columbus to East 59th and

Second Avenue, arriving at the pound full of ideas about soft and cuddly puppies. But as I pass the row of caged dogs, I realize I can't handle the responsibility of a dog when I can't guarantee surviving the week. Cats are more resilient and therefore a much better option for me. Sure, PETA will advise against adopting an animal when you yourself are dying, but in this situation, I can't help it. Moreover, I am metaphorically dying; shutting down, becoming a miserable hermit who wishes each day was her last. A cat feels like an appropriate addition to my macabre future. As I examine the long corridor of felines, I remember that Ben is the only man I know who likes cats. Their little furry faces remind me of him. A surreal panic takes hold. I cannot imagine life without him. I lock eyes with an obese and dandruff-covered cat. His name tag reads Fatty.

"Ahhhh...uh...ahhh...," I mutter.

"What's the matter?" the ASPCA worker, who has been tailing me since my arrival, asks quietly.

"Fatty looks like my ex-boyfriend."

"I'm not sure I understand."

"I...called him...Fatty..."

The rest of the sentence is lost in a loud wail.

"I would like to adopt Fatty, please. This is a sign. Fatty will be my road to salvation. I don't mean to sound evangelical, especially since this is a nondenominational pound. Basically, I just need Fatty...a lot..."

Again, I trail off into unintelligible gasps and squeals.

"Oh my. Your breath."

"What? Is it against the law to forget to brush your teeth? I'm sure Fatty doesn't mind."

The woman inspects me, scrutinizing every inch of my body.

"There is a clause in our charter about mental stability, and I am afraid that I cannot with a clear conscience say that you are of sound mind and able to care for Fatty the cat. I am sorry, but adoption denied. Please see yourself out."

"What?"

"I said adoption denied."

"Who do you think you are, God? Is that what you think? Or maybe Cupid, deciding who gets to have love and who doesn't?"

"Lady, I don't want any trouble. I'm just here to pro-tect the animals."

I realize that I, too, do not want any trouble. I have no one to pay my bail should I get arrested.

Alone, rejected by the pound, I make my way back to the Hudson. As I enter the lobby, I sense eyes from several people—from the concierge to a small child—watching me with pity. I am a broken woman on the verge of total annihilation, and it shows. Back in my room, I climb beneath the sheets and give up. I should call Janice, as a courtesy, and let her know that I can no longer work for her. I must face my destiny to return to Ohio and live with Mother or in a sanitarium. Either way, they won't let me around knives to cook. Oh, thank heavens she's not home.

"Janice. Ben dumped me. I have decided to die—metaphorically speaking—and can no longer be a part of society."

I drop the phone to the floor without bothering to place it back on the cradle. Who cares? I close my eyes, and begin to drift into blackness.

Some period of time later, I hear the click of the door opening and the swish of it closing. Is that the maid again? How many times must I tell her that I don't want clean sheets? I'm not even brushing my teeth; why should my sheets be clean? A bag drops to the floor, followed by the clanging of a chain. I know that sound; it's the sound of a quilted bag with a chain strap.

"How did you find me?" I ask pitifully.

"Sweetie, I'm your Fairy Godmother. I always know where you are. It's called caller ID," Janice says flatly.

"And they just gave you a key to my room? What if you were some stranger off the street?"

"You've made quite the impression downstairs. They were taking bets on whether you'd jump out the window. Trust me, they were more than willing to let you be someone else's problem."

"I'm already dead. Run . . . save yourself."

"Get up!" Janice barks authoritatively. "You've missed three days of work, run up a hotel tab that will take you a year of baking quiches to pay off, and from the smell of this place, I suspect you have done permanent damage to your gums. You need to get up."

"Janice, you aren't listening to me," I yell from under the blanket, "*I am dead!* Go away!"

"I know you are dead inside. I'm not trying to diminish that. I simply want you to continue your journey to gingivitis in my guest room. I can keep an eye on you in case you decide to rethink the metaphorical death for a more literal one."

Janice's guest room is painted a deep crimson, which seems somehow appropriate. I imagine that I am in the center of my own personal bloodbath. Janice tiptoes into the room, goes directly to the window, and flings open the curtains. Sunlight burns my corneas. It's been days since I have seen natural light.

"Please close the curtains," I beg.

"Not unless you take a shower."

"You said you would leave me alone."

"I have left you alone for days. You smell. Either sit in the sunlight or shower. It's up to you."

"I'll shower."

Janice hands me a toothbrush with toothpaste and walks me to the bathroom. She holds my greasy hair back while I brush my tongue vigorously. When I finish brushing, she turns on the shower and shuts the bathroom door.

The shower pressure hurts my skin as it penetrates the protective layer of grime covering my body. My hair is vile and requires two washings to remove the grease. I run my tongue against my newly clean teeth. Only now, as I towel off, do I realize how nice it is to have found hygiene again. I leave the shower dressed in a white terry cloth robe and return to bed.

I wake almost fifteen hours later to Janice. Once again, she leads me through the motions of brushing and washing. This time I change into jeans and a sweater. I attempt to apply makeup but stop after foundation, realizing it will smear when I cry. Who needs the mess?

Alone with the paper, I scan the listings for available apartments. It is a painful reminder of the breakup: we no longer live together because he dumped me. Ben doesn't love me, but I still love him. I want to know what Ben is doing at this very second. Is he eating eggs or reading the paper? Is he thinking of me? Does he miss me? The answer is no. He broke up with me. I am the woman he knows he doesn't want. And what is worse, I can't even blame him—I wouldn't want me either.

Chapter Thirty-three

My downstairs neighbor plays scales on his piano. At first, I found it repetitive and annoying, but now I take comfort in it. This is my first Saturday night in my minuscule studio apartment on the least charming street in the East Village. And yes, I have my own bathroom. I bought a mattress and box spring and covered it with a crisp white duvet. I want to make the apartment as cheery as possible to combat my desperate feelings of loneliness. A few personal items along with posters given to me by Janice add a bit of life to the place. I like thin walls for the first time in my life. I enjoy the piano scales downstairs mixing with the college girls laughing next door. This is the only kind of company I can handle. My mind often finds its way to the lamest question any newly single woman can ask: "I wonder what he's doing right now?" Late at night, when I would normally be driven to violent tantrums by noisy neighbors, I take pleasure in the distraction.

For my first Saturday night dinner, I am preparing a tea party for myself. I have made fig tarts from scratch, coconut macaroons, cucumber sandwiches, chocolate chip cookies, and a pot of English breakfast tea. I lay a small pink and white sheet on the floor near the quiet neighbor and set up my tea party. I haven't heard much from this apartment beside an occasional Enya song.

With my first bite of fig tart in my mouth, Sinead O'Connor's "Nothing Compares 2 U" starts playing next door. It's impossible for me to cheer myself up with this breakup anthem playing. Maybe I should give in and release my sadness through a song. My duet with Sinead O'Connor feels amazing.

"Will you shut the fuck up!" a man screams through the wall. "I didn't invite you to my pity party."

I am too embarrassed to respond or even to stay awake. I chase an Ambien with three gulps of vodka, a recipe passed on from Mother. She claims her doctor recommends the combination, but Barney says she discovered it the old-fashioned way, crank-calling Dad. Apparently, half an Ambien and two large gulps of vodka was not enough to stop Mother from crank-calling Dad in her bad Chinese accent, saying, "I know you at Tiananmen." However, a whole Ambien and three gulps put her straight to sleep.

In this postapocalyptic state, I cannot remember life before Ben and I still can't imagine life after him. There isn't a definition good enough to describe the loneliness I experience. I check my messages, crossing my fingers that Ben has called. I shut my eyes. I pray. Please be Ben. I punch in my password and walk to the fridge to grab a mini Pellegrino. I buy Pellegrino because I like the way it looks in my fridge. It's superficial, especially since it's a mini fridge.

"Anna, call me. I saw Ming at the grocery store. Oh, and I bought you a mood ring so you can monitor yourself. Best, Mother." In the wake of being dumped, I recognize that Mother and I have more in common than I thought. I may not shop on QVC or coin inappropriate racial euphemisms, but I clearly inherited her relationship ignorance. Until Ben dumped me, I never had empathy for Mother and the pain she endured in the divorce. As a scarred woman, I realize that Mother could offer guidance. I need Mother. It's strange to crave the woman I have most tried to escape. As I dial, I feel a strange excitement at the idea of returning home.

"Hello?"

"Mother, I'm coming home," I say immediately.

"To Ohio?"

"Yes, Mother, unless you've moved. Can you have Barney get me at the train station at 6:00 p.m. tomorrow?"

"Yes. Bring dark clothes. We may need to go on a stakeout."

The great lengths to which Mother has gone to harass Dad and Ming continue to shock me. Apparently, Mother and Barney have been participating in stakeouts outside of Dad and Ming's house. They usually happen around 8:30 on a Friday or Saturday night. Dressed in dark hooded sweatshirts, Mother and Barney scope out the house, noting which lights are on. Mother then takes Barney to Dunkin' Donuts before heading back, where they patiently wait for all the lights to go out. While waiting, the two play trivia games by the light of the console. This is family bonding at its most dysfunctional.

On these missions, Mother calls Barney "Yun Lee" and Barney calls Mother "Soon Yi." Mother's reasoning is that if Dad hears them talking, he will think some of Ming's Chinese gang-member friends are casing the house. However, for a couple of sheltered Ohio natives, the names are too hard to remember. More often than not, they call each other "Lee" and "Yi."

Having absorbed this information, I second-guess my decision to go home; however, there are no other opportunities for guidance on the horizon.

After eleven hours on the train, I disembark in Norfolk, Ohio, smiling expectantly as I scan the landing for Barney. After five minutes, I accept that my stupid brother forgot me. I enter the station to call a cab when I spot Barney hunched over, shoveling lo mein into his mouth. He looks up at me, his face racked with guilt.

"Don't tell Mother about the Panda Express. She'll kill me," Barney says with food in his mouth. He's wearing a sweatshirt that says "I Can't Turn This Off." What exactly *this* refers to is totally beyond me.

"Barn, relax. I have no interest in upsetting Mother's strictly enforced Patriot Act."

Mother has declared a ban on Chinese food in protest of Ming. It doesn't matter how many times I tell her that Ming's family is from the Philippines or that Ming was born in the United States. Chinese food is strictly forbidden.

Barney drives Mother's brown station wagon through Norfolk. I stare out the window in silence. I turn toward Barney and realize how far I've come. It wasn't so long ago that I had Barney's profile, double chin and all.

"How's Mother?"

"I suspect she's posting things about Ming on the Internet."

"Why do you think that?"

"I helped her do it. Mother's not very computer savvy."

"Barney, you could get in a lot of trouble."

"No way. We refer to her as Ming and to Dad as Ned

Forton. Get it? We switched the first two letters of his name."

"Actually, if you did it would be Nred, not Ned. Dad's name is Fred, not Fed. See?"

"Semantics, my dear."

"Next time you're on the Internet, look up the definition of *semantics*. I think it might surprise you."

The car returns to silence as we enter Mother's neighborhood. Living in New York, I appreciate the simple magic of tree-lined suburban streets. However, at this moment, I would rather approach someone else's childhood home at the end of a tree-lined street. I am nervous to see Mother. What if she fails me in my quest for comfort?

"Can you open up the glove compartment? I need the Scope and air freshener."

I hand Barney the items. He quickly covers himself with a lilac room spray and swallows some mouthwash. He catches my quizzical look and explains, "You would be surprised how much Chinese food sticks to clothes."

"Barney, this whole Chinese thing has gone too far. I am going to say something to her."

"Anna, I am going to pretend I didn't hear that," Barney responds firmly.

"Barney, Ming's not even Chinese."

"Please don't rock the boat. If you get any cravings, I know a place that will deliver to the back window in a KFC bag."

"I am speechless."

"By the way, sorry about Ben. I spent some quality time with him in the fort, and I really thought he was a keeper."

"So did I, but he ate a lot of Chinese food. It was a deal breaker—out of loyalty to Mother," I deadpan. Sarcasm is my only hope of staying sane here. Not that Barney even takes it in, as he is too focused on the pressing matter of deception.

"Quick, check my breath," he gasps as we pull into the driveway.

Mother's house never changes. The moderately green grass never varies in color and the hedges remain as poorly trimmed as I remember. The one-story dark brown house with forest green trim is a monument to the prefabricated homes built after World War II. Mother's appliances, like the furniture, haven't been updated since the early 1970s. I follow the thin brick walkway from the driveway to the front door. A dilapidated barbecue still sits to the right of the door, waiting for someone to use it. Next to the barbecue is a large potted plant Mother bought for the sole purpose of hiding a spare house key. The entire neighborhood has seen Barney retrieve the key at least twice a week for twenty years. There's no risk of robbery; it's a well-known fact that we don't own anything worth taking. The faded orange curtains in the front window communicate an important message to potential out-of-town burglars: "Cheap people live here."

My memory of home is tied to the smell trapped in these walls; an indelicate odor akin to Aqua Net meets mothballs with a splash of Irish Spring soap. I used to hate this smell, but as I approach the door, I look forward to it. Ben was my foundation, and without him, I must return to my former definition of home.

Immediately upon entering the house, the smell triggers the sensation of cozy depression. This is the place where I sought refuge from the world while simultaneously feeling trapped by my family.

Mother enters the living room in a mint green Jacqueline Smith pantsuit. She is overaccessorized with dangly zirconium earrings and a matching necklace. Before she even says hello, she points to her left hand like a newly engaged woman dying to show off her rock. It's a pink marbled ring that clashes with her fake diamond ensemble.

"Pink means happy! I must be happy you are home!" Mother has yet to hug me or kiss my cheek. Instead, she takes off the ring and shoves it onto my index finger.

"Let's see how you are doing."

"Mother, I'm not really in the mood for—"

"You don't need to tell me. I can see from the dark blue that this breakup is taking a toll on you. Poor little lady."

Mother finally embraces me, patting my back and whispering "there, there" into my ear as if I were crying. It's nice to be hugged by someone other than Janice. Barney didn't hug me at the train station. Maybe he was too preoccupied with the Panda Express.

"Mother, I'm okay. Really. Thank you for the ring."

"Good job getting your sister, Lee," Mother says to Barney.

"Thanks, Yi," Barney responds proudly. "We need to pick up Jennifer on the way to dinner."

Barney is unquestionably a loser, but I was shocked to discover that his girlfriend, Jennifer, is not. Well, at least not the complete loser I expected. She is neither fat nor maimed in any visible manner. She is able to converse fluently in English and she appears to have all her teeth.

Jennifer is short and thin with a lopsided bob courtesy of the Norfolk Hair Shop. She dresses like every other middle-class girl in town: jeans and a sweatshirt. Barney hugs her from behind while we wait for the server to seat us, and once seated, Barney watches Jennifer read her plastic menu with obvious pride. It's actually quite adorable. Barney and Jennifer's cuteness makes me miss Ben. I yearn for Ben to be next to me at the table, holding my hand. However, I know that Ben no longer wishes to be near me; his friends probably avoid mentioning my name. I am going to cry. Sandwiched between Mother and Jennifer in a booth, I cannot extricate myself in time to hide the tears. I cough hysterically as if a large insect crawled up my throat.

"Anna, arms up," Mother says immediately. She slaps my back as mothers always do in films. While I'm sure there is a reason to do this, I haven't found it.

"I'm okay, thanks Mother," I say quietly.

"Jesus, Anna, what the F happened?" Barney asks.

"Barney, don't use the *f* word," Mother reprimands.

"I didn't; I said F."

"Exactly, don't use the *f* word."

"What? *F* is a bad word?"

"It is when it's a place holder for *fuck*."

"Mother, you can't throw away letters that bad words begin with. Plus, you said the real *f* word, so you are not in any position to tell me what to do."

"I am an adult."

"So is Barney, Mother. Can we please drop it? I would like to get to know Jennifer, and the symposium on bad words is getting in the way," I plead.

Barney and Mother eye each other and nod their heads.

"Jennifer, I understand you work at the multiplex."

"I am on concessions. That's how Barn and I met. I gave him the employee discount on his popcorn because I thought he was cute."

"I had been eyeing her for a while. When I ordered the popcorn and she gave me the discount, I just kind of knew."

"I knew, too."

They stare into each other's eyes, dreaming about the popcorn that brought them together. "And then I met Mary and, well, we both love QVC, so we started having shopping dates."

"In the house?" I ask stupidly.

"Usually in the living room, but sometimes if Mary is tired, we'll shop from the bedroom."

Mother's recent addiction to the fast food of art, Thomas Kincaid, is the result of Jennifer's refined eye. Jennifer's proclivity for home shopping exponentially increases her chances of surviving in the family. Being here with them all in Ohio, I see how ludicrous it was for me to try to bring Ben into my world. It's far too pedestrian a place for someone like him.

Chapter Thirty-four

Ben was in my dream last night. I don't remember the dream, but the feeling of sadness and longing remains with me as I sit in my childhood kitchen. I wonder when the exact moment was that Ben stopped loving me. Was it when John told him about the snack visit, or was it weeks or months before? Did it take something jarring for him to admit it? Of course, he may not have ever loved me. He may have simply appreciated me as a companion.

"Why are you crying?" Barney asks from the doorway.

"I'm sad, Barney. Really sad."

Barney stares at me, unsure how to handle my overt emotions. He apparently decides to ignore them and says cheerily, "Not for long. You are looking at the man who made pigs fly, hell freeze over, dogs talk—"

"Barney—"

"And Mother agree to dinner with Dad."

"Are you serious?" I say while blowing my nose.

"I am Stone Cold Steve Austin serious."

"Barney, stop talking like that!"

"Fine."

"Why did you do this?"

"Jennifer and I have been in love," Barney says with a wink, "for a while and it's made me realize that unless Mother buries the hatchet, I will have to have two weddings, two baptisms. It's going to be too rough on the grandkids. Imagine it: 'Hey little guy, you don't mind turning four twice, do you?'"

"Barney, don't you think you're jumping the gun on all this—"

"Anna, I don't know if you've ever been in love, but let me tell you, it's pretty awesome."

"Barney, you know just what to say," I sniff, fleeing the kitchen for a private sob. I wish them every happiness. But maybe not right now, and not in front of me.

Harvey's Restaurant, located on the outskirts of Norfolk, is renowned for its dark interior. On more than one occasion, I have been unable to decipher the food on my plate. Mother insisted that we choose a discreet location. She's worried about being seen with her ex-husband, fueling the town gossip mills. The reality would offend Mother deeply; the Norton family is so inconsequential that no one would waste their breath gossiping about us. Normally in a town as small as Norfolk, a sex scandal including a secretary would be hot news, but not when the people are my parents.

It's 6:30 on an average Wednesday night. I am dressed in what Mother refers to as my "New York funeral attire." She objects to my new style on the grounds that wearing black on black for regular occasions lessens its significance when someone dies. It's crying wolf in the clothing world, or so she says. I am far too nervous about the meal to worry about Mother's disapproval of my outfit.

Clearly, I am not the only one feeling apprehensive. Barney drives erratically while Mother wipes sweat from her brow. "Barney, you need to pull the car over," Mother demands. She steps out of the car, leans into a nearby bush, and throws up. I am jealous that she is able to vomit. I would love to expunge the tension coursing through me. Maybe I should at least try. I stand next to Mother and attempt to translate dry heaves into actual sickness, but it's fruitless.

"Anna, I appreciate the gesture, but I don't think it's going to happen."

"I just—"

"I know."

We get back into the car, both slightly less anxious than before.

"Mother, open the glove compartment. I've got air freshener and mouthwash."

"Barney, you have shown great foresight this evening. Thank you."

Dad is dressed in a white short-sleeved shirt and brown polyester pants that highlight his yellow socks. His hair is grayer and thinner than I remember. It's strange that for Bastard Won Ton, this will be Dad in his prime. He stands as the three of us approach the table. Barney goes in for a strange man hug that involves two pats on the back. I offer Dad a tight hug and a grunt-resembling hello. I'm far too tense to articulate properly.

"Hi, Mary," Dad says quietly.

"Fred," Mother responds.

Maybe this evening isn't going to be horrendous after all.

Barney and I sit between our parents at the four-top. They stare each other down from their respective heads of table. Mother raises the plastic menu in front of her face, prompting us to follow suit. While the positioning makes it difficult to read the menu, it's highly effective in block-ing the view.

"Fred, I am sorry to inform you, but there is no Peking Pussy on the menu, so you will have to wait until you get home for that. Although, they do have fettuccine Alfredo, which you like," Mother says from behind her plastic menu wall.

"Barney, why don't you tell Dad about Jennifer," I lamely interject from behind my own menu.

"Dad, Jennifer is my girlfriend. We met at the conces-sion stand at the multiplex."

"Tell Dad about Jennifer's discount," I continue.

"I will have the fettuccine. Good suggestion, Mary," Dad says sincerely.

The menus slowly lower until we are once again vis-ible to each other. Even though we have spent more time as a family unit than apart, we swim in discomfort. It is unfathomable that the four of us were ever a cohesive, if dysfunctional, entity.

"I'm sure the kids told you, but I'm involved with someone," Mother announces proudly.

Barney stares at me with bewilderment. I mirror his thoughts.

"Actually, we didn't say anything. We thought Dad should hear it from you," I say quietly.

"I am involved in a serious and, occasionally, sexual relationship."

Mother is either lying in a futile attempt to make Dad jealous or has secretly entered the world of Internet dating.

"Excuse me, are you Mary Norton?" a young waitress inquires.

"Yes."

"You have a phone call at the bar."

"Please excuse me."

Mother stands and walks away. She returns a few minutes later to find the three of us sitting in complete silence. She is overwhelmingly pleased with herself for getting a phone call. Never mind that people don't get calls at restaurants anymore. Never mind that she has a cell phone. Mother is desperate for attention.

"Sorry about that. My boyfriend had a quick question about my birthday," Mother says as if she were a schoolgirl.

"Your birthday is not for seven months, Mary."

Mother stares Dad down until he finally looks away.

"The reason I arranged this dinner is that I have some things to tell you."

"The kids arranged this dinner," Dad says defensively.

"The kids work for me, Fred."

"Mother?"

"Fine, Barney is the only member of my team. Happy? Now Fred, how does Chairman Mao feel about you impregnating his unwed daughter?"

"Dear God, it's me, Barney."

"Barney, we can hear you," Mother interrupts.

"I don't care if you can hear me. I want God to hear me, Mother!"

"Barney, pray on your own time," she commands.

Barney stands angrily, prepared to make a dramatic exit, but is only able to do his usual thigh-brushing waddle as he leaves the table.

Hello Fatty,
Run! It's not safe to be alone with your parents!

                                        —Anna

"Fred, this dinner is over. I hope you are happy; you upset the children."

I follow Barney. Mother follows me. Dad remains seated alone at the table.

The familial reconciliation was a colossal failure, and I am okay with that. I appreciate having something to focus on other than Ben.

Memories of my former boyfriend wake me, twisting my stomach into knots. I recall all the mornings that I woke next to him. Did I know how special each one was? As I begin to cry over Ben, the inimitable smell of Mother's special pancakes wafts into my room. It's not the actual pancakes that are special but the syrup, a homemade blend of maple and cherry Robitussin. Mother concocted the syrup as a means to manage our energy level as children. Much of the family's dysfunction can be traced back to Mother's unique approach to parenting. I wander into the kitchen dressed in pink pajamas, aware that the time has come. I need to be honest with Mother. She is seated at the kitchen table, watching Barney shove pancakes into his mouth between sips of whole milk.

"Mother, I did something bad," I blurt out.

"Back on the junk food?"

"No, it's worse. It has to do with Ben."

"Ah, good old brother Ben," Barney helpfully chimes in.

"Barney, this is an A and B conversation. Please C your way out," Mother rudely informs him.

"Anna doesn't mind," Barney insists.

"Isn't it time for your morning conversation with God?" Mother asks harshly.

"I tried him earlier; went straight to voicemail," Barney says snidely.

"God has voicemail?" Mother asks.

"I heard he even has TiVo!" Barney responds.

"Please stop! I don't care if Barney stays," I announce with frustration. "I have done something very, very bad. The guy you saw in New York was not the Ben I fell in love with. When I first met Ben, he was so physically exquisite that women literally threw themselves at him. I was terrified of losing him and—"

"And?" Mother says, anxious to hear what comes next.

"I made him look like that. The clothes, the hair, the fat—it was all me. I didn't mean for it to get out of control."

"You really are Mother's daughter. That is twisted."

"Barney, get out. Your sister doesn't need compliments now! She's trying to confess her sins!"

"I want to hear the rest," he whines.

"Barney, do you hear that?"

"What?"

"God. He's e-mailing you. Go check your computer."

"Mother, you can't hear people e-mailing!"

"If God can e-mail, I can hear it. Leave before I ground you!"

Barney stomps out of the kitchen while Mother looks at me without judgment, offering only kindness. She appears to understand me in this moment, and I am grateful.

"It's not your fault."

"Yes, Mother, it is. I did it. I even created a plan. I called it The Makedown." I cry uncontrollably, ashamed of what I have done.

"When you were a little girl, you were very, very, very

unpopular, and it affected your confidence. As wonderful as you are today, the effects are still with you. It's a classic case of post-traumatic nerd disorder."

"What?"

"As a victim of post-traumatic divorce disorder, I know the signs when I see them."

"I assume you made up post-traumatic divorce disorder."

"I prefer the term *created*."

"Okay. How did you create it?"

"Mostly Tyra, Montel, and a *20/20* special on post-traumatic stress disorder. I'm thinking of writing a book."

Clearly, Mother was a limited resource, with her love of reality television, delusions of grandeur, and racist tendencies. However, I must say I am impressed with the post-traumatic divorce disorder Mother created for herself. She may not suffer from the typical substance abuse seen in PTSD, but she certainly has an addiction to QVC. Whereas Mother sees her PTDD as an excuse for her questionable behavior, I see it as an inspiration. Hiding behind excuses such as PTDD would only leave me paralyzed in an unhappy state in which I'd wait for someone else to guide me out. This is about confronting my life, approaching it from a new angle, one of self-sufficiency. I do not need a Fairy Godmother guiding me through the inferno and out the other side. I will be my own FG. However, as my own FG, I will borrow a few ideas from a staple of recovery—Alcoholics Anonymous.

Having tried the twelve steps for my compulsive overeating in ninth grade, I am reasonably familiar with their tenets. When I review the steps online, I focus on step eight (Make a list of all persons we have harmed, and become willing to make amends to them all) and step nine (Make direct amends to such people wherever possible, except when to do so would injure them or others). My list is short, but that doesn't make it any easier. Lessening Ben's already-tarnished opinion of me is hard to swallow. However, I must do it. It is my only hope.

Chapter Thirty-five

New York is home. On some level, I have known that for a while, but today, as my train back from Ohio approached the city, I said it aloud for the first time. This is where I am meant to live, with or without Ben. I didn't come to New York looking for a man, and I am not going to give up on the city because one man didn't work out. I've been walking around with blinders on, thinking Ben was the only man New York had to offer. This place has endless possibilities. Today I notice hundreds of bankers, stockbrokers, doctors, and lesser-paid professionals as possible dating material. I am going to move on. I just need to handle one last detail, Ben. I pull out my cell phone, breathe deeply, and dial.

"Hello, Ben. It's Anna. Anna Norton...didn't mean to sound all Bond-like. Um, I wanted to see if you had time for a quick coffee. Not to crowd you, but I would really like five minutes, which isn't very much time, seeing as we have twenty four hours in a day. This is beginning to feel like that scene in *Swingers*. Can you call me? Thanks."

Sitting alone in my small apartment, I can't shake the feeling that something is missing. As I change my sheets, wash dishes, or sweep the floor, an odd sense of loss is with me. It's not overwhelming or overt; it's quiet and penetrating. Occasionally, it even wakes me up in the middle of the night. I roll over, instinctively expecting to find Ben. Instead, I discover emptiness. I look forward to going to work with a passion rarely seen in people in my tax bracket.

"Well?" Janice asks the next morning as I glumly enter D&D.

"Better...much better. Still no call, but yeah, I'm feeling...better."

"Sweetie, I think it's best he doesn't call. Let it die with the relationship."

"I...just...don't feel right. My life feels so empty."

"Well, that's probably because it is. You kind of neglected to make any friends after you met Ben. I think it's time."

"You know, I've never really had any friends. I'm not sure if I can make them."

"Book club, tennis lessons, bridge—if you sign up for just one of these, you will meet people."

"Okay."

"And if you're ready, maybe it's time to put up a pro-file on Match, or I'd love to introduce you to Gary's brother—"

"No! I am definitely not ready to date."

"That's fine. You should take as much time as you need."

In the days and weeks that follow, I undergo a renaissance, dipping my proverbial toe into many different arenas. Even though I am double-jointed and wildly uncoordi-nated, I sign up for Saturday tennis, mostly because there are two women in my class whom I consider potential friend candidates. Bridge is a bust, as I am younger than most of the players' grandchildren. However, the book club is the greatest thing since Accutane. I get to hang around with new people without worrying what to talk about. Between classes, reading, and work, a wonderful thing occurs. I accept that it's truly over.

And just like that, optimism sneaks into my life, prompting me to smile at strangers, buy my first expensive trench coat, and generally just go with it as it comes.

"Well?" Janice asks with her usual trepidation one morning as I enter D&D.

"Well what?" I ask, pouring myself a cup of coffee.

"How are you?"

"Good," I say, pulling my hair into a ponytail to get it out of my way before I start chopping vegetables. "You want to see a movie tonight?"

Janice looks constipated with anxiety.

"Anna," she says seriously.

"Honestly, are you still upset about Gary's brother? I promise, when I'm ready to date again, he will be my first call."

"It's not about Jonathan. It's ... it's Ben."

"Ben?" I repeat back to Janice, confused.

"He called here looking for you."

"Did you talk to him?"

"Yeah, he sounds good. I don't know if that's what you want to hear, but—"

"No, he deserves to be happy."

"Oh, Anna."

"Honestly, Janice, it's better he's in good spirits."

"You know, you really don't have to tell him what you did. You both are moving on. Why dredge up the past? Especially since it doesn't paint you in the best light."

"It will help me move on. Hand me the phone; I need to get this over with."

The final flame of possibility is about to be blown out. I expect Ben to say he never wants to see me again. But at least I will know I did the right thing.

"Hello."

"Hey."

He recognizes my voice immediately, reminding me how close we once were.

"How are you?"

"I'm okay. How are you?" I ask politely.

"Good. So what's up?"

"Um, well, I was wondering if we could get a coffee."

"Anna, it's too soon."

"I know, I know. But I really need to tell you something."

"Can't you tell me on the phone?"

"No, I think it would be better—"

"I really don't want to see you. It truly is over between us."

"I know it's over, but I need five minutes. Please, you are the only man I have ever been in love with. Just five minutes." I fight off tears. I don't want Ben to feel manipulated by emotion.

There is a long silence on the other end of the phone.

"How about the Starbucks near the apartment?"

He says "the apartment" as if we still live there together.

"Yeah, that works."

"Can you make 5:30 this afternoon?"

"Thank you, Ben."

This afternoon's actions will dictate the tone of the

rest of my life. This is the first step toward being proud of myself as a person. This is a character-building exercise. However, as dedicated as I am to building character, I maintain a superficial need to look good in front of Ben. Today's outfit must convey my sincere apologies while also highlighting my subtle sex appeal. I know that Ben cannot be lured back into my arms, but this afternoon will be emblazoned in his memory forever. He will never forget what I am going to tell him. He will tell his future wife and children about it, finding laughter in the story as the years pass. At first, I will be a mentally unstable psychotic freak, followed by a neurotic bitch, then a crazy young woman, and finally a sweet but misguided girl. Oddly enough, the less he cares about me, the kinder his description of me will be. Therefore, if I am to be engraved in his mind for eternity, I must look good. Today's outfit will be wide-cuffed black slacks that create the optical illusion that I am both tall and skinny and a low-cut black sweater. It's not too revealing, but it offers a tempting glimpse of cleavage.

Sitting alone at the Starbucks on Spring Street, my stomach wrestles with anxiety and fear. I begin my traditional hand-wiping exercise. My palms are once again a watery mess and my sweat 'stache is rapidly forming.

Ben enters.

I wipe off the 'stache, rub my palms, and stand up. He walks toward me with a serious expression. Remember, what's done is done. I cannot change or redo anything. Ben sports jeans and his Born in the USA T-shirt, the same shirt he wore the first time I saw him. Does he know that? Did he wear it on purpose? It is more likely that he has no idea of the shirt's significance and just happened to put it on today. I prepare for what will most likely be our last hug. I am going to savor the moment as long as possible, without seeming strange. He stands in front of me, but to my great surprise, he doesn't offer a hug, only a handshake.

We shared a life, an apartment, and countless orgasms, and he offers me a handshake? I accept his hand as if he is a perfect stranger.

"Do you want a coffee or anything? I'm buying," I say awkwardly. Why did I say "I'm buying" as if a three-dollar latte is going to sway his opinion of me?

"No, I'm good."

"I don't want any coffee either."

Silence hangs between us. I need to say it, but somehow my mouth remains closed.

"How is your new place?" Ben asks without making eye contact. An unbearable sadness takes over me. If I don't tell him quickly, I may fall apart.

"It's fine. Listen, I need to tell you something."

"That's why I'm here."

"I don't look like the girls you normally date."

"Anna, why are you doing this?"

"No, please let me finish. I knew from the beginning that you gave me a chance because your mother forced you to after Gela. I didn't care. I loved you. Everywhere we went, women smiled at you and scratched their heads when they saw me, wondering how I got a man like you. And when they smiled at you, you smiled back."

"Stop this, please."

"No, you need to know, Ben. I was convinced I was going to lose you to someone more physically appropriate.

This is me at my best—I had to work really hard to get here."

"Anna—"

"I only did it because I was afraid of losing you."

Ben stares at me perplexed. "Did what?"

"I made you gain weight. I was the one who canceled your gym membership and pushed those awful flannels on you. The bald patches were from me putting Nair in your shampoo. I didn't mean for it to get out of hand. I wanted to make you less perfect."

"That explains the fake Nature's Way bars."

"They were Skor bars. How did you find out?"

"Someone gave me a Skor bar," Ben says calmly.

Maybe this will be okay. Maybe he won't hate me.

"Anna, this is a little hard for me to accept. I let you into my life and I loved you. You actively worked to destroy me."

"I didn't mean for—"

"Only a cruel and vicious person could do something like this."

"I loved you, Ben. I love you still."

He stands to leave, revolted by the sight of me. Maybe if he understood the kind of persecution I withstood as a child, maybe he could find an ounce of compassion.

"If you just let me explain what it was like for me growing up..."

Ben turns away from me without so much as a look or a wave good-bye. I am the most putrescent of all scum. The sensation of pain, guilt, and self-loathing is worse than anything I could have imagined. To watch his opinion of me sour is excruciating.

As unscrupulously nasty as people were in my youth, I had always been on the right side of the ethical equation. I was never in a position where I questioned how my behavior affected another person. But I don't regret telling Ben the truth. He has the right to understand the metamorphosis I thrust upon him. And I deserve to feel exactly like I do—devastated.

Chapter Thirty-six

"Are you okay?" Janice asks soothingly.

Her face is etched with concern as she prepares me a cup of tea at D&D. It takes a loyal friend to offer compassion to the guilty. She would care for me if I self-destructed again, refusing to brush my teeth or shower. For that, I am eternally grateful. Thankfully, I don't think it will be necessary.

"Watching him lose respect for me was unbearable, but I feel okay."

"Did you order delivery? Maybe some donuts. It's okay if you did."

"No. It's shocking, but I didn't even think about that. I can't believe—"

"That it's over?"

"That I haven't fallen apart. It feels right; we're supposed to be over. After what happened, it should be over. He deserves to move on... to let go."

"Anna, you don't sound like yourself. It's kind of freaking me out. Why aren't you crying and refusing to brush your teeth?"

"I don't know. I guess I'm okay that it's over."

"Do you still love him?" Janice asks, grappling to understand my calm façade.

"Of course. I'll always love Ben. Always. That will

never change, but I don't want to spend my life feeling insecure that my boyfriend will leave me."

"But you still love him."

"I know this is right. We're both going to be happy."

"You've come along way, baby."

"Nothing says friendship like stealing tag lines from cigarette companies."

"Next time you meet someone, it will be different. You will be different."

"Yeah," I respond.

"On the bright side, you can start eating meat again!"

"You're sweet, but I think being a vegetarian suits me."

The next morning, I wake to a huge surprise at 7:20.

"Hello?" I grumble into the telephone.

"The Won has arrived!" Barney cries rapturously.

"What?"

"The Won Ton fell out of Ming's . . . soup bowl."

"Well, there's a euphemism I haven't heard before."

I'm shocked by the news. I shouldn't really be surprised, seeing as I've had nine months to get used to it, but I still somehow am. I am now the proud owner of an illegitimate half-sibling, Thomas Joseph Norton, weighing eight pounds three ounces. He is the lightest baby ever born to the Norton clan.

"The Won has some grip. He's got my whole finger in his hand."

"So you like him?"

"He's pretty cool," Barney says, trying to appear nonchalant.

"I thought you were waiting until he was two to make a decision."

"I'm not saying he's in my will or anything, but he has that certain Norton something. It's kind of magical."

"Poor kid. Have you talked to Mother?"

"Anna, you have no idea what you are in for."

"What does that mean? Is she drunk? Crying? Lighting things on fire?"

"Call her."

"Barney, tell me!" I shriek.

"Not on your life." Click.

Barney shouldn't withhold such pertinent information from me. This is our mother. She's moderately old with the mind of a circus performer. God only knows what she's done. I can barely dial Mother's number, I'm so hysterical.

The phone rings. Please answer.

"Hello?" Mother says with food in her mouth.

"Mother? Are you okay?" I say frantically.

"Sorry, had an egg roll in my mouth."

"Did you say egg roll?"

"Yes, and let me tell you, it's not easy to find a Chinese place that delivers this early in the morning."

"You're eating Chinese food?"

"A little MSG never hurt anyone."

"So the ban on Chinese food has been lifted?"

"Of course! Didn't you hear? Ming and your father apologized."

"What? They did? I had no idea," I say with astonishment.

"I didn't give Ming enough credit. She may have terrible taste in men, but she's pretty smart."

"What happened? When did they call?"

"Oh, they didn't call."

"They wrote you a note? An e-mail?"

"No."

"Flowers? A Mrs. Fields cookie cake? Balloons?"

"No, it was more of a subliminal apology."

"I'm not following."

"They named the baby after me."

"Uh, Mother, I'm not sure what Barney told you, but they named him Thomas. Your name is Mary. They don't even sound similar."

"His middle name is Joseph, Mary's husband in the Bible. Pretty damn smart. Honestly Anna, I almost didn't get it."

"I understand that. It certainly isn't the most direct way to apologize."

"Anna, I can move on. This is what I've been waiting for."

"Mother, are you still in love with Dad?"

"In love?" Mother laughs. "Oh, Anna, I don't want to upset you, but I haven't been in love with your father in many decades."

"Then why didn't you move on?"

"I may not have been in love with him, but we had a life, and he left that life without so much as an apology. After thirty years, I deserved an apology. I deserved something—a gesture that made me understand that I meant something. And now I have it."

Even though Mother's delusional, I'm thrilled she can move on. Hopefully now she can focus on deprogramming her QVC addiction.

Mother's newfound freedom ignites concern in me. I fret that Ben is consumed by anger over my betrayal. Was telling him the wrong thing to do? I can no longer tell if I did it for his sake or merely to appease my guilt. If only he had stayed and heard what I had to say, maybe it would have helped him. It's too late. To call him now would be another interruption. And what if he's fine; my call will only upset him again. But what if he's not?

The only person I trust to decipher Ben's state of mind is the woman who brought us together—his mother, Milly. I cringe, thinking how she must loathe me. I honestly wouldn't be surprised if my face was pinned to a dartboard somewhere in her apartment. Maybe I should write her a letter cataloging the pain of my youth, explaining the misery I endured over my physical appearance. Or maybe I should simply send her Hello Fatty. The thought of someone, let alone Ben's mother, reading my innermost secrets and criticisms makes me want to vomit. It is the emotional equivalent of a gynecological exam. My intense nervousness and nausea communicate one simple fact—there is no more powerful record of my past than this book.

On a plain white paper, I craft a note to Milly. I don't ponder long and hard about the words. I force them onto the page. I cannot allow myself time to waver, so I write as fast as possible.

Milly,
As Ben's mother, I suspect you must hate me. I understand. I only write to you today because I worry that my actions have had a lasting effect on Ben. I won't contact him, for I don't want to upset his life any more. I send this to you, on the off chance that you think he needs it

to let go of the anger. If he's okay, please just throw this
away. It doesn't mean much, but I'm sorry.

—*Anna*
P.S. I'm still a vegetarian and I voted
for a Democrat in the last election.

In mailing Hello Fatty to Milly, I am finally free of the past; everything from Weird Fat Bear to FG to Ben to The Makedown is behind me now. I have my whole life ahead of me, and for once, I'm ready to embrace it. I open a blank page in a journal and address it "Hello Anna."

Epilogue

Two Years Later...

Seated in a café a couple blocks from Union Square, I sip my latte patiently, occasionally looking at my watch or rubbing my diamond against my sweater. The jeweler mentioned I could damage the rock through improper cleaning, but somehow I doubt that. I pull the seating chart out of my bag and again count how many tables will act as a buffer between Dad and Ming and Mother.

"Anna?" a familiar voice beckons. I slowly raise my eyes, trying to place the voice.

"Ben."

I am speechless. In two years, I have never run into him or even heard so much as his name mentioned in passing. On the rare occasion when I think of him, he feels distant and fuzzy, as if from a dream.

"You look great," Ben says kindly.

"Oh, thank you. So do you." And I mean it. He's lost the weight, and he looks like the Ben I first knew. But...kinder somehow.

We both continue to stare at each other, mirroring each other's shock. Ben looks down at the seating chart, then up to me.

"Are you getting married?" he asks, devoid of any

identifiable emotion. I look at the seating chart, then back to him.

"Oh...this is for Barney's wedding."

A man comes up behind me and kisses me on the cheek.

"Hi, sorry I'm late," Anthony says in his friendly way before extending his hand to Ben. "Hi, I'm Anthony, Anna's fiancé."

Ben shakes Anthony's hand. "Nice to meet you. Congratulations to both of you—and to Barney, of course."

A young blonde girl grabs Ben's hand, pulling him away with only a quick smile toward Anthony and myself. Clearly, she has no interest in an introduction.

"Thank you," I say graciously as I try to place the blonde girl's familiar face.

"See you around, bastard," Ben says with a wink.

I return the wink as Anthony whispers in my ear, "Did he just call you a bastard?"

"Yeah," I say, wistful about the past—a time before I eschewed fairy tale ambition for the more practical fairy tale-in-progress.

Then it hits me. Coffee Slut #1!

And to think he denied he was flirting with her!

About the Author

I was born in Los Angeles to an Iranian father and an American mother. As a child I talked incessantly, feeling the need to comment on everything around me. While at first charmed by my verbose nature, my family soon tired of the constant chatter. This is how I found writing—it was like talking only I didn't need anyone else to participate.

After graduating from high school, I moved to Paris to study French, but left a year later fearing I was missing out on my *Felicity* era. After returning to the United States and enrolling at UC Davis, I quickly realized that dorm life and frat parties weren't what the WB (now the CW) cracked them up to be. Depressed by the view of the freeway from my dorm window, I transferred to UC Santa Cruz. It was an odd choice for someone who didn't smoke pot, loathed incense, and openly shopped at the Gap, but somehow it worked.

Upon graduation in 2000, I moved back to Los Angeles and began working in the film industry. I went from intern to assistant to assistant to assistant to creative executive to director of development before I finally decided to write full time. In addition to *The Makedown,* I have a four-part young adult adventure series, *School of Fear,* debuting from Little, Brown for Young Readers in fall 2009. The film rights to my neuroses-inspired series were optioned by Warner Brothers and GK Films.

I currently live in Los Angeles. And, yes, I still talk too much.

Lisi Daneshvari

5 Signs That You Need an FG Intervention:

1 You still use your SAT score as a conversation piece...twenty years after taking it.

2 Brushing your hair is reserved for special occasions.

3 The invitation list for your birthday party doubles as a family tree.

4 You consider watching television and the pursuit of happiness as one and the same.

5 The last time you had a boyfriend "going all the way" meant holding hands.